WRITTEN IN BLOOD

WRITTEN IN BLOOD

ANKITA VERMA

JAICO PUBLISHING HOUSE

Ahmedabad Bangalore Bhopal Chennai
Delhi Hyderabad Kolkata Lucknow Mumbai

Published by Jaico Publishing House
A-2 Jash Chambers, 7-A Sir Phirozshah Mehta Road
Fort, Mumbai - 400 001
jaicopub@jaicobooks.com
www.jaicobooks.com

WRITTEN IN BLOOD
ISBN 978-93-91019-59-4

First Jaico Impression: 2021

Page design and layout: Inosoft Systems, Delhi

Printed by
Nutech Print Services - India

1

Srinagar, Kashmir
January 6, 1991

It was nearing 4:00 p.m. in Srinagar and because of the weather warning for the day, most employees of *The Kashmiri Times,* a leading local daily, were busy winding up their day's work. It was almost closing time and they were a bit distracted. But it was not so for the lead reporter, Sana Sikander Sheikh, who was locked in an intense verbal spat on the phone.

"No, I will not change my report," Sana screamed into the phone, the color rising under her porcelain skin. "You can tell them that *The Kashmiri Times* is not for sale. Truth will be reported as it is. And I don't care for your reasons." She banged the phone down and looked up to find the entire office staring at her, shocked by the outburst. They knew the call had been from an influential politician. Sana cast a wary glance around and absentmindedly tucked a thick strand of hair behind her ears. The call had left her in no mood to interact with anyone. She hurriedly hoisted her tote bag, adjusted her head scarf and stepped out of the office into the biting chill.

Sana walked at a brisk pace, trying to clear her head while also reminding herself to stop by the grocery store on her way home. She was brusque with the friendly shopkeeper during her purchase of kesar and spices and other staples. Hoping yet again that her brother was home for dinner, she picked up her pace against the January wind howling through the bare branches of tall chinars. She felt queasy with hunger and she struggled under the weight of the grocery bag. She wanted to get home soon. The unmistakable sound of an AK-47 reverberated through the trees and caused her to stumble in shock. It had sounded disturbingly close. She had been hearing gunfire a lot more regularly in recent months as the presence of *Hizb-ul-Mujahideen* and the rising militancy was slowly but surely turning her beloved valley into an unpredictable death trap.

The short winter day darkened quickly. Most residents had retreated into their homes and warm lights twinkled across the snow-flecked landscape. Sana walked as fast as the crusted, slippery road allowed her and sighed with relief as she finally entered the porch of her handsome double-storied house. She stomped her feet on the mat, pulled out the key and twisted it into the lock.

Stepping into the quiet house, she pulled off her scarf and let her luxurious mane tumble down. The wooden floors of the old house creaked under her feet. She inhaled its familiar scent of old wood and spices and walked to the kitchen to put away the groceries and fresh meat she had picked up to prepare rogan josh, her younger brother's favorite dish. But once again, Awais, her brother was not home. He was the only family she had and even though he was younger by four years, they were more like twins. Sana found the empty house forlorn and depressing. It was one of the reasons why she had started spending so much time at her office—she loved that tight space teeming with humans. None of her fellow reporters would ever guess that their senior reporter, Sana Sikander Sheikh, a popular Kashmiri beauty was trying to find an escape from her loneliness. They all admired her, not just for her skills as a journalist but for her inimitable spirit and courage.

Sana washed the meat and marinated it in hung curds, deviating slightly from the traditional rogan josh recipe that she had inherited from her mother. A nostalgic smile crept up on Sana's lips as she remembered her mom fussing around in the kitchen. They had always been a happy family, up until the fateful day five years ago, when her parents had decided to take an unfortunate drive on a snowy morning to a nearby town. The car had skidded on the ice-sheeted road and the crash had been fatal for both. It was like a bolt out of the blue for her and Awais but they had lived through it together. Sana knew that it had been especially hard on him, then in his early teens. Awais withdrew into himself and started spending more and more time alone, away from the house. And it had only increased after he turned eighteen a couple of years ago.

Her parents had always wanted her to pursue higher education and work. They were a fairly well-to-do family and their progressive sensibilities had influenced Sana more than her brother. But at times she felt a gnawing feeling of unrest within her. *How would her progressive parents have really reacted to her being in love with Anurag, a Kashmiri Pandit?*

She had dealt with this guilt by throwing herself relentlessly into her work and between her work and her passionate affair with Anurag Kaul, a local Kashmiri artifact dealer's son, her relationship with Awais had suffered. She often wondered if his detachment from home had coincided with her selfish obsession with her own life. She also knew that cooking the occasional pot of meat was not going to remedy anything. She needed to make more of a real effort in her relationship with Awais.

Suddenly, Sana was overcome by a need to throw up and she rushed to the bathroom. She retched into the sink for a few moments but nothing came out. She splashed her face with cold water and toweling off, noticed in the mirror the dark circles under her large eyes. They stood out prominently against her porcelain complexion and made her look melancholic and vulnerable.

Over the past year, her relationship with Anurag had borne the brunt of the ongoing crusade against Kashmiri Pandits. She knew he loved her but she also knew that their love was as fragile as the survival of Kashmiri Pandits in the valley. Their future was uncertain but in Kashmir, women didn't make the first move. She had already committed to him by giving herself to him without any promises. Now, she was waiting for him to take a step. She was giving him time but the fact that he hadn't contacted her in three months was beginning to bother her. Her calls to his house had been politely deflected by his otherwise doting mother.

Anurag had changed a lot in the past one year since *Hizb-ul-Mujahideen* had announced jihad against all non-Muslims in Kashmir, which were mainly Kashmiri Pandits. She missed her happy, careless Anurag who would do anything just to see her smile. Sana's confidence in their love had led her to his doorstep one evening, even after all her calls had been unreciprocated. It was a rather bold move and though no one had answered the door, she had spotted Anurag's father on the terrace. She had turned and walked away quickly, never once looking back.

Sana was jolted out of her reverie by the telephone's ring echoing through the cavernous house. Few people called at this time of the day. Her heart leapt at the thought that it might be Anurag. *Don't be a fool,* she admonished herself. *He hasn't called in three months. And his parents have literally turned you away from their doorstep.*

Slightly panting, she answered the phone and was thrilled to hear Anurag's voice.

"Hello, Sana?" his voice was unsure, as if expecting someone else to pick up the phone.

"Yes Anurag, I am so glad you called. Can we meet?" Sana was frantic.

"Sana, my dear, listen to me carefully. We are leaving tomorrow. We can't stay here any longer." He paused before adding, "And I have called to ask you to come with us."

After a moment of confused silence, Sana was able to respond.

"Leaving? Come with you? Where?" she sputtered, dreading the inevitable.

"We are leaving Kashmir," he spoke in a hurried whisper. "Dad has sold all our properties and even our business. We only got half the price of what it's worth, but we have no choice. We are moving to Delhi and I want you to come with us. My parents are okay with it as long as we are far away from here." He sounded almost impatient.

"Anurag, this is my home, this is where my roots are. My people are here. I can't just get up and leave." She struggled to hold back tears.

"I know, Sana. But I love you and I need you with me!"

"I love you too, Anurag. But how can I leave my people?"

"Your people are the ones out to kill us, Sana." Anurag spat out the words sharply.

Hurt, Sana replied, "Don't say that Anurag."

"You have to hear this, Sana! Exactly a year ago today, your people declared a war against us. And you know what we found painted in black yesterday morning on our showroom shutters? It said, 'Be one with us … Run … or Die.' What do you think we should do?" he huffed.

"Please stop it, Anurag! You knew my family. These terrorists are not *my people*. I love you." Sana sobbed.

"Then come with me, Sana. Things here in the valley are going from bad to worse for us Hindus." His voice was suddenly soft. "Staying is not an option for my family. And I can't imagine my life without you."

Sana held back a sob.

He continued, "Some of us have gotten together and hired an entire bus. If we leave at 6:00 a.m. tomorrow, we will be in Jammu by evening. The very next day, we take a train for Delhi. I promise you Sana, we will have a great life together."

"Okay, Anurag." Sana felt weak and drained. "But what about Awais? I need to tell him. He should come too."

There was a noticeable pause at the other end before Anurag spoke again. "Sana, I'm sorry. I know what he means to you, but ... it's best if we keep Awais out of it. I've somehow convinced my family about you. But it's going to be a bus full of Kashmiri Pandits. These people are being forced to leave behind everything—all that they've owned and known—*just because they are not Muslims*. Some have even lost their families. I can protect you because you are my girl. But how do you think they'll react to Awais?"

Sana didn't reply. After a beat, Anurag added, "I promise, once we're settled, we'll convince Awais to come to Delhi. I'll see you tomorrow morning at six at the bus station. Be there, Sana. Please."

The line disconnected and Sana stared at the phone's receiver, stupefied by the enormity of what she had agreed to in the name of love. She would have to write what would be the most difficult note any sister could ever write to her brother.

2

Srinagar Bus Station
January 7, 1991

The old tea shop owner, probably older than the bus station itself, curiously eyed the young and pretty Kashmiri girl who stood huddled with her single piece of luggage. His gnarled fingers were expertly preparing tea for the drivers hanging around in the bone-chilling winter morning. Buses for Jammu had left half an hour ago and the next lot weren't due for another couple of hours. His wise, permanently crinkled eyes once again swept the deserted bus station.

"Are you waiting for someone, *beti*?" he called out to her.

Sana turned to him with a forced smile and nodded. "Have a cup of kahwa. It will warm you up," he invited.

"Thanks, *chacha,*" Sana replied, settling on a rickety bench by the shop and accepting a clay cup steaming with spiced aromas.

"Where are you off to?" he asked as he resumed cleaning his counter.

"Jammu," Sana lied.

"You're too early," he remonstrated, eyebrows raised. "Jammu buses aren't due for the next two hours."

"It's a chartered bus."

The old man stopped cleaning. Hiring an entire bus was rare in Srinagar. "Are you talking about the bus hired by the Kashmiri Pandits?"

"Yes," said a startled Sana.

"*Beti,* that bus left last night. There was a tip-off about militants planning to attack them today. So they changed their plans. Did no one tell you?"

Sana felt her world spin out of control. She set the cup aside and gripped the bench so hard that her knuckles went white. As she turned to her side and retched violently, the chaiwalla came up to her quickly and patted her shoulder until she settled down. "Someone very close to you was leaving on that bus?" His voice was low and sympathetic. It was a while before Sana could stand up. The tea seller hailed a rickshaw for her and she waited, shivering. His crinkled eyes watched the rickshaw until it vanished from his view.

It was a short ride and Sana was still, numb, until she was standing in front of her beautiful house. The sight brought fresh tears to her eyes. Only a few hours ago, she had left the house for what she thought would be the last time. Yet, here she was again. Sana climbed the four steps and noticed wet, muddy boot prints on the floorboards. Awais was home!

Sana raced through the front doors calling out, "Awais! Awais!" Her farewell note still lay on the wooden cabinet and she rushed over to take it back. "Awais!" she called out again, receiving no reply.

And then she saw it. An innocuous looking white envelope from the government hospital was tucked beneath her note to Awais. It was her medical report. Her heart thudding fast, her fingers trembling, she pulled out the single piece of paper from the envelope. Sana's tests were positive—she was pregnant.

And, scribbled on top of the report was a note from Awais, "Hope I never see you again. Burn in hell, *kafir!*"

Sana shivered involuntarily. Within a single morning, she had lost everything. She was left alone among the ruins of her life while a grave responsibility grew slowly in her belly. She heaved deeply and then howled like a wild animal, her pained cries reverberating through the empty house.

3

State Guest House, Tel Aviv
February 25, 2005
8:00 p.m.

Head of Personnel, Rotem Tishby was inspecting the state guest house for the final time that day. Her watch showed it was just past 8:00 p.m. The Indian diplomat, Mr. Faisal Umer Naqvi and his wife weren't back for dinner yet and had not called ahead with any information. This was unusual and was fast becoming a matter of concern. A typical Israeli beauty, Rotem was a fastidious woman. She dressed impeccably and her manners were groomed to the hilt by her years of serving diplomats from around the world while they visited Israel. And even though she was a thorough professional, she was secretly upset that her Indian guests were to leave the next day. She was going to miss the young boy who had accompanied his parents on an official trip. Rotem was not crazy about kids but this boy was a joy to be around. The staff loved him too, especially when he attempted to speak stray Hebrew words. She made a mental note to check up on the boy.

Briskly, she walked through the charming Mediterranean-style villa, inhaling the salty breeze from the nearby beach. She checked the lounge and study, the entertainment center, the parlor and the utilities rooms. Everything was quiet and orderly. Finally, she climbed up to the residential floor and knocked on a door, behind which, she knew, were Shezii and his gaming console.

"Come in," answered young Shahzaib Naqvi.

Rotem found him in a dim room, his face illuminated by the blue light from a screen as he concentrated on battling digital foes in a virtual world

"Hello, Mr. Shahzaib," she said softly.

Shezii looked up from his gaming console and flashed his charming smile, complete with a set of recently fitted braces. He simply loved being called by his formal name.

"Would Mr. Shahzaib care to take a break from his PlayStation and have his dinner? I shall lay the table."

"Nah, I'll wait for mom 'n dad. Thank you, Ms. Tishby," Shezii lisped through his braces and went back to his game. In the short time that he had known Rotem, they had formed a comfortable bond.

Rotem smiled indulgently and exited, closing the door behind her. She headed for the kitchen to warn the staff that dinner would be pushed back. As she climbed down the staircase, she noticed that the ground floor seemed unusually quiet. *Where was everybody?* She headed noiselessly to the kitchen and opened the door.

The kitchen seemed empty too.

"Keren?" she called out, hoping the Head Cook was somewhere close by. The pots on the stove were bubbling with delicious smelling sauces and the air smelled of za'atar. *Why is no one attending to them*? Rotem thought exasperatedly. She slowly rounded the counter, calling out to Keren again. And then she stopped in her tracks.

At her feet, Keren lay face down on the floor, her body at an unnatural angle, her face in a pool of blood. Rotem sprang into action. She was reaching for the security intercom when powerful hands grabbed her and covered her mouth. As Rotem clawed against the suffocating grip, she felt something sharp slide across her throat. She felt no pain, just a warm burning sensation in her throat. But she couldn't breathe and her screams came out as strange gurgling sounds. She clutched her throat and her fingers felt warm and slippery. Hot black patches swam in front of her eyes as she collapsed on the cold white tiles. The last thing she saw was the Indian couple entering the guest house, looking happy and laughing carelessly. And then, there was just peaceful darkness.

4

State Guest House, Tel Aviv
February 25, 2005
9:00 p.m.

Shaziya Naqvi bounded up the stairs to their residential suites feeling exhilarated. The sun, the sea and some rare quality time with her beloved husband had done her a world of good. She felt alive, radiant and happy, even though her skin felt sticky and her hair smelled salty. She would need a shower for sure, but first she had to see her precious Shezii. After all, this was war-torn Israel and they had been gone for longer than anticipated.

Shaziya opened the door to his room and stood still. It was empty. Shezii's gaming console was on standby mode. It was rare for him to abandon his PlayStation mid-game. Her mind reeling with doubt and fear, she returned to the master bedroom. There Shezii sat, on the large couch, his hands folded over the PlayStation controller. Shaziya cheerfully took a step further, intending to surprise him, but then slowed down. Something was off. The mother in her sensed Shezii's fear and unusal stillness.

"Shezii? Are you alright, baby?"

That last word came out as a cry—someone had pushed her roughly to the ground. She landed face down on the soft carpet. Shezii's terrified scream cut through her. She clumsily tried to get up.

Only then did she see Faisal kneeling on the other side of the couch, his hands tied behind his back. A gun was being held to his ashen face and his mouth was covered with duct tape. The assailants must have nabbed him as soon as he had entered the master bedroom. Four large men in loose black jumpsuits and masks loomed over them. Their eyes reflected an angry hatred that Shaziya would never forget. One of the men pulled her up roughly and dumped her on the sofa next to Shezii. He grabbed her by the hair, spewing profanities in Arabic about the oldest profession in the world. Shaziya let out a pained cry. Faisal desperately made an attempt to reach her, but his holder hit him across the face with the butt of a gun. Faisal toppled sideways and a nasty gash bled across his forehead. Shezii sobbed uncontrollably.

The leader among the four tormenters approached Faisal. He pulled up a cushioned stool, sat down, and with marked deliberation removed a dark blue booklet from Faisal's jacket. Faisal saw the Indian emblem etched in gold and recognized, with dismay, his diplomatic passport.

"*Hindustani*?" the man asked in an oily, nasal tone.

Faisal nodded.

"Then you are a friend? Hind's *hukumat* supports our cause."

Faisal stared at him uncertainly.

"Too bad. We thought we could play with a *Yahoodi* or *Ameriki* rat! But, you are a *Hindustani* and a *musalman*. You are our brother, no?"

The terrorist paused as if considering his options and then ripped off the duct tape covering Faisal's mouth. Faisal gasped and tried to stay up on his knees.

"Faisal Umer Naqvi," the man spat. "Do you know the significance of this name, brother?"

Faisal caught a whiff of sandalwood as the man bent close to his face. He shook his head. He was beginning to realize, to his utter horror, that he was facing the members of the Islamic Jihad, a Palestinian militant organization.

The leader held Faisal's eye in a steady gaze. Then he turned slowly towards Shezii.

"See, this is the problem," he said, looking at the boy. "Our own brothers don't know about Islam. They have forgotten the teachings of the Prophet."

The leader got up and slowly made his way to the sofa. Shaziya drew her son closer and tried to turn his face into her embrace. But the man grabbed hold of Shezii's chin and tilted it up firmly, even as Shaziya futilely clawed at his arm.

"What about you, son? Do they teach you such things at your *angrezi* school?" he hissed.

"They teach him this much about Islam," Faisal spoke, trying to draw the madman's attention away from his son, "that it is wrong to hurt and kill innocents."

In a flash, the jihadi had caught Faisal by the tie and smashed his face into the floor. Pulling him back by the collar, he grinned as blood trickled from Faisal's broken nose.

Shezii screamed and Shaziya pulled his face back into her embrace so he wouldn't see any more. Faisal groaned as the terrorist wiped the blood from his face with the same tie.

"This is all it's good for, this western neck rope," he spat. "Oh and you should know, Naqvi Muslims get their name from Imam Ali Naqvi, one of the twelve Shia Imams and the direct descendent of the Prophet's own daughter!"

He let Faisal go and backed off a little. Turning to one of his accomplices who stood by the window, he asked, "How much longer to the event?"

"Al-Basr should be getting in place this very minute. Not very long for him now," his comrade responded almost cheerfully.

As soon as the words were spoken, the leader moved like lightning and grabbed his comrade's neck.

"Take his name with respect," he growled. "Al-Basr is a *Mujahid* who fights for the Prophet and Islam. His place awaits him in heaven."

"What are you planning?" Faisal didn't know what gave him the courage to speak. Shaziya's eyes widened in fear.

The leader turned sharply towards him, his face seething with a volatile dark anger, and Faisal flinched. But then, in an instant, his expression melted into an indulgent and patient smile.

"You will be proud to hear of it. We brothers are going to teach these *Yahoodis* a lesson. Gaza, the West Bank and *mashallah* all of Israel shall once more be the land of Islam. And we shall rule it. Today, your brother will sacrifice himself. He will wipe out those Israeli soldiers—those *kafirs* who want to enjoy the abominable Western culture in that club. They dance and sing as they kill our people and rule our land. But not anymore! Soon they will turn into a mound of blood and bones. Al-Basr will sacrifice himself for Islam. *Inshallah*, our brother will be successful and will reach the heavens."

Faisal froze. The jihadis had planted a suicide bomber at the beach-front night club frequented by Israeli soldiers and innocent civilians. He couldn't contain his anger and spat through bloodied lips, "He is not my brother, no murderer can be my brother."

A broad hand connected with Faisal's jaw, dislocating it. As he fell forward, he heard the distinct sound of a blast. Everyone froze. The leader checked his watch, and then the wall clock. *Half past eleven*.

The men moved towards the French windows and stared towards the distant beach promenade. They consulted in whispers. Then, the leader returned to Faisal and slipped the passport back into his breast pocket.

"Al-Basr is a *shaheed* now. He has sacrificed himself for the rest of us. I am letting you live, brother," he murmured close to Faisal's face. "Do you know why?"

Faisal swallowed hard.

"So that you can read the Quran and understand it. Use the remainder of your life as a gift from Allah, to know and love His Word. Realize the true cause and someday you may join us ... join Al-Basr in Jannat."

And with that, the men slipped out into the dark night.

5

Current Day
Delhi, India

The woman ran fast. She ran as fast as she could towards the edge of an abyss, falling several times on the way. She was cold and her legs were giving away. Her lungs burned, yet running felt urgent, as if her life depended upon it. She had to do something important but she could not remember what. The farther she ran the more she stayed in the same place. She cried for help but she couldn't hear her own voice. Suddenly, it came to her—she had to save someone. Someone she loved. And then it began to rain. An oily, thick rain.

The skies rumbled and through the deep thunder, it became clear to her. She now knew. She reached the edge of the abyss and peered into the dark gorge and into the scared eyes of a very young man hanging onto a single rock. He was screaming. Her hands felt clammy and slick with oil. He reached out for her desperately and she gripped his hand. But then, slowly, he started to slip away from her slick grip, until she felt the tips of their fingers finally losing touch.

Awais falls away silently and Sana's throat chokes with fear.

With a start, Sana sat up in her pristine queen-sized luxurious bed, gasping for breath. It wasn't the first time she had had this nightmare in the past 15 years. She reached for a glass of water on her bedside table, her eyes refusing to focus. Finally, she looked up to see her daughter, Aliya, standing at her bedroom door, giving her a strange look. Aliya was Sana's spitting image when she was younger but Sana was probably the only mother who hated this resemblance. Her daughter's beauty had an added ethereal, haunting quality, and she always looked slightly aloof and a bit sad.

"Are you okay?" Aliya asked hesitantly.

"Hm. You need anything?" Sana was brusque as she got out of bed and reached for a bottle of Scotch.

"Nothing. I am playing at the college today, at an art festival." She tilted her head towards the case holding her Carlo Lamberti violin. "Will you come?" she asked, already knowing the answer.

"No, you go ahead. Have a busy day today. Another time maybe?" Sana dismissed it and lit a slim cigarette. As Aliya was beginning to turn away, Sana said, "By the way, next month there is a violin workshop in Vienna. Would you like to attend? I could ask Tracy at the office to organize everything."

"It would be difficult," Aliya shook her head. "I have lectures to attend and the second semester starts next month. Remember, I told you?"

"Hmm. Okay." This was the only response Aliya could elicit from Sana. Aliya turned and walked out of her mother's room—a familiar pattern since her return from London.

Sana sighed with relief and gulped down the neat peg of single malt out of the crystal tumbler. Then she switched on the TV, which was already tuned to *India Truth*—a leading news channel which she had painstakingly built into a name synonymous with credible reporting. As if on cue, her mobile phone chirped with an incoming message and she smiled. The prime-time slot the previous night had once again topped the target rating point charts. *India Truth* boasted of shows that garnered phenomenal TRPs on a regular basis. But it had all come at a cost.

For Sana Sikander Sheikh, it had been a long journey, over a decade and a half, from the charming, unpolluted alleys of Kashmir to Delhi's vicious power corridor. And her only child, Aliya had grown up at various expensive boarding schools, before leaving for London University as a young adult.

Sana looked at herself in her bathroom mirror and saw a face with fading beauty, hardened by the rigors of time and betrayal. But there was no anger or disappointment in it, only acceptance. She pulled herself out of her thoughts and called her driver.

"Get the car out in 20 minutes. Have to visit the minister's office first," she ordered and then busied herself with selecting the ensemble for the power-packed day ahead. The less she thought about herself, the better it was for her.

6

Meera looked up from her phone and clucked disapprovingly. Shezii had promised to meet her at the main hall at 9:00 a.m. sharp but there was no sign of him. Meera Bakshi, daughter of a senior IFS bureaucrat, Rajeev Bakshi and granddaughter of a retired Army General, had been taught punctuality before she was out of diapers. But it was a virtue unknown to her childhood friend Shezii. She still remembered him smiling at her broadly with braces on his teeth, when he had first visited their house almost a decade ago along with Shaziya Aunty. Even back then, as a keen little girl, she had found his strange foreign accent very intriguing. The braces and accent both were long gone, but that open charming smile still had the same effect on her.

She glanced morosely at the surging crowd of visiting students from other colleges. They were here to attend the popular college festival MeRIT, an apt acronym devised from Madhav Raje Institute of Technology, associated with the premium Madhav Raje University in Delhi. A final-year student of architectural engineering at MRIT, Meera hated what the crowds did to the peaceful and serene campus of her college. She impatiently scanned the crowd once again for Shezii. Across the crowd, he had spotted her already. With her tall ramp-worthy figure and peaches and cream complexion, Meera was hard to miss. Shezii smiled mischievously as he typed a message and pushed the send icon before starting to move towards her.

Meera's phone beeped with a cryptic message from Shezii. *Gonna be late. You go ahead.* They were late for the lecture. *Where was he?* As she looked up from her phone, she saw him scurrying towards her through the crowd and her heart lifted.

"Hey!" Shezii was breathless by the time he reached Meera. He smiled sheepishly as she held up her phone questioningly.

"Damn! You and your pranks. Come on, we are already late." She started hurrying towards the lecture hall.

"By the way, the lecture venue has been changed to hall number seven. It's that way." He pointed in the opposite direction with an impish grin.

"What? Really?" Meera eyed him closely, half suspecting another prank.

"Don't worry your smart head, I just checked the updated notice board on the way here." He flashed a teasing smile.

"But tell me, why this sudden interest in Dr. Kamran Khan's lecture. Can't believe *you* want to attend a lecture by a visiting faculty. You do know we are missing two regular lectures to attend this one," Meera changed the subject.

"Come on, the guy is a PhD in ancient architecture. He is the Robert Langdon of the subject."

Shezii smiled and continued, "By the way, do you know the topic of today's lecture?"

"Of course, The Era of Exotic Architecture between Nineth and Eleventh Century," she answered innocently.

"Interestingly, the era coincides with the golden era of Islamic architecture."

"So? What's the problem with that?"

"Nothing, as long as one remembers that it's not possible to turn back time. If some people think they can bring back the Islam of the seventh century, then they must understand that it can only be done by looking forward. And with an open mind."

"Shezii, how long will you keep locking horns with people over religion? Why don't you just let it go?" She knew of the Tel Aviv incident and how it had affected Shezii, even though he stubbornly refused to acknowledge it.

"I don't lock horns with everybody, Meera. But yes, closet extremists worry me. Especially if they have political aspirations and a large band of followers."

"What do you mean? *Professor* Kamran Khan?"

"Yes, our esteemed lecturer for today. He's floating a new political party. Have you read or heard any of his discourses online? He sounds progressive and reasonable, but there is always a subtle appeal about 'injustice, exploitation and suppression' aimed at the minorities. You know, that usual victim card. And nothing riles up a group of people more than the idea of being wronged."

"So, then, why do you want to attend his lecture?" Meera frowned.

"Well, no harm in having a little bit of fun while we learn. Come on, I want to be on one of the front benches." He chuckled and picked up the pace.

"Oh no, Shezii! Don't you dare do it again," Meera exclaimed, her eyes widening as she hurried after him.

7

The lecture hall was buzzing with excitement as students murmured among themselves. Finally, Professor Kamran Khan turned to face the audience, his arms folded. It was a sign that he was ready to begin and silence descended upon the class.

Dr. Khan had an imposing personality. He was popular with students for his interesting style of discourse and his vast knowledge on the subject of architecture. His lectures were always packed to capacity and today was no exception. He surveyed the lecture room once, as if he owned it and then started, "Good morning everybody! As you all know, today we will be discussing exotic architecture between the nineth and eleventh century."

Shezii raised his hand.

Dr. Khan chuckled, "I haven't even begun and there are questions already. I am going to love this class." Only nervous laughter met his response.

"Yes, young man?"

"Dr. Khan, sir, are we going to exclusively discuss Islamic architecture today? I was curious, it wasn't mentioned explicitly in the summary." Shezii asked the question with a straight face but Meera instinctively shifted in her seat next to him. They had managed to squeeze into the third row.

"Yes, because the era we are discussing was primarily known for the rise of Islamic architecture," the professor replied coolly and turned his attention to the class. "Let's begin with the Abbasid dynasty consisting of Arab, Egyptian and Persian lands. It's where the Islamic architecture thrived, until," he paused, "it was invaded by the Mongols around 1258, which caused the fall of the Abbasid dynasty and destruction of Islamic architecture largely."

Shezii's hand went up again and Dr. Khan nodded, although sternly.

"But wasn't Islamic architecture, to begin with, influenced by Persian, Roman, Byzantine and other lands conquered by Muslims in the seventh and eighth centuries?"

"Yes, such influences can be seen in some places," Dr. Khan said impatiently.

"Pardon me, sir, do you then mean to say that Islamic architecture wasn't original?"

"No, I certainly do not mean that." Dr. Khan glared at him. "In fact, it was unique in its subtle and artistic nuances. Which reminds me of the beautiful decorative art technique used in Islamic architecture called the arabesque. A very complicated technique with twisting patterns of vines, flowers, leaves or even geometric patterns that were carved in stone during that period."

Dr. Khan had curtly deflected Shezii's observation but Shezii was not ready to let go. Not yet at least. This time he intervened without permission.

"Was the exclusive use of flowers, leaves and geometric patterns due to religious reasons? Because the Prophet had warned the artists to not make images of living things, lest they may imitate the creator Himself?"

"You seem to have some keen insight into the subject, young man. What's your name?" Dr. Khan changed his tack. He knew he had a troublemaker in the class.

"Shezii ... uh, Shahzaib Umer Naqvi," Shezii hurriedly added after Meera nudged him in the ribs.

"Well, you have made a relevant point, Mr. Naqvi."

"But doesn't that curb free thinking? I mean, the head of the largest group of followers of that time, the Prophet himself, had instructed them to not think out of the box. Isn't that the cause of decline of any socio-cultural structure or religion for that matter? When you stop thinking, you stop growing. I would have expected a far more progressive outlook from the world's youngest religion at that time." Shezii smirked.

"That is a subject for an entirely different discussion, Mr. Naqvi," Dr. Khan said frostily. "This presentation is not about religion. But while we are at it, let me assert that societies and religions decay and decline when more powerful forces trample on and destroy them." Dr. Khan's good-natured humor was vanishing swiftly.

"Are those powerful forces also responsible for Islam parting ways with science?" Shezii responded in a level tone. "Is that the reason the numbers of scientists and engineers are so low in Muslim countries? Or is it that the Muslim world is still largely stuck with the directives given in the seventh century? Just making an observation, Dr. Khan. I apologize for my interjection."

Shezii sat down, conscious of the furtive glances coming his way from across the lecture room. His message had been delivered.

"Well Mr. Naqvi, I believe you have made your point, although entirely irrelevant to today's subject." Outwardly calm, Dr. Kamran Khan was seething inside with an anger he could not afford to display. "You have quite efficiently wasted a lot of my time. May I now request you to leave my class?" He pointed towards the door.

The class was silent. Nobody moved.

"Mr. Shahzaib, please. I would like to get back to my presentation." Dr. Khan looked serious.

Meera stared ahead expressionlessly and Shezii smiled at her discomfort. Then, he collected his stuff and sauntered out of the lecture hall.

Meera watched him walk out while Dr. Khan resumed his discourse with gusto. But he had lost his natural tempo and, for the first time in his teaching career, his lecture room was edgy and unresponsive.

8

As he exited the lecture hall, Shezii allowed himself a soft chuckle. He had wanted to needle the professor but hadn't anticipated such fireworks. He paused in the quiet, empty corridor and checked his watch. There was still time for the next lecture, so he decided to tackle a long-pending visit to the library.

He was about to turn when he heard the faint sound of music emanating from the far end of the corridor. It was an instrumental piece played on a violin. He wasn't much into classical music but what he heard sounded beautifully sad, like an angel's lament. It was the kind of music that willed you to stay and listen to its story. Shezii knew he had to meet the musician.

He followed the music to the main auditorium where MeRIT's performances were being held. But the music didn't sound amateurish, it sounded like a maestro's rendition. As he entered the auditorium, he was spellbound. A wraithlike girl—almost too delicate to carry the weight of the powerful music she was creating—played the violin as if in a trance. Dressed in a black off-shoulder gown with matching black opera gloves, she looked like a beautiful painting in motion. Her piece ended to deafening applause. Shezii stood mesmerized, charmed by the girl's self-conscious smile. And then he turned and almost bumped into Meera who had sneaked out of the lecture to follow him there.

"Who is she?" he spoke softly, as if to himself.

"No idea," Meera responded, eyeing the musician curiously.

9

Dr. Kamran Khan walked purposefully towards the office of the university's vice-chancellor, Anandita Devi. He was already running late for the Haj Committee's board meeting but his reason for meeting the vice-chancellor was far more important. He got there just in time to witness an awkward situation. Anandita Devi was telling off an aging custodian, who Dr. Khan recognized as the meek, long-time head librarian of the university. The mousy man left, his eyes glued to the floor. Dr. Khan knew enough to know that Anandita Devi wasn't going to allow the inefficacies of a low-life to affect her chances of soon becoming the chancellor of the university.

"Bad timing," Dr. Khan muttered softly to himself. But without losing a beat, he flashed a charming smile at the secretary who was watching the scene avidly. She quickly buzzed the intercom, "Ma'am, Dr. Kamran Khan is here."

"Send him in please," came the prompt reply.

Dr. Khan breezed into Anandita Devi's office.

"Hello, Dr. Khan." She got up and shook hands with him. "How was your class? A big hit as usual?" She smiled, adjusting the perfectly pinned *pallu* of her designer cotton sari.

"I cannot take all the credit. The students here are quite enthusiastic," he smiled back, remembering his pesky interrupter.

"Do have a seat. Would you like some tea?" She poured him a cup from the silver service beside her.

"Thank you," he said, accepting the cup.

"You were saying about your class?" she prodded.

"If only all my other efforts were met with such enthusiasm."

"What happened, Dr. Khan? I hope everything is on track for your political venture."

"Oh yes, it is. But you know how it is in politics. It's a tricky game."

"Well, I can't say that I understand this tricky game called politics." She sat back.

"In my opinion, everybody understands politics. Humans love to plan, plot and polarize. What is that, if not politics?" He paused to smile. "The only other structure that allows them to do this methodically is religion."

"Hmm interesting point. So what is it for you? Politics or religion?" She was ready to challenge him.

"Ananditaji, actually I am here to seek your support," he expertly deflected.

"My support? I have no political experience and you know that."

"That's hardly an issue. How does a Member of Parliament seat sound to you?" He peered at her.

"Dr. Khan, I appreciate your herculean attempt to launch a new political party. But I think even the established opposition can forget about being elected into power next term." She was unimpressed by the offer.

"We don't want to form the government. We just want to create a voice that can't be ignored." He continued with a knowing smile. "We are talking of minorities, Ananditaji. We have powerful minorities in our country. Yet, no one is representing their concerns. You yourself have a diverse youth body under your control. Do you not owe it to them?"

"Your point being?" Her academic mind was curious now.

"People constantly need an issue to discuss and debate about. And they love to form opinions."

"And I imagine that you would want that opinion to be against the ruling government."

"Yes. We can correct all the wrongs in society only if we have the 'power' of the 'position'."

"How can I be of help?" The words power and position had piqued her interest. Political muscle would surely aid in her run for chancellor.

"Right now, we need all the support we can get. And you are already sitting on a powerhouse." Dr. Khan sensed that he had made the crucial breakthrough with the vice-chancellor of Madhav Raje University.

"What do you mean?"

"The strength of the student body."

"Dr. Khan, I am sure you are not looking for a voter base, because the numbers here won't excite you."

"You are an incredibly smart woman, Ananditaji, but not all games are about numbers."

He knew that the fish had caught the bait. Anandita Devi was right about one thing—he wasn't looking for a voter base. Madhav Raje University, in the heart of Delhi, the political headquarters of the nation, pulsed with raw energy, like a powerful sleeping beast. And he had big plans for it.

10

The guard shut the hood of the Mercedes with a bang and Sana winced from the sound of it. He cross-checked the license plates once again with the register in his hands. Finally, with one last scrutinizing look at the occupant of the car, he nodded at Sana's driver. Sana took a deep breath as the car rolled into the heavily guarded residence of the Union Minister of Defense, Arjun Jaisinghani. She got out of the car outside the main residence entrance and absentmindedly responded to the head of security's crisp greeting.

For the first time that day, Sana smiled. She had spotted Prasanna, personal secretary to Jaisinghani, approaching to receive her. His appearance this early meant that she would not have to wait too long for her meeting with the minister.

"Good morning, ma'am. Come, he is waiting for you." Prasanna turned and led her across the long corridor to the main residence. He was a short, nondescript man, but he was one of the rare, honest ones in the world of politics. She had instinctively liked him when they had met for the first time, almost a decade ago. He was an old-timer with Jaisinghani.

Sana followed him closely, even though she knew the way to the main guest room from her numerous previous visits. But, she also knew she had to follow protocol while visiting a union minister, even if it was in his residence.

Just as Prasanna had said, Union Minister Arjun Jaisinghani, dressed in a crisp cream-colored kurta and brown jacket, was already seated in the guest room waiting for her. His face broke into a smile as he looked up from the file he was browsing through.

"Sana, my dear, where have you been? *Aao baitho.*" He gestured at the sofa across from him.

"Recent months have been very hectic, *bhai sahab.*" Sana frowned and added, "But, you seem to have lost weight. *Rajneeti ka pressure*?"

"No, no, nothing like that. You worry too much, Sana." He chuckled.

"I can't believe it's the Union Minister of Defense saying this to me. You need to take care of your health now."

"What do you mean, *now*? Do you mean I am getting old? What do they say nowadays—50 is the new 40 or something like that?"

"*Arre baba,* I meant with the added responsibility of the Defense portfolio."

"I agree. The previous portfolios of Information & Broadcasting or even External Affairs were a cakewalk compared to Defense."

"I guess they couldn't find a tougher cookie than you to handle it."

"Our government is under tremendous pressure, Sana, due to both external and internal factors. If I can be of any help, in any way, to serve the nation and the party, then I won't back off."

"Always the nice, modest man." Sana pursed her lips.

"Anyway, we shall discuss all that later. So, tell me, did you get it?" He spoke conspiratorially, making sure that Prasanna was still at the far end of the hall, busy in a discussion with some officials.

"You are going to get me into a lot of trouble with Prasanna one of these days. You know you are not allowed all this." Sana sighed and pulled out a small box from her tote bag. "Here are your favorite besan laddoos. And you are getting them only because of this," Sana held up a delicate rakhi. Jaisinghani plopped a laddoo in his mouth and extended his right hand. He beamed at her as Sana tied the rakhi on his wrist. "Next time, make sure you don't miss the day," she chided him.

"Thanks to the Home Ministry, Kashmir is now top priority. So, when Pakistan's External Affairs Secretary chose Raksha Bandhan to visit for talks ..." He shook his head regretfully. "I could not say no. Or the opposition would have pounced on us, citing 'lack of dialogue' as the cause of all the trouble in Kashmir."

"What is going on with the party and government? I hear religion is the new buzzword with the opposition," Sana asked sardonically.

"You tell me," laughed Jaisinghani. "Television is the new religion and media rules. People form political opinions in their drawing rooms, right in front of their TV set sand mobile screens."

"Oh, come on, you know that's a very small percentage of your voter base. But the opposition is labeling Jagrut Bharat Party as a pro-Hindu party."

"Honestly Sana, this doesn't bother me too much. Just talk to any grassroots voter for a few minutes—all they want is a better life and equal opportunity. Religion is just an easy weapon to use." He sighed. "This is a development and progress-oriented government. People will eventually see it, as they experience the positive results."

"But that will be in the long term and we need to start preparing for its next term now. The opposition is already accusing JBP and its coalition government of overlooking the minorities and its rights. I think the party should issue a statement clarifying its stand on religion-based issues."

"See, that's the problem. If we don't talk about religion, we are avoiding the subject and playing it safe. If we talk about religion, we are trying to influence the innocent masses." He smiled wryly. "But the fact remains that this government has not issued any policy or passed a single law that exclusively benefits Hindus."

"Hm, do you know of Dr. Kamran Khan, head of the Aware Indian Muslim, or AIM? It's a social service and awareness organization."

"Of course I know Kamran, and also that he has plans to float a political party soon. And he has my best wishes if he intends to do good for the citizens of this country."

"Well, he is planning to keep Delhi as his base. And he will attack JBP and its coalition on minority issues. He wants to establish credibility fast. And the best way to do it is to discredit others. He already has substantial support and is working hard to get like-minded organizations together."

"Such boutique political parties have no long-term agenda to offer, Sana. They are mostly driven by personal motives. They eventually fizzle out." Arjun Jaisinghani exuded calm. He wasn't one to react instinctively. Reclining on his couch, he almost looked like a powerful feline.

Sana replied, "I know, but I hate this religion-based, divisive politics they play. It only causes death and destruction."

"Do you know something I don't?" Jaisinghani asked thoughtfully.

"Nothing for sure, but the religious divide in the country is fast widening, thanks to people like Dr. Kamran Khan. My instincts are telling me he is up to something."

"If he is, we will find out."

"I hope it's not too late by then."

Jaisinghani's hawk-like eyes peered at Sana, but he chose not to comment. A powerful man himself, he respected the strength Sana Sikander Sheikh carried within her, even though the circumstances under which she had left Kashmir often came back to haunt her. Anyone else would have buckled under such heavy emotional baggage, but she had chosen to leave it far behind. Or so he thought.

11

Nikki Rajpal blew a kiss at her own reflection in the glass door of her office. *You are the best, Nikki*, she almost said out loud. Her latest television report, exposing a renowned religious guru's nexus with politics, had gone viral with close to three hundred shares and more than ten thousand likes within hours of being aired. Nikki was damn good at what she did—investigative features and live reporting on politics. She was youthful and easy on camera and had a knack for sniffing out political scoops. For three consecutive years she had been the star performer on *India Truth*, a top-ranking news channel.

It was time to pay a special visit to the boss. Adjusting her perfectly coiffured hairdo, she stepped out of her office and straightened her shoulders. Sana made her more nervous than any camera. Because, unlike the camera, Sana could see through people and Nikki didn't like this one bit.

As she reached Sana Sheikh's cabin, she saw her personal secretary, Tracy, at the front desk, talking animatedly into the phone. She seemed hassled but her easy body language told Nikki that Sana wasn't in the office. Nikki popped a fresh strip of gum in her mouth and approached Tracy.

"Hey Tracy, she isn't in I guess." Nikki gestured at the cabin door.

"Ma'am is expected anytime now. You wanted to meet her?" Tracy had disapproval written all over her face. Nikki knew that Tracy didn't like people chewing gum in the office.

"So, is that property manager in Kashmir giving you grief again?" Nikki asked, casually perching herself on Tracy's desk to irritate her further.

"How did you know?" Tracy was confused.

"Sweetheart, did anyone ever tell you that you get very loud over the phone, especially when you are talking to that Kashmiri jerk." Nikki smirked. "Did you ever ask your ma'am why she still needs to keep that house in Srinagar? She hasn't been there in years and it doesn't seem like she ever intends to. At least allow the staff to visit there for a holiday."

Tracy was mentally preparing a barbed response for Nikki when she spotted Sana entering the office and went quiet. Nikki sensed it too and got off the desk. She swallowed the gum she was chewing and faced Sana as she approached.

"Nikki, good, you are here already. Could you come in for a moment?" Sana spoke airily, nodded at Tracy and Nikki followed Sana into her office.

"Come, sit. You wanted to see me about something?" Sana deposited her mobile and iPad on the large desk.

"Uh … nothing. I was in the office so thought I should drop by," Nikki spoke hurriedly and mentally abandoned her plan to discuss her promotion to bureau chief. Sana always had that effect on her.

"Good, I wanted to give you this. Check it out." Sana pushed an elegant envelope across the table towards Nikki. It was an invite for a formal event, to be held at the prestigious Roshanara Club in South Delhi.

"Dr. Kamran Khan has invited us to his political party's official launch. Since you cover the political beat, it's best you attend it. Just make sure you find a fresh angle for the story you cover."

"This is an interesting development. But won't you be attending?" Nikki's curiousity was piqued.

"It's scheduled for next month. Too early for me to know my travel plans. I will see if I can join at the last moment." Sana was already looking at her phone, scrolling through the contact list. It was a signal that the meeting was over.

Nikki left the cabin smiling. She knew that Sana's aloof response to the invite had to do with her affinity for the current ruling government. But Nikki had been closely following Dr. Kamran Khan's career. He was suave and sophisticated and she often wondered how the young female students reacted to this charming professor of ancient archaeology. Even in his late forties, Dr. Kamran Khan was a tall, good looking man, with sharp features and salt and pepper hair. She looked at the invite again, now excited at the prospect of meeting this charismatic man.

12

Cairo, Egypt
Current Day

As he walked the dusty corridors of the infamous Tora prison in Cairo, Ashraf Shaheen shivered inwardly. The dark memories of numerous years spent in prison made him uneasy. And the 30 feet high walls of this prison, more than a century old, made him feel claustrophobic. He had dedicated his life to fighting for his beliefs and for the principles of Islam, and his jihadi group took good care of him. He didn't know where the money came from or what their connections were but they always got him out to continue his jihad. In return, his life was mortgaged to them and he was ready to willingly forsake it, if asked to.

But thankfully, today he was at the Tora prison only as a visitor. He was there to meet Mustafa Al-Gazzar, the aging head of *Tehrik-e-Islam*, a devout arm of Egyptian Islamic Jihad. In fact, he had been surprised to receive the message asking him to visit Al-Gazzar in prison. It was an unwritten policy that the group's operatives were never to be seen together publicly. He also knew that although Al-Gazzar was the mastermind of the group, his chances of getting out of the Tora prison alive were next to nil.

As they took the next turn, the prison guard escorting him slowed down, pointed towards the end of the corridor and whispered, "That's his cell. You have 15 minutes. Outsiders are not allowed in solitary confinement, so make it quick. I will get you out before the shift changes." The prison guard turned away, busying himself with his phone. He was paid well for the simple task of looking the other way.

Ashraf Shaheen approached the cell tentatively. It was a clean but small rectangular room with high walls and no windows. The only natural light came from a small square opening almost 15 feet up. By the Tora prison standards, notorious for holding up to 30 prisoners in squalid 20 square feet cells, it was almost luxurious. In the corner, propped against the wall, was a walking crutch. Al-Gazzar had lost one of his legs when their secure camp in Lebanon had been bombed by the security forces. It was the only victory *Mukhbarat*, the Egyptian intelligence agency, had enjoyed over Mustafa Al-Gazzar. They had managed to keep him in prison, but this hadn't deterred Al-Gazzar from running his jihadi army and suicide squads from within the prison with equal efficacy.

"*Salaam-Alaikum,*" Ashraf whispered reverently to the old man sitting still on a stone bench facing the wall. Mustafa Al-Gazzar slowly turned his head sideways and Ashraf stiffened. It was believed within the jihadi group that Al-Gazzar had eyes on the back of his head.

"*Wa-Alaikum-Salaam*," he responded, as if in a blessing, and turned towards Ashraf. His bearded face was smiling as if it had nothing to do with the hundreds of jihadi bombings and the death of thousands, including Muslims. Ashraf bowed his head in respect and waited for the leader to continue.

"Welcome. And thank you for coming, Awais Sheikh."

Ashraf Shaheen tensed and his face turned white. Nobody had called him by that name in 15 years, ever since he had left Kashmir and moved to Sudan. He had almost forgotten that Ashraf Shaheen was his acquired Arab identity. The sound of his real name knocked the wind out of him. But Al-Gazzar had his ways.

"Do not worry," Al-Gazzar smiled. "I know everything about you since your Kashmir days. You have been of great service to us, to *Tehrik-e-Islam*."

"*Shukran, sidi* Al-Gazzar," Awais said softly. He still wasn't sure about the purpose of this meeting.

"You have served Allah and Islam very well till now. But I have a special job for you. And your past is the reason I am talking to you." Al-Gazzar paused.

"I am ready for anything."

"Then you have to go back to Hind, to Kashmir." Al-Gazzar gazed at Awais's calm face. But Awais kept quiet and the master continued.

"Your connection to Kashmir is of crucial importance. You know that area very well. We are planning a special operation for *Azaad Kashmir*. And, if everything goes well, this could be your final jihad." He smiled proudly.

"What do you wish me to do?" Awais's voice was resolute. He didn't want to go back. That place had reduced him to a wanted name in the records of most non-Muslim nations' anti-terrorism hit lists. But the call to a final jihad was something he couldn't turn down. It was time to do his final bidding for Allah and become a *shaheed*.

"May his blessings shower upon you," Al-Gazzar pointed a long, slender finger to the heavens and continued with a smile, "Plan your departure for Dilli. You will go as Ashraf Shaheen. Other comrades will join you there soon. Get there and await instructions to activate our sleeper cells."

Awais nodded. "May he keep you in his protection until you achieve your purpose on this mortal earth."

Awais quickly exited the cell and spotted the prison guard pacing impatiently at the other end of the corridor. He whispered urgently, "Let's get out of here quickly." Awais too wanted to get out of there. He wasn't sure if he was ready to face whatever lay on the other side of the door that he had shut tightly so long ago. But he could sense that his story was about to end in the very place where it had begun, a decade and a half ago. Strangely, he felt at peace.

13

"Must say, Sana has done a fantastic job with her news channel," Rajeev Bakshi said, eyeing the crème de la crème of Delhi who had graced the party celebrating another landmark year for *India Truth*.

Faisal raised his glass in agreement and swirled the aged scotch as he assessed the powdered and perfumed crowd spreading over the lawn of Sana's expansive Haus Khaz villa. "She is setting an example. It's tough to be unbiased in today's times and still be a successful media honcho—especially when you are in Delhi."

"Well, not entirely unbiased perhaps?" said a charmingly attired Shaziya. "She has some political clout with the Jagrut Bharat Party. I hear—oh there they are!" she broke off as she spotted Meera and Shezii.

The three turned to see their children engaging in banter with a group of other youngsters. To their adoring eyes, Meera and Shezii formed the most beautiful couple.

Faisal mused, "Can't believe it's been a decade since we moved back to Delhi. They've both grown up so fast."

Both friends were quiet for a beat as their thoughts were drawn to the Tel Aviv incident. By tacit agreement, they never discussed it. But Rajeev knew how it had affected the Naqvi family.

"By the way, Sana has a daughter," remarked Shaziya, trying to lighten the moment. "She just told me. With such a pretty name too—Aliya. She has just transferred from King's College, London to Shezii and Meera's university."

"Didn't know Sana had a daughter!" Rajeev said, surprised.

"Now, how did you miss *that* bit of info, Rajeev?" Faisal chuckled.

Even though they were now in their late 40s and placed in high-ranking bureaucratic posts, Rajeev and Faisal's relationship had remained strong. While Faisal had quit his bureaucratic career for good after the Tel Aviv incident, he still served on various panels on international affairs. Rajeev Bakshi was currently Additional Secretary with the Ministry of External Affairs, heading India's counter-terrorism division.

"They are all in their final year. And guess what, Aliya also teaches violin to fellow students as part of an exchange program."

"She sounds talented," said Faisal, taking another sip from his glass.

At the far end of the lawn Shezii, tired of the bonhomie, was looking for an opportunity to make an exit. He spotted Aliya. All evening he had been stealing glances at the mysterious girl but she was constantly surrounded by people, smiling politely at the unending number of guests. She looked almost ethereal, in a pastel pink full-length gown that enhanced her delicate frame.

Finally, as Aliya took to an empty seat, looking grim and resigned, Shezii found his opportunity.

He walked up to her, smiling. "Hello," he said in a low voice, settling down next to her.

Aliya eyed him warily. Her "Hi" was dismissive and she looked away.

"You play the violin beautifully."

"Is that so?" said Aliya in a tone she hoped would discourage him from further conversation.

"I saw you perform at MeRIT. We are in the same college. I am Shezii." He extended a hand.

She ignored it.

"Oh Aliya, there you are!" came Sana's voice. Aliya looked up to see her glittering mother bearing down on her with her coterie. "Everyone, come meet my wonderful daughter, Aliya. She's just back from London."

Shezii and Aliya rose as the group formed a bubble around them.

"We hear you play the violin very well, Aliya?" an elderly man said politely.

Shezii watched Aliya squirm.

"Play us a piece," exclaimed the gentleman. "Yes, play for us Aliya," chorused the other voices.

Shezii saw Aliya's eyes light up. She was about to respond when her mother lay a restraining hand on her shoulder. "Now, now, I didn't bring you here to bully my pet. She's a bit shy you know, unless she's on stage, and then she is fantastic. Positively electric!" And Sana was already moving away.

Aliya's eyes dimmed even as she continued to smile like a doll. She turned her gaze as her mother herded the disappointed group away to the next attraction.

Shezii waited till they were alone again.

"Will you play now? Your music is like magic."

Aliya turned and stared at the only person left by her side. Shezii saw something strong and wild in her deeply defiant eyes. *Just like a caged bird.*

"I am tired. I need to call it a night," she said flatly.

With that she got up and walked away, leaving Shezii alone, staring blankly after her receding figure.

From a distance, Meera watched the scene unfold. Her heart felt as if it was being squeezed. When Aliya had vanished inside the house, she approached Shezii with an overly bright smile.

"Hey, you ready to leave? I am kind of done here."

Shezii got up with a nod and she held onto his arm. Together they moved towards the gate, their hearts crushed by the weight of their own expectations.

14

Aliya called her driver's cell phone once again and was met with the same audio message. The phone was switched off. She called her mother but disconnected before the call could go through. Typical. The only thing Aliya appreciated about her mother was her brutal honesty in telling her about her father leaving them. Sometimes Aliya wondered if both of them would keep punishing each other for a mistake committed by someone who had long been out of the picture. That was the price one paid for being foolishly in love. Aliya had resolved never to fall prey to such fallacies, and it was one rule she was unlikely to break.

She looked around the college campus impatiently. Her lectures for the day were over and she had cancelled the violin class due to low attendance. She started walking towards the college canteen to wait but immediately regretted having the violin case with her, which attracted unnecessary attention. Aliya was never comfortable with attention. She preferred the anonymity of her life in London and was still coming to terms with being in the social spotlight in Delhi due to her mother's professional life.

The canteen was almost empty, with only a few groups spread out across the hall. The low voices echoed across the room as she got herself a chilled can of Diet Coke from the counter and settled at a corner table. She was deeply engrossed in her phone when there was a tap on her table. She looked up to find three guys standing in front of her table, blocking it from three sides. Despite their aggressive body language, they were smiling at her.

"Helloji, I am Krishna Sahu, student leader of Madhav Raje College. You seem to be new here." The aggressor held his polite smile. He was dressed simply and looked like any other student. Only his age didn't seem to match.

"Yes, I just got admission this year." Aliya was cold and aloof, hoping to quickly end the conversation.

"You didn't tell us your name. See, I introduced myself with my name." His loud laugh reverberated across the room.

"Aliya Sheikh," she answered and looked back down at her phone.

"Oh, Sheikh *sahiba*, do you play this or is it just for show?" Krishna Sahu pointed at her violin case.

"Yes, I do play." Aliya's staccato answers were beginning to bother Krishna Sahu who was used to polite respect from students.

"How about strumming a few strings for us?"

"Violin is played with a bow, not fingers. This is not a guitar." Aliya's irritation was beginning to surface.

"Yeah sure, whatever," he guffawed and sat down at her table without an invitation. His flunkies continued to stand. Aliya started collecting her things to leave.

"Sit down, Sheikh *sahiba*, let's have a chat. What's the hurry? Aren't you the daughter of that famous channel owner?" Krishna Sahu's smile had lost its benign quality.

Aliya was about to retort when suddenly Shezii breezed in and sat down next to Krishna Sahu. He spoke brightly, "Hello Krishna, how are you, buddy?" He patted him and continued, "Haven't seen you around since the college festival." Shezii gestured at the canteen boy for tea and added, "Hey Aliya, I have been looking around for you."

There was an instant change in Krishna Sahu's demeanor as his smile turned friendly, "I was out of town for the last couple of weeks, Shezii *bhai*. You tell me? What's up with my handsome Student of the Year?" he finished with a laugh.

As minutes passed, Aliya watched them talk animatedly, fascinated by the sudden change in the environment. She clearly remembered the strikingly attractive yet reticent guy from her mother's party last weekend. Suddenly, Shezii turned towards her and spoke, "Aliya, are you leaving now? I think I saw your car arrive. If I could get a lift with you ..." He smiled, his expression requesting her to comply.

Aliya slowly got up from the table, her manner a bit subdued. Krishna Sahu too got up and said, respectfully, "Sheikh *sahiba*, if you ever need anything, please let me know. Krishna Sahu will be at your service. You are after all our Shezii's friend." Aliya nodded at him and even mustered half a smile. And after a few more pleasantries between Krishna and Shezii, they walked out of the canteen together.

Neither of them spoke for a while until Aliya mumbled, without looking in Shezii's direction, "I would have handled him myself."

"I know," Shezii said simply.

"I don't need your help." This time her voice was sharp.

Shezii chose to ignore the bait. Instead he asked, "Where's your driver?"

Remembering her predicament, Aliya pulled out her phone and redialed the number. The monotonous message repeated itself. She sighed.

"He may be a while yet."

She and Shezii stood awkwardly in the empty parking lot.

"Do you have a place around here? Like where you can be yourself?" asked Aliya restlessly.

Shezii was lost momentarily but recovered quickly. "Yes, I do."

"Don't tell me about it. Just take me there."

"Yes, ma'am!" grinned Shezii. He extended his hand and took the violin case from her.

At the touch of his fingers, Aliya let go instinctively, then grimaced. But Shezii didn't notice. He was already thinking about his favorite place. He couldn't wait to see how Aliya would respond to it.

Together, they walked towards the open wooded area

behind the campus. Not many students ventured into this secluded area and as a result, it was like a patch of wilderness in the middle of the city. After wading through the densely growing shrubs and trees for 15 minutes on a narrow trail, they arrived at a clearing. The cool air smelled of wild flowers. The thick growth of trees around the patch blocked any direct sunlight, muting the natural light and leaving the spot cooler than its surroundings. It was a small circular natural garden, with a charming pond and lilies snuggled in one of its corners. It was already past four in the evening and the birds were chirping happily and the sound of the lightly swaying trees was adding to their music.

Aliya stood mesmerized. Shezii kicked of his shoes and she followed suit eagerly. The grass was velvet soft beneath her feet, dotted with sprigs of white and pink inflorescence.

"You like it? This is my secret place."

"Can we stay here for a little while?" She spoke as if in a trance.

"Yes, of course. But unfortunately, we don't have much time. It's going to be dark soon."

Aliya nodded and walked up to the small pond. She perched herself on a small stone boulder on its shore and dipped her toes past the flowers into the water.

"You said you wanted to hear me play?"

Shezii couldn't believe how his day was turning out. Without a word, he handed over her violin case. Aliya opened the case, lifted her beloved instrument, inhaled deeply and began playing.

The notes were soft yet powerful, transporting him to another realm where time ceased to exist and days and nights were of no consequence. He sat mesmerized in equal measures by her music and her beauty, fighting the immense desire to hold her, drink her in and immerse himself into her. To be one with her.

When she stopped playing, he had no idea of the time. It was past five in the evening. The shadows of the thick trees were darkening and the sound of the birds was fast getting replaced by the shrill ruckus of crickets.

"My car must have arrived by now," Aliya spoke, finally breaking the spell.

Shezii started leading the way back carefully across the dark trail. Twice, Aliya hesitated in the darkness. He casually reached out for her hand to help but she pointedly pulled it away.

"What's the matter?" he asked.

"I told you, I don't need your help," she snapped.

Shezii wasn't sure what he had expected out of this short evening with Aliya, but it had left him pining, almost aching for more.

It would have been fairly easy for him to chase and court a girl who was playing hard to get. Even if it wasn't his style, he would have done it for Aliya. But it was impossible to fight the invisible enemy—the seemingly insurmountable walls of defense she had built around herself. There wasn't a chance of a fair fight here, unless he figured out the reason behind those walls. *One step at a time,* he mentally chided himself.

15

Nikki was thankful for the valet service at Roshanara Club because she was running behind schedule. She grabbed the invite from the glove compartment and hoped the official briefing hadn't already begun. Her camera crew had been calling her every few minutes. Not only was *India Truth* a highly professional network, but she personally wanted to make a good impression on Dr. Kamran Khan. *Thank God Sana isn't attending this event,* she thought.

As she entered the main lobby, she saw, right there, Dr. Kamran Khan. Dressed in a handsome black suit, with a cool, purposeful gait, he looked like a younger George Clooney. As their eyes met, Dr. Khan smiled politely.

"Aren't you Nikki Rajpal from *India Truth*?" He smiled a charming smile.

"Yes," Nikki nodded, practically tongue-tied as her heart thudded loudly.

"Hi. I am Kamran Khan." He extended a hand. "I hope you are here to cover our Aware India Muslim Party event. I was half-sure *India Truth* would give us a miss." He laughed as he held her hand in a masculine grip.

"Oh absolutely not, Dr. Khan! In fact, I was rather

upset just now thinking I might be late," she gushed nervously.

"Well, you're kind of late. But you haven't missed the interesting part, which is me." He winked. "I am up next. See you in the hall." With that, Dr. Khan walked away.

Nikki entered the auditorium and was relieved to see that her team had a prime spot up front. She felt a rush when Dr. Khan nodded at her before starting his speech. He was a gifted speaker and held the crowd in thrall with his well-articulated thoughts on the state of the Indian government and the need for a political party like Aware Indian Muslim—a party that could give voice to the minority community of Indian Muslims. It was time, he thundered, that they became a part of mainstream politics without being apologetic about it. 'Minority' as a tag was no longer justifiable for the Indian Muslim of today. As he ended with this last statement, there was a hearty round of applause. The media representatives clamored to have their questions heard.

"So, Dr. Khan, how did the concept of forming AIM come to you in the current political scenario?" asked a reporter from the crowd.

"Let me start at the beginning." He smiled for the benefit of the camera. "AIM is more than a political party. It is more a sense of awareness and a new form of thinking. And its aim is to bring about corruption-free progress and development in this nation. To build an equal society, without any class- or religion-based discrimination, mind you."

Nikki joined the conversation. "But then why name it Aware Indian Muslim? Doesn't that convey a favorable bent towards a certain religious group?"

"Because we need to be unapologetic about being Muslim. There are so many politically associated Hindu organizations doing fantastic charitable social work, across all classes and segments of India. Nobody ever asks them this question. And you are asking me this question because of the name of my party?"

"Dr. Khan, my question is—are you trying to build a religion-based vote bank?" countered Nikki.

"Oh, come on! I have already said this officially. We need to get out of this deprecatory mindset when it comes to our heritage. There is a considerable Islamic population in India. The time has come to bring it to the mainstream."

A scatter of applause ran through the audience.

"So, you do agree that AIM has been formed on the basic premise of bringing people of a certain religion under one banner, for the sake of politics?" Nikki pressed.

"I am not breaking any rules; I am only breaking mindsets. The democratic structure of this country allows for it. AIM will work towards a balanced and safe society. You will agree that in a secure environment, development is a fast process. Peace and progress go hand in hand." He flashed another debonair smile.

"Are you saying that the current government is not able to maintain a peaceful and secure environment?"

"Did I say that? You are the media, you have all the news," he laughed. "But on a serious note, I do feel that the minorities in our country have been feeling a bit threatened lately. And we need to change that."

"Do you not think that the extremist Islamic outfits worldwide are responsible for this feeling?" pitched in a new reporter.

"I am concerned with the Muslims of India. They are the ones who chose to stick with this nation, back in 1947. Their presence has given our country a unique wealth of culture and belief systems. The Muslims of India are integral to the nation."

Dr. Khan spun and wove around the reporters' questions—a consummate politician, he avoided direct answers. As he wound up his speech, the crowd of socialites and media people dispersed and re-grouped around the cocktail counters. Nikki smiled. It was the first political event she'd seen where they served alcohol. It was the 'liberal' thing to do, and true to the gutsy style of the founder of AIM. As the atmosphere turned informal, Nikki's eyes skimmed the crowd, trying to spot Dr. Khan. She heard her name called and turned to see the man himself, standing with two glasses of white wine in his hands.

"I prefer to start with white. I hope you do as well." He extended a glass to her.

Nikki accepted the glass with a meaningful smile.

"So, how did I do?" he asked, confident of praise.

"I thought you were great!" Nikki responded with a smile. "I wish there were more political leaders with your kind of gumption."

"And I wish there were more journalists with your kind of spark."

He scrutinized her face and continued, "If you weren't in such a good position with *India Truth*, I would have gladly offered you a media relations position with AIM. That too at the price of your asking."

"Thank you for the compliment, Dr. Khan. Yes, *India Truth* is the reason I am here talking to you," she said, brushing imaginary dust off his shoulder.

"I hope Sana Sheikh is doing justice to your talent." He took her hand from his shoulder and kissed it flirtatiously.

Nikki laughed away the back-handed offer Dr. Khan had made. Her career was at a sensitive stage, and one wrong move would unravel it completely. All the hard work she had put in over the past few years would be thrown away for nothing. She wasn't going to risk it so easily.

Dr. Khan gazed shrewdly at her. He needed more people like Nikki on his side. She was young, sharp and had a large following. And, she was falling in love with him. He smiled enigmatically, preparing to exert himself in pursuit of his prey.

16

Hey! So are you coming to Jaipur? Shezii finally mustered the courage to send the message to Aliya. The lecture hall was already buzzing with students. He fidgeted nervously with his phone until he spotted Meera making her way through the hall towards him. He couldn't help but notice the number of heads turning in her direction. It had taken him a while to get used to the way other guys reacted to her every single time she passed by. But he also knew that they could not possibly appreciate her for all she was. She was perfect in every sense—the kind of friend you would want by your side for eternity.

Shezii smiled at Meera but was met with a frosty glare. Dropping her journal on the desk, she sat down beside him and hissed, "I can't believe you took her to our spot!"

It took Shezii a few moments to register what she was saying and he looked at her, speechless.

"The canteen boy told me he saw you two come out of the woods at the back of the college."

"What? Oh no, no. It's nothing like that. She wanted to play her violin, alone. I just accompanied her," he spoke hurriedly.

"Shezii, it's not about what you were doing there with her. You and I also go there to just study. But it was our exclusive, secret spot. Didn't we agree not to tell anyone about it?"

"I went with Aliya only because she seemed very sad and lonely," Shezii said guiltily. It had indeed been thoughtless of him. And lying to Meera now didn't make him feel any better. Just then his phone pinged. Both of them automatically looked at the screen. It was a text message from Aliya, simply saying *Yes*.

What timing! groaned Shezii inwardly.

Meera searched Shezii's face for a few moments. She was curious about this girl who Shezii seemed so taken with. She spoke as if coming to a conclusion, "Look, why don't you ask her to join us for that Jaipur architectural study tour. It's open to students from all streams. We will get to know each other better. Maybe we can even become friends."

"Seriously?" Shezii eyed her warily, not revealing that he had already made the suggestion to Aliya—and had already received an answer.

"Yeah, she's new after all. And you say she's sad and lonely? Perhaps she's having trouble adjusting. A trip will be good for her. She might find friends among our lot."

Even as she spoke, Meera felt a deep yawning emptiness threaten to engulf her. She had wanted Shezii all to herself! They had been inseparable for so long, he was a given in her life. Now some random woman was threatening their bond? *What the hell are you doing, Meera?* She kicked herself for extending the invitation.

No, this is good, said another voice in her brain. *Know thine enemy*. She would see what this Aliya was made of. Meera made a show of getting busy setting up her notes for the lecture, not looking in Shezii's direction.

On the other end of campus, in the quiet confines of the library, Aliya was facing her own dilemma. She stared at her phone, which lay in silent mode on the table. She picked it up and looked again at Shezii's invitation to a weekend trip. With friends, as he promised.

Aliya ran her hands through her hair. It's just what a guy would say. Why had she agreed? *He's sweet, sensitive and handsome—nothing like other guys,* replied her traitorous mind.

But it wasn't just that. Shezii had been texting her constantly since their evening together. *Romantic evening,* whispered her irrepressible inner voice.

She sat up resolutely. She had to cut this off, once and for all, and let him know that there was no space in her life for any love interest.

Aliya rang his number.

"Hi, Aliya?" Shezii's voice was a mixture of hope and disbelief.

Aliya couldn't repress a small smile. Then she shook herself mentally and said, "Yeah, it's me. Hi. Listen, um, about the trip ..."

Sensing a rejection, Shezii cut in, "I'm so glad you agreed. It's gonna be a great tour. Meera and I are starting out from my place. Do you wanna meet us there?"

"Oh," said Aliya, taken aback by the curve ball. "You see, about that—"

"She's really looking forward to meeting you, you know," Shezii cut in again. "We both want to get to know you better."

"There is nothing more to know than what you already know. I am Sana Sheikh's daughter, I play the violin very well, and I have returned from London to complete my computer engineering here."

There was a short pause.

"I want to know why your eyes are sad even when you smile," Shezii said softly.

"Listen Shezii, I am not looking for any emotional entanglements."

"I know. I just want us to be friends. Can we work on that?"

"I can't promise anything."

"Hey, it's just a weekend study tour, a beautiful old city, a group of chums from college. How about giving this friendship a try?"

"I will have to check my pending assignments and I also have to ask my mom," Aliya stalled, as her heart and head sparred with each other.

"That's great. It's best if you come over to my place in the morning. We'll all grab some breakfast and set out together."

Aliya realized after she hung up that Shezii had more or less assumed she was going. Well, at least there'll be plenty of time on the trip to set him straight.

But she had already started thinking of reasons to not go. Her only challenge was to stick to them. She didn't want to add more chaos to her already complicated life. He was a good guy. And she knew she wasn't ready to handle *good*.

17

Sana punched in the programming head's extension and impatiently waited for the call to go through. As per the program chart in front of her, Aware Indian Muslim's launch event capsule was scheduled to be aired at 9:00 p.m. that evening. This primetime slot was always reserved for the panel debate by their star news anchor and was never disturbed unless there was breaking news of national or international significance. Kamran Khan's pre-recorded event did not qualify on either count. Finally, a harried sounding voice answered.

"Hello, Shanbag?" Sana barked into the phone.

"Yes, Sana," the programming head answered pointedly. Sana never intervened in his job unless it was something important.

"Did you put AIM's launch event into the prime slot?"

"No, *you* did."

"What do you mean?"

"Well, that's what Nikki told me," he answered cautiously.

"Nikki? She asked you to put it in the *primetime* slot? At *my* behest?"

"Yes. Is there a problem? I can put it on hold and replace it, if necessary. The telecast is still three hours away."

"Yes, let's move it to one of the feature slots in the morning. Show me what you've got to replace it. And Shanbag, in the future, please speak to me before changing the primetime piece." Sana disconnected the phone and immediately dialed her secretary. "Tracy, please ask Nikki to see me now."

Sana tapped her pen impatiently and stared at her phone. After a beat, she picked it up and called Aliya's number. But as expected there was no reply. Lately, Sana had hardly seen her daughter at home. She wondered if Aliya was deliberately avoiding her. Sana had once ignored her brother's prolonged absences from home with dire results. She wasn't going to make that same mistake with her daughter. She was lost in thought when there was a knock on the door and Nikki entered.

"Nikki, did you ask Shanbag to air Dr. Khan's event at primetime today?" Sana did not ask Nikki to sit.

"Yes, I did." Nikki hesitated and then continued, "I think he spoke quite well on behalf of the minorities."

"Prime slots are fixed and can be changed only in case of big, breaking news and ... on my instructions alone," Sana emphasized, staring hard at Nikki.

Nikki chose to stay quiet.

"Next time, please seek my permission before airing anything pertaining to Dr. Khan or AIM. Am I making myself clear?" Sana's voice was low but stern.

"Yes, I understand," Nikki answered timidly.

"Please send me the details of all the stories you intend to cover in the next fortnight." Nikki simply nodded in response and exited the cabin without another word.

Sana stared after her. Nikki was always a challenge to handle. She was fiery and unruly, with little respect for authority or norms, and her talent came with the baggage of unpredictability. Sana had barely managed to keep Nikki in line all these years.

Uneasy, Sana dialed Arjun Jaisinghani. The call was answered by Prasanna, who immediately took the phone to the minister.

"Hello Sana, how are you? I hope you aren't calling with some breaking news." The Minister of Defense answered in his usual relaxed tone.

"Nothing so bad, but nothing too good either. Dr. Kamran Khan's press interview launching AIM will be going on air soon. I'm sending a preview link to your private email. Will you take a look? Something feels off, though I can't quite put my finger on it."

"Thanks for this, Sana but I already know what he has been talking about." He spoke casually and Sana could hear the smile in his voice.

"You mean his claims about the government's inability to maintain a safe and peaceful environment? Or that he's playing the minority card and attracting a lot of support?" Sana persisted.

"He is already feeling the pressure. He doesn't have a clear objective or agenda and it is making him desperate. Obfuscation and attack are his best defense, you see. And I have no issues with him playing the minority card, as long as his endgame is the betterment of his people, who are after all Indian citizens."

"I don't know Arjunji, my gut says there's something fishy and he's catfooting all around it. He *sounds* liberal and *talks* of social causes, but then he creates a political party with a religious bent?"

"It's alright, Sana. Don't worry. Whatever he is planning to do, let it play out. We can't stop him, but I will be keeping a close eye on AIM and Dr. Khan."

"You mean he is under surveillance?" Sana quizzed, a little surprised.

Jaisinghani laughed jovially at the other end. "Oh no, no, no. Of course not. That would be illegal. All the same, we'll know if he's up to something. At the moment Sana, he may just be a good guy who wants to work for his community."

"His political move is too sudden yet too well-planned for that. I am curious to know, how is he planning to fund his party?"

"Ever the skeptic, Sana." Jaisinghani laughed again. "Just wait and watch. If I have any updates, I will let you know. By the way, how is Aliya doing?"

"She is fine and busy with her computers and violin. But ever since she came back, she has been kind of withdrawn. She hardly talks to me," Sana lamented.

"It's okay, she is a young adult now. It's a phase and she will come out of it. Her childhood wasn't perfect and you know it, Sana. After years of being away from her for the sake of a career, you of all people shouldn't be complaining. Just give her some time." He paused and added as an afterthought, "Maybe you two should take a holiday together."

"Hm. Sounds like a good idea."

Sana hung up and looked thoughtfully at the phone. Then she tried Aliya's number again.

The phone connected and Aliya's cool voice said, "Yes?"

"Aliya? Are you in a lecture? Am I disturbing you?" Sana asked, feeling oddly defensive.

"No, I am done for the day," Aliya's reply was almost irritable.

"Oh great! I was worried. I tried calling you so many times, but you never answered."

"I must have been in class."

"And by the time I get home, you'll most likely have retired for the day. That's what the servants have been telling me for the last I-don't-know-how-many days."

"Yeah, I've been feeling a bit tired lately," Aliya said off-handedly.

"You need a change of scene. We both do. How about a week-long trip to Bali? I have everything planned. The weekend after next there's the International Music Conclave happening there. You can have your music and also get some sun. While I get to see you play. What do you think?" Sana asked enthusiastically.

"Weekend after next? Um ..." Aliya paused. Suddenly, unexpected invitations were coming her way. *First Jaipur and now Bali?* "Actually, I have already committed myself to a college trip to Jaipur for that weekend. Maybe some other time?" Even though Aliya was telling the truth, to

Sana it sounded like a last-minute improvisation to stall her invite.

"Oh alright. No problem. I can plan another time." Sana's heart sank. This rejection felt like her brother's all over again.

18

India Truth ran a non-smoking office so strictly that it did not even have a designated smoking room. All those who couldn't curb their urge for a cigarette had to literally exit not only the office but also the building itself. This irked Nikki even more than her boss' subjugating persona. Especially on that cold winter evening, when she was in the middle of filing the online version of a news story. She looked around. The office was humming quietly, most desks were lit up by their monitors. The night shift executives were on their 24x7 vigil of the fickle world of the internet, typing away on the keyboards and clicking through search after search. Online news always spread like wild fire and *India Truth* had a dedicated quick-response team for this. Their job was to simply raise an alarm if they sniffed out anything worthwhile.

Nikki was bored with the monotony and humdrum. It was time to try out that washroom experiment. A few quick puffs in the toilet with a handheld fan to blow away the smoke before it could reach the smoke detector would do the trick. Any remaining smoke would be gone by the morning. The plan was certainly better than the prospect of stepping out into the bitter cold winter evening. Pocketing the smokes, lighter and a small battery-operated fan, she exited her cabin. Just as she was about to turn towards the ladies' room, she noticed that the lights were on in Sana's cabin.

Nikki had seen her leave a couple of hours ago. *Was she back again?* Nikki slowly approached the office and saw Tracy's handbag on the desk, along with a pile of paperwork. More folders and dockets lay strewn on the floor and even on Tracy's desk. Sana was nowhere in sight. Only Tracy was standing behind her desk, deeply engrossed in a heavy file, thumbing its pages back and forth.

Something caught Nikki's eye. On the side desk was a half-open cloth docket yellowed with age. It was simply marked *Srinagar—1991*. That part of Sana's life had always intrigued Nikki and she could not rein in the investigative journalist in her. With a quick sweeping glance around, she approached the docket and gently tilted its contents out. She quietly spread them out using the tip of her finger, keeping an eye on Tracy the whole time. Most of it was dull—utility bills, receipts of an antique shop, expired permissions, an old bank passbook and other faded papers from almost two decades ago.

Her eyes stopped at a tattered old college ID bearing the black and white photo of a handsome boy. Government Degree College, Srinagar (GDC), and on the reverse was the year 1989. Tucked inside the inner fold of the ID was a small photo of Sana with the same boy, sitting on a park bench. They were smiling at the camera, their hands locked intimately with each other's. Something about that man's name and face felt familiar. Nikki shoved the ID into her pocket. She noticed an envelope from GDC for Sana. It was clearly a medical report. She folded the envelope and a few other papers from the docket and hurriedly put them in her pocket too.

Just as she was leaving, Tracy called out her name. Stunned to a halt, Nikki slowly turned to face Tracy, who was looking pointedly at her pants pocket. Nikki couldn't dare look down at her own pockets, and the color left her face at the prospect of the public humiliation she would be subjected to for trying to spy into the personal life of her employer.

"I can't believe you're up to something like this now," Tracy's brow was crinkled and her tone, disgusted. Nikki's mind went into overdrive thinking up excuses.

"You know smoking isn't allowed in this office, not even in the washroom."

"What are you talking about?" Nikki blurted out and finally dared to look down at her pockets. The cigarette packet and the little fan were peeking out of one pocket.

"You walk around not bothering to hide your intention to smoke and you think nobody will notice? I am warning you Nikki, if you smoke in here, I am informing HR."

"It's okay, Tracy." Nikki laughed in relief. "I wasn't going to smoke here. I was heading out, I promise, sweetheart. I just saw the light and dropped by to say hello. Is Sana in there?" She knew that she was pushing her luck.

"No, she is not. I am just trying to locate a few documents she needs tomorrow." Tracy eyed Nikki suspiciously; Nikki wasn't usually so nice to her.

"Okay then, good luck with your search. See you tomorrow." With that cheery greeting, Nikki quickly walked back towards her cubicle. Her heart was hammering against her chest and she was acutely aware of the stolen documents in her pocket. She pushed the cigarette pack further into her pocket along with that college ID and folded envelope. Smoking was the last thing on her mind.

19

The CCTV clip playing on the computer screen was black and white—and horrifically silent. The grainy footage of a shopfront showed two uniformed cops beating a young boy, repeatedly and ruthlessly, with batons. The boy's bent and bloodied body convulsed with every strike. Nikki could almost hear the boy's spine-chilling cries even without the audio feed. He didn't look like he could last much longer. The video made even a hardcore journalist like Nikki Rajpal wince.

She looked up at Dr. Kamran Khan with a mix of disgust and anger. When he had called her for an urgent meeting in his office, she had anticipated another political announcement.

"What the hell is this?" she demanded.

"I received this video from a party worker in Muzaffarnagar. The boy is an employee at this small jewelry shop. The owner called the cops on him, accusing him of stealing a few of the gold pieces."

"False charge?" Nikki asked.

"Yeah. The owner had no proof."

"So? Were they trying to extract a confession?"

"No." Dr. Khan sighed, "According to my party worker, there was no theft at all."

"What do you mean?"

"The boy and the owner's daughter were in a relationship. Dad didn't approve."

"Oh, the same old rich-poor divide." Nikki shook her head.

"It's not as simple as that. The boy, who is now missing, is Muslim and his boss is Hindu. What you just witnessed is a hate crime. After beating the lad almost to death, the cops took him away to an undisclosed location. That was three days ago." He paused for impact and whispered, "I fear that he is dead already."

"Oh my God." Nikki looked at the screen, horrified.

"Which God would that be?" He smirked.

Nikki collected herself and snapped back, "Why wasn't this reported to the authorities? They could take action against these cops."

"The boy's family tried. The station in-charge denied the incident and said that those cops were with him at the police station at that time, giving them a solid alibi. They are covering it up. This footage was leaked to us by another employee at the shop. We suspect the original has been erased by now." Dr. Khan's tone was impatient. "This is what happens when an extreme, right-wing government sends the wrong signals to its office bearers. This is a threat to our democratic institutions, to the secular fiber of our nation."

"What are you trying to say?"

"Don't you see it for what it is, Nikki? It's a hate crime against a Muslim, committed by a Hindu and encouraged by this very government who is willing to turn a blind eye to the plight of its minorities."

"What do you want to do? If there is no proof …" Nikki was hesitant.

Dr. Khan lifted her hands into his warm grasp. "Trust me, Nikki. In the current circumstances, a legal inquiry is out of the question. They will suppress all the facts. The only way justice can be ensured is by making this video go viral. The weight of public opinion will force the government to respond." Dr. Khan looked deep into her eyes, which were steadily widening.

"Oh, no … no! If I run this without any substantial proof or back-up evidence, two things will happen. I will be thrown out of my job and the country will burn in a violent rage. I am not looking forward to any of those."

"Nikki," Dr. Khan almost purred as he rubbed small circles on the back of her hands. "Have some faith in your judgment. You are the only one who can do this! You have the moral compass and the media face to pull this off. Besides, if the case opens up and these cops are proven guilty, this news would make a major national impact. It would be a huge boost to your career. You just have to trust me. I will get you the proof and back-up evidence."

Nikki was staring down at their intertwined hands as her thoughts strayed to the possibility of hitting national headlines for her daring journalism and being nominated for India's Outstanding Woman Mediaperson award, if not the Pulitzer Prize. Dr. Khan's warm, firm grip was an added incentive. He was a very powerful man, and he was asking for her help. She felt giddy.

20

Shezii had been dragging his feet from the time he had woken up. He couldn't wait to see Aliya and dreaded that she might not show up. Breakfast was under way and there was no sign of her yet. Meera had arrived and was chatting animatedly with his parents. She had been ignoring him though. He sighed inwardly and pushed the food moodily around his plate.

"What's up with you? You aren't eating," Faisal observed.

Shezii looked up to see his father gazing at him with a mixture of amusement and concern. Before he could respond however, the doorbell chimed.

"That must be Aliya," exclaimed Meera with a meaningful look at Shezii. The little exchange caught Shaziya's attention.

Chand Bibi, the devoted caretaker who had been with the Naqvi household for three generations, entered the dining hall followed by Aliya. Aliya was dressed in a white shirt and blue jeans. Her gelled hair was pulled up by a band, and it highlighted her delicate cheekbones and light brown eyes. The clean, scrubbed look made her seem even more delicate and vulnerable. Shezii fumbled as he got up from his chair and pulled one out for her.

Aliya greeted everyone politely as she took the proffered seat.

"How is your mother, Aliya?" Shaziya asked.

"She is fine. Just too busy for family breakfasts, as I suppose most media bigwigs are." Aliya spoke with a matter-of-fact resignation. An awkward silence engulfed the table.

"*Beti*, what's your full name?" asked Chand Bibi as she placed buttered toast on Aliya's plate. Her simple question surprised everyone at the table.

"Aliya Sheikh."

"You must be from Kashmir," Chand Bibi continued excitedly.

Aliya nodded.

"Had to be. Such glowing beauty must come from Kashmir," Chand Bibi gushed, looking at her lovingly.

"Bibi, let the poor girl eat," Shaziya laughingly admonished. Shezii felt a warm glow watching Aliya at the family table. With Aliya next to him, he was finally able to smile. But it wasn't for long.

"Sadly, Kashmir is beautiful no more," Aliya stated softly, looking hard at her plate. "Its beauty is now confined to poetry and old calendars. Even tourists are scared of going there. Kashmir is scarred and bleeding. And nobody cares."

Shezii stared at her, wondering if the word Kashmir was something of a trigger.

"I agree, Aliya *beta*. Kashmir is a problem. But our government is trying its best. Give it time," said Faisal.

"It has already been four decades. We have run out of time." Aliya shook her head.

"Still, I am positive we can arrive at a peaceful solution." Faisal could sense the turmoil in the young girl. He knew about her mother's Kashmir days.

"A peaceful solution?" Shezii scoffed. "Not possible! Until this nonsense about 'my religion is better than yours' stops, there can be no peace."

"It's not just about religion. There is a long political history behind it and people who stand to benefit from the conflict," replied Faisal.

"An entire state is under siege and people are dying. Only because a few Muslim leaders believe that they don't belong to India? They are making it about religion," Shezii countered.

"A large part of any religion is how it is interpreted by people. And there lies the problem," said Aliya.

"That's why the only religion that remains relevant in today's times is nationalism." Shezii was almost huffing now.

"So, what is nationalism to you? Internalized anger, group discussions and social media rants? Don't over-simplify." Aliya challenged Shezii.

"I just know that killing in the name of jihad is utter madness. Any religion advocating this thought, even in a small part, needs to be reformed."

"And you think that is easy?"

Shezii was on edge and also a bit irritated with Aliya. "I simply refuse to subscribe to any religion. Because when you believe in a religion, you are willing to defend it no matter what, even if it takes blood. I am happy being an atheist. At least they don't go around killing people in the name of religion."

"Hm, renouncing the faith. That's the easy way out," Aliya said nonchalantly.

Shezii was about to retort when, thankfully, Chand Bibi wisely decided to mediate in the spar.

"Shezii *beta*, don't be so angry. Religion is the way to find *sukoon*, peace of mind, you see. These jihadis don't understand Islam. They understand only a part of it and base their thoughts on it, just like blind men would judge the shape of an elephant by touching just its ears or tail."

And before any further discussion could ensue, Shaziya intervened to diffuse the situation.

"Chand Bibi, I think the kids are getting late. Shezii, is your bag ready?" Her husband took his cue.

"Yeah, you guys should get going now if you wish to beat the traffic. Need any help with the luggage?" Faisal asked, getting up.

The trio politely denied the offer and soon they filed out of the house. The atmosphere was a bit charged. Aliya once again withdrew into herself and Shezii was seething internally. Meera was the only one who warmly hugged Shaziya and Faisal goodbye.

This wasn't exactly the start Shezii was hoping for the trip but with Aliya nothing was standard procedure, ever. As he slipped into the driver's seat, there was an awkward confusion about who would take the front seat next to Shezii. Then Aliya simplified the matter by casually dumping her bag and violin case on the back seat and climbing in after them. Meera, used to riding shotgun with Shezii, shrugged and climbed into her usual seat. Shezii adjusted the rear-view mirror and glanced at Aliya in the back seat. She was wearing dark glasses now and as always, he couldn't figure out what was on her mind.

21

Meera woke up with a start and stared into the pitch darkness. She reached over to switch on the bedside lamp and picked up her mobile. 6:30 a.m. Half an hour till her alarm was set to go off. She dropped back onto her pillow, her eyes wide open. She had slept fitfully the whole night. The idea that her room and Shezii's let out on to the same terrace had filled her mind with possibilities. Giving up on sleep, she got off the bed, threw a shawl over her PJs and stepped on to the terrace. The cool dawn air hit her, mildly smoky from a bonfire burning somewhere on the premises. Meera's dad had used his ministry connections to put them up in Diggi Palace, the century and a half old royal palace converted into a heritage hotel. She had raved about it all through the drive. It was an apt stay arrangement for an architectural study tour, even though a bit too luxurious by student standards.

She was strolling, marveling at the *Rajwada*-style verandahs, massive columns and high ceilings decorated with exquisite adornments, when she caught sight of a flash of a colorful skirt vanishing around the far corner.

Intrigued, Meera rounded the corner and stopped in shock. In the distance, Aliya was walking gingerly, almost tiptoeing, her eyes focused on a broad ledge ahead. Sitting regally on the ledge was a grand peacock, eyeing the surroundings curiously as its head moved rhythmically in all directions. And then she spotted Shezii following Aliya closely.

Meera caught her breath. *What were these two doing alone on the terrace so early?* Aliya's shawl was hued like the peacock's feathers—an iridescent kind of blue-green. The bird cast a fleeting glance at her as Aliya pulled out her cell phone. *She wanted to photograph the peacock?* But just then, the majestic bird flapped to lift its large frame and flew heavily away to a more secluded ledge. Suddenly, Aliya turned in Meera's direction, irritation writ on her face. *Damn! Did she see me?* Meera thought, quickly receding into the dusky shadows of a pillar.

She watched as Shezii approached Aliya. He wore an obviously smitten look on his face and they were speaking softly. Then he placed a hand on her shoulder and Meera winced. He was telling her something very urgent but from Aliya's response she seemed uninterested. Finally, Shezii moved away in the direction of his room, but not before he brushed Aliya's cheek lightly. Aliya stood unmoved but Meera's heart sank. Finally, no longer able to contain herself, she approached Aliya.

"You like watching birds?" Meera said.

"I do," she had a strange look on her face. "They aren't restricted by any boundaries we humans decide to draw on this land." She perched herself on the ledge where the bird had been sitting.

"But we do capture them and cage them."

Aliya stiffened.

"You ever been to Kashmir?" Meera prodded further.

"No. Mom never wanted to go back. Bad memories. I guess she didn't want to face them. It was the early 90s and Kashmir was turning into hell."

"I know, it must have been tough for her."

"Oh, you can never know unless the father of your unborn child deserts you overnight."

"I guess we all have our own demons." Meera shook her head and sighed.

"You too have demons?" Aliya crossed her feet at the ankles and finally smiled.

"Hm, are you planning to join me and Shezii for the study tour?" Meera deflected.

"No, you guys go ahead. I have no interest in buildings."

"Yeah ... good thing you aren't coming. You would have probably gotten bored stiff. Architecture is not even your subject. And Shezii has no interest in your computers," she added sharply.

"Well, he wants to meet me for dinner tonight. He said he wants to talk," Aliya said coolly.

"I will be surprised if he comes. He isn't the 'let's talk over dinner' type of guy." Meera bristled.

"You know Shezii very well, don't you?"

"Well enough to know when he is about to get blindsided." Meera opted to be direct with her.

"Good for him. You should probably keep him in your back pocket," Aliya answered in her trademark aloof style.

"Maybe I will. He likes it there, at least he did, until now."

"Good luck with that. From what I can tell, back pockets aren't a very comfortable place to be." The girls locked eyes. After a few long seconds of a standoff, both smiled knowingly and moved away. There was nothing more left to say. For now.

22

Aliya snapped her laptop shut and stared out at the falling dusk. She pondered over her options for the evening. She could stay in, order room service and continue with her never ending cycle of books and TV shows late into the night. Or she could meet Shezii over dinner. Strangely, for the moment, the latter felt more appealing. *If he comes,* that's what Meera had said. Well, the challenge was worth taking up. Thoughts about Shezii had been distracting her all day. *It must be the damn hormones.* She chided herself, walked over to the closet and deliberated on what to wear. Normally, she just wore whatever caught her eye first. Finally, she chose a pretty lemon-colored cold-shoulder top with skinny blue jeans.

Aliya reached the terrace restaurant of the hotel. The weather was perfect with just the right amount of chill, which was probably why the venue was packed to capacity. *Oh no!* She groaned inwardly. She hated crowds.

"So what do you think?" Shezii asked, sneaking up behind her.

"Too many people." Aliya winced.

"Yeah, I wasn't expecting this either."

"What's that?" She turned, eyeing the brown bag in his hand.

"Well, it's my favorite wine. Was going to get it served at the table. Hope you like white."

"Only if it's a chardonnay."

"Bingo." He smiled.

"So, your room or mine?" Aliya's tone was light.

He stared at her.

"What?" She raised an eyebrow. "This place seems like a village fair and we need a place to squat. We can order room service. Come on." She started to walk away.

"My room?" Shezii said and followed her, shaking his head.

In Shezii's room, Aliya got comfortable on the couch while he poured the wine.

"You said you wanted to talk?" she said, accepting the wine.

"You in a hurry?"

"Nope."

Shezii stayed silent.

"By the way, sorry about my behavior at your place. I didn't mean to upset you or your parents."

"You didn't."

"Then tell me, why are you such an extremist?"

"Extremist? Me?"

"Theoretically speaking, blindly denying religion is as conceited as blindly accepting it."

"Do *you* believe in religion?" Shezii searched her face.

"I am a believer. Religion and its form doesn't matter."

"Well, my experience with religion hasn't been that great."

"Hm, want to talk about it?" She settled her chin on her palm. *He is kind of cute.*

Shezii inhaled deeply and looked at Aliya. Her eyes were already fixed on him.

"I was with mom and dad in Tel Aviv when the Islamic jihadi group from Palestine took over our guest house."

Aliya sat up and took a large swig from her wine glass.

"Trust me, it's not easy for an 11-year-old to watch his parents beaten and humiliated."

"You were just 11?"

"Yup, it was in 2005. They slaughtered the entire Jewish staff. Slit their throats with a knife."

"Is that why they had come?"

"No. They had come to blow up the night club nearby and our guest house was a convenient hideout. The Jewish staff was just collateral damage." He shivered involuntarily.

"Did they succeed in their mission?"

"Yeah, pretty much. I looked it up on the net much later. Fifty-one people died in the bombing that night."

"How did you guys survive?"

"Well ..." he responded with a twisted smile. "You know why they didn't kill us?"

Aliya watched him silently.

"Because we were Muslims. Just like them." Shezii downed his wine and poured some more, before settling back into the pillows of his bed.

They sat silently, staring into nothingness, until finally Shezii spoke with a light smile.

"You know, you are the first person I have spoken to about that evening." This time he fixed her with a stare.

Aliya got off the couch and moved towards Shezii, and then stopped. Shezii looked at her expectantly. She moved again, closer and stood gazing into his eyes. In that moment, an eternity of understanding passed between them. Finally, as she was about to speak, he pulled her closer to him. She didn't resist, falling easily into his embrace. As their eyes met again, an urgent, smoldering fire consumed their bodies. Aliya lifted her face, offering her parted lips to Shezii. A sense of restlessness stirred within Aliya, screaming at her to stop before it was too late. But she hushed it up quickly. *I am not responsible,* was her last sane thought. And then, the night turned into a hazy smoke of passion.

23

In the soundproof meeting room on the top floor of the defense HQ, Rajeev Bakshi scanned the faces of his classified team. Faisal Umer Naqvi was there in a special advisory position because of the firm finger he kept on the diplomatic pulse of the Middle East. The team was certainly up to the mark, both in expertise and experience. And even though it had been swiftly put together within 72 hours, it was far better than he had hoped for. They were all hand-picked and thoroughly vetted before being assigned this project.

The silent buzzing of Rajeev Bakshi's unlisted cell phone alerted him that an important call was incoming. He answered the call and after listening intently for a few seconds, disconnected with a crisp "Yes, sir." Then he eyed his team once again.

Project leader Major Ram Arya was a seasoned operator from insurgency and war zones. At 40, he already had a string of successful covert operations behind him. Talks were underway of his nomination for the Shaurya Chakra, although this made Major Arya uncomfortable. He preferred staying under the radar, which allowed him to function with lethal efficacy. He was a first-generation army officer … and most likely the last as he was still a proud bachelor. He had lost his parents to the bombings by Bodo militants in Assam when he was barely in his teens.

Heading the cyber monitoring cell was Akshara Swaminathan, a merit ranker from MIT. In her mid-20s, Akshara was a wizard who could break through any firewall and decode complex encryptions in record time. She was known to have refused jobs with Facebook, Google and Microsoft to work for her country's Department of Counter-Terrorism. She proudly wore a miniature enameled metal tricolor on her lapel at all times.

Then there was S. Anandan, retired Commissioner of Mumbai Police, who was renowned for tackling problems hands on. He was famous in the department for refusing to accommodate politicians or celebrities, and for breaking the backbone of Mumbai's underworld. But more specifically, he had become famous for slapping a Bollywood actor during an interrogation. After the 2008 Mumbai terror attacks, he was brought in to restructure the country's external and internal security provisions as an active member of the National Security Council. He was as seasoned as they came.

Finally, Rajeev Bakshi's eyes met Faisal's. They were ready to roll. Clearing his throat, he announced, "Well, we couldn't have had a more encouraging start. Mr. Arjun Jaisinghani himself is joining us for our first briefing session. I welcome you to Project Jai Hind, my friends."

24

On the record, Arjun Jaisinghani had arrived at the defense HQ to preside over a dull, inter-departmental policy meeting. But once inside, he made his way to a soundproof room on the top floor. The door had a simple nameplate—Classified. Prasanna held it open for the minister and then quietly stood guard outside.

As the minister entered, Rajeev and his team stood up in respect.

Jaisinghani gave them a broad smile but came straight to business.

"So, what news do you have, Rajeev?"

"I'm afraid it's not very good news," replied Rajeev. "Our intel in France has detected hostile activity in Egypt. A major action is underway, but we aren't yet sure of the specific target. From the skeletal information we have, it's most likely to be in either Delhi or Kashmir."

"Any idea about the group involved?"

"We know for sure its *Tehrik-e-Islam*. The name Mustafa Al-Gazzar is making the rounds."

The minister frowned.

"Isn't Al-Gazzar's current residence a maximum-security prison?"

"Yes, he is in Tora prison. But that's hardly a deterrent for him. He has been efficiently running his jihadi army from within the prison. He is very well funded."

Jaisinghani closed his eyes and rubbed the bridge of his nose with his fingertips. "How far along are the plans?"

"That's the point. We aren't sure if he's planning a public shootout, a suicide bombing, an assassination, or something else. One of their key assets is already on Indian soil. He or she is supposed to be activating sleeper cells, right here in Delhi."

"What are the threat levels as per your evaluation?" the minister asked warily.

"Mass scale. *Tehrik-e-Islam* is known for its large-scale civil targets. They could hit a mall, movie theatre, a school or even a government building." Rajeev sounded tired.

"Hm, how are they communicating? Have we been able to track it?"

"Akshara will brief us on this. She represents the cyber cell." Rajeev nodded at her.

"Sir, we have been tracking all the key operators of *Tehrik-e-Islam*, but they have been strangely quiet on their known channels. They could be relying more on physical and offline communication methods. It takes longer to get the message across, but it is harder for external parties to track. Also, they seem to be in no hurry. Having said that, I have found something unusual in the chat room of a website selling Qurans with gold-plated covers."

"Yes?"

"There has been a repeated mention of *Rub-el-Hizb* and its delivery to Hind along with the Qurans."

"*Rub-el-Hizb*?"

"*Rub-el-Hizb* is a widely used Islamic symbol. It looks like an octagram and is used as a marker for the end of a chapter in Arabic calligraphy. The Quran has sixty *hizbs*, which means roughly sixty equal parts. You can also see variations of this symbol on Islamic flags. We are still figuring out its relevance to our case. The term could refer to a person, a message, a signal or something physical. It is difficult to judge how deep or far this network runs," Akshara concluded.

Anandan was watching her keenly. The kid was delivering on her part but he knew that things weren't as simple. She needed concrete leads and verified information to offer a solid action plan. "What about firepower?" he asked, steering the subject into operations.

Jaisinghani nodded. "Yes. This kind of plan will require weapons, bombs, etc. How do they intend to get them across India's tight borders?"

Major Arya responded, "With all due respect sir, we have over 15,000 km of land borders and 7,000 km of coastline. Our border security focuses on the Indo-Pak line, which is about 3,323 km, and round-the-clock manning of all the remaining land and sea borders is very difficult, especially considering the unpredictability of our enemy."

Major Arya glanced at the retired police commissioner who had first-hand experience of an attack on Mumbai via sea. The Major was met with an imperceptible nod of acknowledgement from the veteran.

"I understand, Major. Any suggestions?" This time Arjun Jaisinghani looked at Rajeev Bakshi pointedly.

"We will be relying on intel, both domestic and international, and will be looking out for suspicious chatter in the cyberworld. Porous border areas, even with friendly nations like Nepal are under close observation. On-ground resources have been deployed to keep an eye on every single person even remotely connected to any terrorist activities in the past. And some of the people we are tailing are rather high-profile residents of Lutyens' Delhi."

Rajeev looked meaningfully at both the minister and Faisal. New Delhi housed some of the biggest power brokers and their political reach posed a nightmare for any officer attempting surveillance or investigation on them.

"Rajeev, you and your team have full jurisdiction over the complete activity spectrum of Project Jai Hind. You have total control over all actions. From intel to investigation, to arrest or targeted killing of anyone who is a proven enemy of the state." Jaisinghani looked around the table and finally his eyes settled on his trusted commander. "Do whatever it takes, Rajeev, but I don't want even a single innocent person dead, just because we fell short."

25

The guy at the check-out desk smiled politely and extended the bills for Shezii to sign. Shezii pored through the bills unsmilingly, his mood a bit prickly. He had been tormented by a thousand thoughts since he awakened alone in his bed in the morning. It was obvious that Aliya had left sometime during the night. But that didn't bother him. That was typical of her. It was that eternal question about their relationship—*What now?* He so badly needed some answers.

Meera was still finishing breakfast when Shezii had offered to get going with the check-out procedure. In reality, he just wanted to catch Aliya alone.

Shezii pulled out his wallet for the credit card when the manager stopped him.

"It's alright, Mr. Naqvi. Your bills have been settled in advance, for all the three rooms."

"By whom?" Shezii asked with a raised eyebrow.

"I believe Mr. Rajeev Bakshi has spoken to the owners directly. Do you need any help with your luggage?" The manager deftly maneuvered the conversation.

"No thanks, we have it here already." He pointed towards his and Meera's bags.

"So, should I have the valet bring in your car?" the manager asked cheerily, eager to see off another satisfied patron.

"Not yet, we are still waiting for our friend." Shezii distractedly looked at the staircase behind the reception.

"Pardon me, sir?"

"Our friend Aliya is yet to come down."

"But sir, Ms. Aliya Sheikh checked out late last night."

"What?" It was Shezii's turn to be confused.

"Yes, she mentioned something about an emergency. I called a cab for her."

Shezii could barely form his words, "Why didn't you tell me this before?"

"Sir, I assumed you knew."

"Did she say where she was going?"

"Ma'am just asked me to get a cab. She didn't confirm the destination." The manager spoke meekly and looked beyond Shezii to see Meera approaching. Relief flooded his face as he greeted her, happy for a break from the intense conversation.

"Hey, what's up?" Meera eyed Shezii and the manager, instantly sensing something wasn't right.

"Aliya already checked out last night." Shezii answered flatly and then addressed the manager, "Please ask the valet to bring the car."

"What do you mean? You know where she went?" Meera wasn't surprised. That girl was cuckoo and such behavior was not beyond her.

Shezii simply shrugged in response and Meera could sense his disappointment. They did not speak again until the car was cruising on the highway.

"You think we should call and ask her mom if she has reached home?" Meera suggested softly.

"She didn't go home." Shezii stared straight at the road.

"How do you know?"

"Because ... she came with us to avoid her mother." Meera stared at him. There was a heavy silence until she spoke again.

"So, you don't know where she went last night but you do know that she wanted to avoid her own mother?"

Shezii didn't respond but the veins in his hands bulged as he tightened his grip on the steering wheel.

"Shezii, why do I get a feeling that you think you understand her but in reality, you know nothing about her?" Meera's tone was icy as she continued, "She is playing the victim card with you, just because she has Kashmiri roots. She has no real reason to do so, given her highly privileged background! She is just a typical, self-entitled rich kid."

"You think she is playing the victim card just because she is Muslim? Or are you simply unwilling to recognize the emotional loss she and her mother experienced? They too lost their home just like any Kashmiri Pandit at that time. Don't tell me that your humanitarianism is reserved for Kashmiri Pandits alone," Shezii shot back.

"I can't believe you are saying this, Shezii. How did the Muslim part come into this? This isn't about religion and *that's* what I have been trying to tell you." Meera blinked back a tear.

"In the end, it is always about religion, isn't it?" Shezii stared hard at the wide empty road.

26

Dr. Kamran Khan's Mercedes E Class was reduced to a crawl through the bustling old gully approaching Jama Masjid. It was becoming increasingly apparent that his luxury sedan wouldn't make any further headway in the jam of buses, autos, cycle-rickshaws, hawkers and seething pedestrians. *Should have called a cab,* he berated himself. Time was running out. He had received the cryptic text message with an instruction while he was having his breakfast, which he could no longer finish. He was to reach Jama Masjid just after *Asr,* the afternoon prayer call, at the Masjid and wait till the sun started to turn orange. There was no way he could have ignored the message. He had their money and even though it was channeled in a way that couldn't be tracked, they owned that money. Along with him. There was no turning back now. Not if he wished to live.

Dr. Khan made a quick decision. Shrugging off his jacket, he ordered his driver, "Drop me off here and find some place to park. I'll call you when I'm done."

He stepped out and watched the car inch away amid the sea of dented vehicles and perspiring humans. But, it was the sudden onslaught of street sounds that disoriented him the most. He didn't know what to expect next. Dr.

Khan pulled out a pristine while skull cap from his pants pocket and put it on. He now belonged.

Just then, the *azaan*, the call to prayer echoed loudly. Around him, swathes of men in white kurtas and skull caps went down on their knees in unison. Places for *namaz* were reserved outside shops, small openings by the road—everywhere. The cool and collected professor now panicked, not knowing what to do. But then, his phone buzzed with an incoming message, *Khari Baoli, above shop no. 21.*

Dr. Khan wiped the sweat off of his forehead. He memorized the address, erased the message and set about identifying the shop. After jostling through the hot malodorous soup of people for a good 15 minutes, he found himself standing outside shop no. 21. It was no different than any other in Khari Baoli, only it sold nuts, all kinds of them. Gunny sacks full of cashews, almonds, dried apricots and dates were displayed under the glaring lights of the busy shop. Dr. Khan noticed a narrow gully adjacent to it, probably an entrance to the old single-story building above the shop. He hesitated, and then entered the passage, and was relieved to find a staircase at the end of it.

The first-floor landing was a long corridor with six doors side by side at equal distances. All of them were shut tight, sporting old large locks. Just one door was half open, revealing a bright green curtain with leaf motifs. This had to be his destination. He walked up to the door and pushed it open to step into a single room, barely ten feet by ten in size. It was musty and smelled of scented oil.

Sitting erect on a wooden diwan by the wall was a large, clean-shaven man in a white silk Pathani suit and gelled-back hair. He looked up from his phone and gestured towards the seat in front of him. Dr. Khan could feel his dark, penetrating eyes on his skin and wondered if it was because of the hint of *surma* in them. He sat down without a word.

"Khan ... Kamran Khan?" the man asked.

"Yes," Dr. Khan replied, sweating under his collar.

"I have a message for you from Egypt. Mustafa Al-Gazzar sends his greetings. He asks about your well-being."

Dr. Khan nodded nervously.

"He also wishes to remind you about the unending dollars he has been sending to fund your party."

Dr. Khan sat unmoving, his eyes fixed on the floor.

"You must remember, Al-Gazzar has been very speedy in organizing every help you have wanted."

"I am thankful for that," he stuttered, "and I am very much on the job. My party is ready and I will clinch enough political power soon and then—"

"Your time has come now," the man growled to cut him off. "You need to make yourself useful soon. Or else, do not expect any mercy from Al-Gazzar."

"Yes, I know. I will not fail you." Dr. Khan shivered.

"But you already have, Khan." The man chewed the words. "We funded you so that you can fill every self-respecting *Musalman* in this country with so much hatred and anger that they stand by us when the call for jihad is made. But you did nothing ... nothing!"

"I wanted to be careful ... for the sake of secrecy." Dr. Khan's face was turning white and he wanted to get out of there and puke.

"You think we are fools?" The man chuckled. "Khan, you be careful. Those who make false promises to Al-Gazzar beg for their own death. Understood?"

Dr. Khan shook his head and wiped off more sweat. He was a staunch pro-Islamist but he wasn't a mercenary. Fanning radical emotions and dreaming of a Muslim world was one thing but he hadn't imagined a situation where he would be made to take actual extremist steps.

"The mission is underway. You will provide safe houses, documents and transport for our operatives."

"Yes it will be done."

"They will also need arms and ammunition. Here in Delhi and Kashmir. You will use your carriers to make it all reach the right places. I assume your sources for automatic guns, semtex and C-4 are active." The man's hard eyes were narrowed in query.

"Yes, yes for sure," he affirmed enthusiastically, already thinking of a group of Islamic youth under his influence who would be proud to be of use.

"Now go distract your government." He fixed Dr. Khan with those penetrating eyes again. "We'll be in touch soon. Meanwhile, get rid of this phone and get a burner phone for communicating with us."

After a pause, he added in a low voice, "And Kamran Khan, don't you dare fail. Or we will skin you alive and leave you for the vultures. They will feed on your live flesh piece by piece, while you scream. You understand?"

Without another word, the man got up abruptly and left. Dr. Khan still didn't know the name of his tormentor.

As he crossed the dark gully of the building and stepped back into the crowded street of Khari Baoli, Dr. Khan could feel his pulse racing. His head swam. Things had changed very quickly within the last 15 minutes. He had planned and prepared for a game of political chess to be played from his air-conditioned office. But what they wanted now was an actual war on the streets, involving blood and gore.

27

The cavernous library of Madhav Raje University was exceedingly quiet. It was late in the day and its young and eager librarian was in the process of closing up. He shut down his computer terminal and then cursed in annoyance. A girl laden with books was walking towards him purposefully. He eyed the wall clock, which showed it was still ten minutes short of closing time. He shook his head and powered up the computer again. But his vexation turned into curious interest when he noticed that the girl was pretty.

"Wow those seem heavy." He smiled as the girl dumped the books on his desk.

"I need to sign them out for a week." Aliya gestured at the books coldly.

"Sure." The guy got the message and started punching the details into the terminal. Her tone had ensured that he wouldn't try to chat her up again. Collecting the books, Aliya walked to the far end of the long table and settled down. The librarian left quickly, without a look in her direction.

She pulled out her laptop and cast a cursory glance around. The only other person in the library's study hall was a nerdy boy hunched over his journal. This suited her because she intended to spend the next two hours there. She wasn't there to study. The final year computer science syllabus was something she could master within a month, but she had to keep up the act. In reality, she was there to work. *On her real project*. She powered up her laptop and logged into a secure network.

Just as she finished signing in, she was startled by a presence. Shezii quietly sat down next to her and said, "Hi." Aliya slammed her laptop shut and stared at him silently.

"I thought you were just getting started. What happened?" He pointed at her laptop.

"I thought I should finish talking to you first?" she said coolly.

"Really? That's quite considerate of you, especially after vanishing from Jaipur without a word." His tone was bitter.

"Something urgent came up. Had to leave."

"And this 'something urgent' had nothing to do with your mom or your studies. I checked." He crossed his arms.

"Listen Shezii, you are not my boyfriend," she said sharply.

"I know. But when you come out with me, I am responsible."

"No, you are not. I am free to act as I wish."

"Seriously? Is that your explanation for leaving in the middle of the night?"

"Come on, Shezii. Both of us are adults who chose to spend some quality time together. So, stop acting like a dad to me," she hissed.

"Sure I will. When you stop acting like a kid on a fantasy trip."

Just then Aliya went quiet. From the corner of her eye, she caught a stealthy shadow move at a distance. Her instincts heightened as she quietly looked at the partition door, which was still moving. Someone had just passed through them into the common area where the ladies washroom was located. But she was the only girl in this section of the library.

"Oh, so now you don't want to talk?" Shezii was exasperated by her sudden silence.

"I need to use the washroom." And Aliya stood up without waiting for his response.

She walked softly towards the door and entered the small open area outside the washroom. It was empty. She cautiously approached the washroom cubicle door and pushed it open lightly. The washroom was empty too. Just as she was about to turn away, her eyes noticed the glint of metal on the white sink.

A thick metal ring was kept primly next to the bottle of hand wash. Aliya picked it up and instantly froze. It wasn't just any ring left carelessly on the sink by some girl running late. It was *the* ring. As she turned it around in her hands, she could see the symbol etched on it—the two overlapping squares, one tilted over the other to make an eight-pointed star. It was more than a thousand years old Islamic symbol of *Rub-el-Hizb*. In Arabic calligraphy, it marked the end of a chapter.

This was the sign she had been waiting for. It was time for the next chapter of the mission to begin. Securing the ring in her jeans pocket, she walked back to her seat, thinking of ways to stall Shezii. There was no time for distractions now. But the seat next to hers was empty. He was gone. But on top of her closed laptop was a piece of paper. The handwritten note simply said, *You are all that I could ever wish for, right in front of me. Only if you let me find you.* It was signed by Shezii.

Aliya sank in her chair and placed her head in her hands. Shezii was making an already demanding task more difficult for her. He was a mistake that could cost her years of groundwork and forethought. She squeezed the ring in her pocket, feeling its edges push agonizingly against her palm.

28

Shezii smiled as he spotted Meera at the cafeteria. She was hunched over a book with a steaming mug of coffee by her side. He walked over and quietly sat down opposite her. She looked up and smiled. They knew each other too well to play games.

"Where were you? Looking for Aliya again?" Meera closed the book and smiled wistfully.

"She is turning into quite a mystery." He shook his head, ignoring Meera's obviously disapproving remark on his interest in Aliya. "She doesn't hold her violin sessions anymore and she is missing most of her lectures."

"Hm, dad spoke to Aliya's mom yesterday. She seemed normal, as if nothing was amiss. Didn't say anything about Aliya." Meera shrugged.

"So she's fine, but not attending college for some reason?"

Shezii's eyes strayed towards the parking lot and stopped on a large man who stood with predatory stillness, leaning against a Maruti sedan. *Not a student and not a professor for sure,* Shezii thought. *What is he, a driver? Or perhaps a bodyguard for some visiting dignitary?*

Shezii followed the man's fixed gaze and froze. The man was watching Aliya. *But what was she doing in the parking lot*? As he watched, she settled into the driver's seat and backed her car out.

"What the hell!" Shezii exclaimed softly.

Meera looked up and followed his gaze. Aliya was pulling out of the parking lot. "Looks like you just missed her."

"Not her. *Him*!" Shezii snapped.

Meera scanned the lot and noticed a jacketed brawny man getting into a car and starting the engine, his eyes fixed on Aliya. His movements were calm and measured, as if he had done this a thousand times. He pulled out, trailing Aliya's midnight blue Honda City down the college road.

"I've got to go." Shezii pulled out the car keys from his pocket.

"I am coming with you," said Meera in a tone that left no room for discussion. In less than a minute, they were exiting the campus.

As he merged with traffic on the main road, Shezii realized he hadn't noted the number of the white Maruti that had taken off after Aliya. His brow creased in concentration as he willed his memory to throw up some tidbit at him, anything to make him remember something about the car. And then, as his eyes rested on a Pepsi billboard, something flashed across his mind. He could now distinctly remember the red, blue and white band on the windshield of the car.

His eyes scanned the traffic moving slowly in front of him. Five cars ahead, crawling in the second lane was the Maruti Swift Desire with a red, blue and white band on its rear windshield. Aliya's deep blue sedan was a few cars further ahead.

"That's him."

"Are you sure?" Meera craned her neck to spot the car.

"Absolutely."

"I mean, are you sure he is following Aliya?"

Shezii did not respond.

The three vehicles headed north, joining the increasingly jammed roads that led to old Delhi. By then it was evident that the white sedan was following Aliya, maintaining a safe gap of three to four cars. Not more, not less. Aliya too had been maintaining a steady pace within speed limits. It seemed like she was in no hurry to get to her destination. Shezii had never seen Aliya drive before. *How was a girl, who had lived in London a good part of her life, maneuvering a car so deftly through Delhi's complex and congested roads?*

They were now technically outside Delhi, driving through Haryana and approaching the Cyber Hub Business Center in Gurugram. Shezii was beginning to wonder how long this chase was going to last. He checked the fuel indicator and cursed. He had less than half a tank of gas and there was no time to stop and refuel.

Meera had been quiet for a while, her shoulders rigid as she sat upright with her hands clasped tightly. As they left Gurugram behind, the sparse traffic forced Shezii to fall back a little. After another 15 minutes of steady driving, both cars in front of him turned right onto a road branching off the main highway. It was a relatively quiet interior road, probably connecting to a smaller town or a village. After dropping the speed considerably, Shezii too turned, hoping to see them in the distance. But the road ahead of him was empty, apart from a tractor trudging along, far ahead. Shezii and Meera exchanged confused glances, but they were too wired up to say anything. *The cars had simply vanished.*

Shezii picked up speed. He was determined to go to the very end of the road if required. After ten minutes of aimless driving, Meera opened her mouth to say something but stopped as Shezii braked hard. In front of them, Aliya's blue Honda City was emerging from a dirt road on the side. With a sharp turn, it levelled with the road's kerb and stopped, just like Shezii had.

Both of them got out of the cars, strode belligerently towards each other and stopped a few feet apart.

"Why are you following me?" Aliya asked, low and hostile.

"I was worried! I saw a car with a strange man in it following you from college."

"I don't see anyone." She looked around. "Apart from you, that is. Also, it's not your job to be worried about me."

"Aliya, stop it. Stop being so stubborn."

Aliya scoffed and looked away.

"Anyway, why are you driving in this wilderness?" He pointed at the muddy trail from which her car had emerged.

"Bird watching! Not that you need to know." She lifted her chin towards the large green board across the road.

It held an arrow and read "Way to Sultanpur National Park & Bird Sanctuary."

Then she scanned his face and said in a flat tone, "Listen Shahzaib, what you are expecting from me is not possible. Never. Ever. The faster you accept it, the better it is. Understood?"

"So that night in Jaipur—," Shezii was cut off even before he could finish.

"That night in Jaipur was a mistake on my part. I thought you would be grown-up about it."

And then she walked off towards the driver's seat. She revved the engine once before driving away.

Shezii stood still for a few moments and then got back in the car and started the engine without saying anything.

In the car, Meera buckled her seat belt and sat quietly. She had unwittingly become witness to her best friend's most private moments. She had heard every last syllable of their shouting match and didn't know what to say to Shezii. In her heart of hearts, she hoped this would be the end of Shezii's obsession with Aliya. *Even if it meant that he would hurt for a while,* whispered her guilty conscience. She stole a glance at him. Shezii's face was set in stone as he revved up the engine and turned back home.

Aliya too was driving back to the city—this time choosing a circuitous route. When she was convinced that no one was following or watching her, she picked up the brown paper bag beside her and emptied its contents on to the seat. It had a cell phone, a sheet of paper with instructions and a fat bundle of ₹2,000 notes. It also had a shiny black Glock 43, a favored hand-held gun for women. Small enough for easy concealment and suitable for shooters with small hands. She had spent some serious time at the shooting range with this particular model.

Aliya unbuckled the seat belt and stepped out into the shadowy dusk. She leaned against her vehicle and exhaled, her breath condensing in the winter chill. Today's courier-drop had almost been compromised. Thank goodness she had spotted Shezii's car in time. She carefully looked around in the darkening night, as the cold wind whistled past her down the open road. It would be time to move once winter let up. With a shiver, as much from the cold as from the anticipation and apprehension, she got into the car and drove off.

As the tail lights of Aliya's car faded away, a man stepped out from the dark shadows of a rusting SUV nearby. He clicked his neck to shake off the stiffness from standing still for too long. His eyes narrowed as he watched the car speeding away. Then, he pulled out a cell phone and punched in a number. He spoke into the phone in a steady voice, "The package has been delivered," and disconnected the call.

29

Sana hadn't slept in the last 24 hours. She finally logged off from her computer but continued to stare at the blank monitor. It had been 24 hours since she had officially apologized on air as the head of the channel for the fake video. Yet, the situation was continuing to escalate. The clip of cops beating up a Muslim boy had gone viral, circulated by lakhs of people in a mad frenzy. Muzaffarnagar was burning with communal riots. The media coverage of burning vehicles, empty roads strewn with footwear and stones, closed shops and the scared, hurt faces of children and women tore at Sana's heart. The town was under Section 144, as the administration had been forced to issue a curfew order to control the situation.

Sana's face sank into her hands. Nikki Rajpal—blindly ambitious, easily manipulated—had run amok. She hadn't bothered to verify the facts. The boy had been finally identified by the local police as Ramkanwar Singh. He had confessed to stealing jewelry from the shop, which actually belonged to his own uncle. The cops had definitely given him a brutal beating, but they let him go once he agreed to return the items.

In no way was it a hate crime. But nobody wanted to hear the truth. Political opposition had stoked the flames, drowned out all other voices as fake news, and were holding the clip as proof of the government's pro-Hindu ideology.

Ironically, Sana knew that the unscrupulous mastermind behind Nikki's actions and the source of the video was one and the same.

Suddenly, Sana was gripped by mad fury. She stormed out of her office, ignoring the meek queries of her secretary. She reached Nikki's cubicle and tapped on the partition harshly. Startled, Nikki looked up from her phone and stood up hurriedly. In the process, she toppled over the crystal timepiece gifted to her by Dr. Kamran Khan.

"Is that phone issued by the company?" Sana asked, pointing towards Nikki's hands.

"Yes."

"Hand it over."

Sana took the proffered device and switched it off.

"I believe the iMac is company property too. You are not to touch it. Other than that, take your personal belongings and get out. I'll wait till you're done."

Sana settled on one of the guest chairs.

"I ... I don't understand," Nikki stuttered.

"What part of *get out* don't you understand?" Sana shot back. "Leave!" she roared, jerking Nikki out of her stupor. Nikki didn't bother to pick up anything apart from her tote bag. As she shuffled out of the cabin, Sana followed, saying, "You will be searched before leaving the premises. So don't even think of carrying any data in soft or hard format. And Nikki, don't bother to come back. Your dues will be settled electronically. That is, if the company decides not to sue you. And it will be wise of you to not use *India Truth*'s credentials in any future job interviews."

Without meeting Sana's eyes, Nikki quietly left the cabin. But she banged the door shut with added force. Inside the Nikki-less cabin, Sana sighed and sat back. *This should have been done long ago.*

Dr. Kamran Khan had officially and conveniently denied meeting Nikki or sharing any video with her. Sana knew that he was lying, but there was nothing that could be done at the moment. A small part of Sana pitied Nikki, who was about to get into a whole lot of trouble.

30

Through a haze of inebriation, Nikki stared at Kamran Khan's chiseled face, set in deep thought. She felt like a mess and his silence was making her wonder if she had committed that one irreversible error of judgment. Finally, the clouds across Dr. Khan's face cleared and he spoke decisively, "You should have called me earlier. It's never a good idea to drink alone."

His voice soft with concern, he added, "It's entirely my mistake. I should have verified the video before I handed it to you. I am sorry, Nikki."

He looked away with a sigh.

This show of concern was enough for Nikki's bottled up emotions to escape in relentless sobs. Almost an entire bottle of expensive vodka had failed to soothe her frayed nerves. Instead, it had brought her current circumstances into sharper focus, making them even more unbearable. Dr. Khan embraced her in one fluid motion, his muscular arms engulfing her slender frame.

"Sshhh ... it's okay. I will fix everything. Don't worry," he crooned against her soft hair.

"How?" she murmured into his chest. "I am an untouchable in the industry now. *India Truth* has disowned me. No way will I be able to find a decent position with any media house. My career is over!" she sobbed.

"No, it isn't. You will work with me and AIM now. Together, we will re-define reporting and journalism. I mean it." He looked down at her and added with a chuckle, "And, I think I can afford a top journalist like you for the sake of my party."

Nikki smiled weakly. She wiped her cheeks with the back of her hand and sat up. The odds were stacked against her, but she still had a powerful man on her side.

Then, with a start, she reached for her tote bag. *Did she still have it?* After fumbling for a bit, she sat back with a relieved sigh. The documents she had taken from Sana's office were safely in the inner pocket of the bag. She silently thanked her stars that she hadn't left them behind in her office drawer and that the security search had not discovered them.

Dr. Khan was looking at her quizzically.

"I have something you must see," Nikki sounded grave. She picked up the tattered ID, the photo and the medical report and handed it to Dr. Khan. "Have a look."

Dr. Khan stared at the photos. Unmistakably, the girl was Sana Sikander Sheikh, the head honcho of *India Truth*. There was no mistaking that face. A young Sana Sheikh was sitting with a handsome man, most likely a boyfriend. The accompanying envelope held a yellowing report from 1991 confirming Sana's pregnancy.

"I think you must have deduced by now—Sana Sheikh's daughter, Aliya is an illegitimate child!" she said with a triumphant smile.

Dr. Khan sighed. "Nikki, get a grip on yourself. I know you are angry, but this is personal stuff. Talking about this publicly will only hurt your image further."

"You don't recognize the man?" she said smugly. When he didn't rise to her bait, she continued, "That is Anurag Kaul, the biggest exporter of Indian cotton fabric ... and husband of your favorite dean and your party's future MP, Anandita Devi."

"What?" Dr. Khan sat up.

"Yes, and I am going to destroy that bitch. This scandal will pull Sana Sheikh down from her pedestal for good." She looked at her paramour, hoping for his support in seeking vengeance. But once again, he was lost in deep thought.

"Dr. Khan?" She nudged him, slightly hurt by his indifference. He turned towards her with a sweet smile and said, "Mind calling me Kamran?" He moved closer to her, this time his arm found her waist. Nikki didn't object.

"What do you think? I want to leak these online as early as tomorrow. I want to hurt her really bad."

"Hey, hey. Easy, babe. Relax." He placed a finger on her lips. "Sometimes, when fate hands you a trump card, you should wait to play it at the right time." Their eyes met and she melted into his arms in an instant. There was a twinkle in his eyes as he stroked her back. It may not be the card that would win him the game, but he was sure that he had been dealt an ace. He smiled and pulled Nikki closer, almost crushing her in his tight embrace.

31

Sana was deep in her research verifying a Kashmiri human rights story when her landline began to ring. She picked up the receiver, her eyes still glued to the screen.

"You bitch! How *dare* you!" snarled a man's voice.

"Excuse me?" Sana responded, shocked.

"I've already told you, I am not the source of that video. You think lodging a police complaint will scare me?" the man growled.

"Oh, Dr. Kamran Khan?" Sana's voice assumed a cool, amused tone. "I was expecting your call. And to answer your question, yes, I think you're scared. You'd be a fool not to be! I have handed over your IP address and service provider details to the police. Right as we speak, their cyber cell must be getting a court order to confiscate your laptop and computer. And don't bother cleaning out the data Dr. Khan, because that will work against you. My advice—don't mess with the cybercrime department."

"There is nothing on my computers. And if the police so much as touches me, I will sue you and your channel to the extent that it shuts down permanently."

"Do your worst, Dr. Khan! What do you think *India Truth* is, huh?" Sana growled back. "My channel is not a plaything for you power-mongering politicians. And you better watch out—because when the police are done with you, you'll be facing charges under Sections 153A and 295A for causing communal unrest. You've committed political suicide, Dr. Khan. And I will cheerfully cover the death of your career on primetime on my channel. You will be our next breaking news, you murdering bastard!"

Dr. Khan gave a humorless laugh. "I will make you pay for that comment, Sana. Remember that."

The line went dead.

Sana sat back and took a deep breath. Then she quickly dialed a number from memory. The call was promptly answered by the Defense Minister, Arjun Jaisinghani himself.

"Sana?" The minister was a bit surprised. It wasn't like her to call him on his direct number during official hours.

"Arjunji, I know you are busy but can you spare a few seconds for Dr. Kamran Khan?"

"That's okay, Sana. I have half an hour until my cabinet meeting."

"He already knows that I filed a complaint against him," Sana said without preamble.

"Well, he is a politician. He is bound to have some insider information. But don't worry, his knowing it won't change a thing."

"But he will try to delete or modify the data on his computers." Sana knew she had bluffed about this to Dr. Khan.

"No, he can't. Not anymore. Cybercrime officials were

at his door when he called you. By now, they must have taken his computers in their possession."

"How do you know he called me?"

"As I said, Sana, we are keeping an eye on him and many others like him. I am hoping to find much more than the proof of that video on those hard drives. All I can say for now is that there is a security threat looming over our country and I am going to turn every stone to find the links that will lead me to the culprits."

"Alright. I hope you do." Sana sighed.

"What's the matter, Sana?" The minister's instincts were as strong as his empathetic sense.

"Nothing. All this is getting so tiresome. I was just researching a story on human rights violation in Kashmir by an international news agency. It's so lopsided and preconceived." Sana sounded frustrated. "Even if you want to help solve the problem they won't let you."

"Sana, when a problem becomes too complex, the only way to handle it is to do it in a straight, simple manner. And that's only possible on ground zero, in Kashmir. By listening to the problems and grievances of the people there, face to face."

"You mean talk to the separatists, people who don't want to be a part of India? Those who incite Kashmiris to throw stones at their own army? They just want to paint a bad picture about the government in the international media, using human right violations as a card."

"And that's not possible for them to do if we, as a government, have transparent, open talks with the Kashmiris."

"You aren't thinking of going to Kashmir, are you?" Sana asked cautiously.

"Well, Kashmir is a part of our country. So if that's the only solution available, then I will go." Then, as if on cue, the desk phone at the minister's end started ringing. He excused himself and disconnected the call.

Sana had a sinking feeling in her gut as she wondered if she had failed to warn the well-meaning minister, who was practically family, enough about the risks and threats that Kashmir posed. *Was it because that was her home once? Was she so selfish? Or did she still wish for peace in the valley she had left behind long ago.* She had no answers, only a jumbled web of questions threatening to unravel her.

32

Akshara's eyes were staring hard at the screen while her fingers tap-danced over the keyboard. She had already established a link between Dr. Khan's IP address and the origin of the controversial video. For the last 48 hours, she had been looking for his connection to the Middle East. Layer after layer, the firewalls collapsed before her matchless mind. Her table was littered with chocolate wrappers and empty coffee cups. Project Jai Hind's team members were taking turns to be with her in the Sit Room. The faster they unearthed their enemy's plan, the higher their chance of stopping its execution. The clock was ticking, and fast.

It was close to eight in the morning when Anandan gazed around, bleary-eyed. Having spent many sleepless nights interrogating criminals, he was used to it. But his age was steadily catching up with him. Shakily getting to his feet, Anandan announced, "I am sick of the pantry coffee. Heading out to the deli. Anybody want some fresh coffee and something real to eat?"

Major Arya raised his hand with a smile but before he could speak, Akshara banged her fist on the desk with a *"Yesss!"*

For the first time since she had received Dr. Khan's laptop, Akshara Swaminathan had a smile of triumph on her face. But as Major Arya and Anandan hurried to her desk, her face wilted.

"Damn," she whispered. "It's that website I mentioned earlier. The one selling gold-plated Qurans and referring to *Rub-el-Hizb*. Dr. Khan has been visiting its chat room regularly for the past year. Look!"

She made space for them to join her at the desk. As they peered at the monitor, she continued, "The encrypted messages come from an IP address in Egypt. There is a mention of *Rub-el-Hizb* and of its arrival in India. There is also a reference to a young operative who is supposed to be the carrier of a ring marked with the *Rub-el-Hizb* symbol. Apparently, this operative is here to lead an important mission. I could possibly establish a further link to *Tehrik-e-Islam*, but I need a little more time. But in any case, Dr. Khan's involvement in this is as good as confirmed."

"Any reference to the operative's age, sex, location … anything that can help with identification?" Major Arya asked.

"Nope. They are being discreet. I only know that this operative is key to the mission—in all likelihood, a suicide mission."

"Suicide mission?" Anandan's sharp mind was already sifting through the information.

"Yes. The ring is hollow and holds a lethal dose of a fast-acting poison. Something like cyanide, I imagine."

"Do these chats tell you how far the operation has advanced?" asked Anandan.

"It's clear they have been moving resources. If the key players are already in the country, they may well be executing their plans soon."

"Any reference to the nature of the operation?" Major Arya asked.

"No," Akshara said in a dismal voice, as if she were personally responsible for the lack of such information.

"Alright. Send me the transcript of the conversation on my secure email ID. And go home and get some sleep, Akshara. You did good." Major Arya smiled at her and then said to Anandan, "Our turn's up. It's time to report to Mr. Bakshi. We need a plan of action and fast."

33

By noon, Rajeev Bakshi was in the Defense Ministry's waiting room. Outside the office, a spacious meeting room was buzzing with an eager, hand-picked set of media correspondents. They were milling around the government-issued tea and biscuits, waiting for the scheduled press conference, all with a decided air of self-importance. And, they were all looking for an exclusive interview with Arjun Jaisinghani after his press conference, where the minister was supposed to make an important announcement.

Bakshi stood up as the minister entered with an open file in his hand. He was followed by three somber office bearers. He snapped the file shut and issued quick instructions before dismissing his staff. He nodded at Rajeev to take a seat and settled into his chair.

"Rajeev, what do you have for me?"

"We've confirmed that Kamran Khan is in touch with an Egyptian group—possibly *Tehrik-e-Islam*. His laptop contains some evidence of collusion in activities against India. We're also considering the possibility that Dr. Khan is the handler of a key operative who has already arrived in India."

The minister contemplated this information for a brief moment before commenting, "Any other names that have cropped up, besides his?"

"None, as of now, but we are still digging. Minister, as per our earlier request, can we now bring in Dr. Khan for questioning? It is time that we find out the nature of the hit. We don't even know if it's civilian, political or against the armed forces."

"If you go by *Tehrik-e-Islam's* SOP, he is too low a rung on the ladder for that kind of information. The moment you bring him in, they will simply cut him loose. And you will lose a vital thread. We need more substantial leads. In my opinion, let Kamran be for now. Just intensify your watch. I mean, go all out. I will get you all the surveillance permissions. Sooner or later, the rat will lead you to the cheese. Other than that, it's your operation." The minister shot him a tense smile.

Silence fell between the two men. Then the minister's phone began to ring. He smiled when he saw the call was from Mahmoud Raza, the popular defense analyst of the country and an old ally.

"Hello, Raza. To what do I owe the pleasure of your call?"

"Your damned stubbornness!" the sturdy voice on the other end said.

"And your timing is impeccable as ever. I am all set for the press conference."

"Call it off while you can, my friend," Raza said.

"Your sense of humor is still intact," the minister laughed in response.

"So is your penchant for needless adventuring, Arjun. This isn't worth it. Going to Kashmir to hold talks with the separatists just doesn't make sense. You are the Defense Minister of India. It's too damn risky."

"Come on, Raza. It's my job to secure our borders against Pakistan. And that can only happen if Kashmir is at peace."

"Do as you wish," he sighed. "But do you really think they will let the peace talks happen? The people who don't want peace in Kashmir can go to any extent. And why must you announce it? Once it's part of the program, you will have to go or else the opposition will rip you apart. So, when you go, take enough security with you." Mahmoud Raza used the warning as a last salvo.

"I know what you are trying to tell me, my friend. Let's meet soon." He sighed and disconnected the call. He looked up at a worried Rajeev Bakshi staring at him in disbelief.

"Sir, you are planning to visit Kashmir? When?"

"Next month. To meet with the Kashmir Liberation Front."

"Sir, don't mind me saying this, but isn't this a rather sensitive time to be doing so? With the border tensions, terrorist threats and other human rights issues flaring up in Kashmir. Our intelligence reports aren't favorable."

"I know, Rajeev, but I must go. The time will never be perfect unless someone is willing to take the necessary steps. Besides, I have the Project Jai Hind team to keep an eye out for me." He stood up and shook hands with Rajeev. "And do keep Kamran Khan on a tight leash.

He will get you your answers." And then the minister exited his office and stepped into the hubbub of clamoring journalists.

Rajeev Bakshi was left standing alone in the office. *What was holding back the minister from going at Kamran Khan? What was the minister not sharing with his team … and why?*

34

The time for evening prayers at Tora prison was fast approaching. It being Friday, the auspicious day of the week, the inmates were allowed to offer prayers facing eastwards on the open square. Not a single prisoner wanted to miss out on this little slice of freedom. As a result, the corridors along the prison cells were empty.

A prison guard padded softly to Al-Gazzar's cell. He saw the criminal mastermind standing eerily still, without his crutch, facing the guard. He silently extended his hand, palm turned upwards. The guard fumbled under his jacket and drew out a bulky sat-phone and handed it over. Al-Gazzar nodded and the guard immediately stepped away.

Leisurely, the old man punched in a number and held the phone to his ear as the phone rang all the way in India.

"*Salaam-Alaikum, janaab,*" Awais Sheikh, alias Ashraf Shaheen, answered reverently.

"*Wa-Alaikum-Salaam*, my Shaheen, may Allah bless you. Hope the winds of Hind are suiting you."

"Yes, I am keeping my head down."

"The time to rise has come, my son. You will make contact with our key operative, who is already in Hind.

You will be assisting in our mission Valley of Death. Our Muslim brothers in Hind are relying on you."

"As you wish, *Sayyid*. Any more instructions for me?" Awais addressed Al-Gazzar with his favorite title—that of a royal person and a supposed descendant of Muhammad himself. He knew this pleased Al-Gazzar.

"Stay safe, my child. You are my special offering in the service of Allah. Your instructions will reach you in Hind soon, along with the operative's contact co-ordinates. Be ready. Your cause is great and the rise of Caliphate is as certain as the rise of the sun each day." With that, he disconnected the call.

A conniving smile crept on his lips as Al-Gazzar punched in another number immediately. He spoke urgently in fluent Palestinian Arabic for a few seconds, shooting crisp instructions and listening keenly. All the while, his eyes never left the guard who was making a show of not listening by staring into his cell phone. Al-Gazzar disconnected the call and handed over the sat-phone to the guard with a knowing smile—a smile that reflected such evil that it was capable of curdling the blood of any sane being.

The guard locked the door to the cell and quickly walked away, as if chased by a dark force wanting to claim him. He exhaled only after he had stepped out into the evening sun filtering on to the prison ground. But even the rising sound of the evening prayers failed to calm his disturbed soul.

35

"What do you mean, Dr. Khan?" Anandita Devi snapped, her eyes blazing with a mix of shock and anger.

This wasn't the agenda she had in mind when she had accepted his invitation to meet for a discussion over dinner. Dr. Khan primly placed his fork on the napkin and with a polite smile gestured to the attendant who quickly refilled their glasses with the expensive champagne they were consuming at an exclusive Italian restaurant. Then he focused on Anandita Devi and spoke.

"I mean that I am from the minority community and I don't feel safe anymore in this country."

He sipped the champagne and continued, "And I need you to help me. I can assure you that this will also confirm a Member of Parliament seat for you."

"You want me to prove India is unsafe for the minority community by staging a mini riot in my college? You must be out of your mind," she replied.

"No, not a riot. Just a planned targeting of a student. Something akin to a ragging gone rough, leading to a skirmish maybe?" He shrugged.

"I believe you have identified the student too," she smirked.

"Oh yes, it has to be a Muslim of course. Aliya Sheikh, a third-year student of computer science. And if it makes you feel any better, she is fairly new to your college."

"You mean Sana Sikander Sheikh's daughter? The one who arrived from London this year?" Disbelief was etched on her face.

"Of course, it has to be a known name. Just so that people know that even the privileged members of the Muslim community aren't safe anymore. Makes tactical sense," he said, concentrating hard on selecting a piece of antipasti.

"It makes no sense whatsoever, Dr. Khan. And I shall now leave you alone with your delirious thoughts." She stood up and threw her napkin on her plate.

As she was retrieving her purse, Dr. Khan spoke again, "Sit down, Ananditaji. I need to talk to you about your husband as well."

She froze. He insisted again, pointing politely at the chair, "Please."

"I didn't want to do this, but you leave me no choice." He sighed and then retrieved the old photograph from his jacket pocket and handed it to her. "Take a look. Maybe this will change your mind."

With a single glance at the picture, Anandita Devi's expression changed from haughty to confused. She knew both the individuals in the photograph. One of them was her husband, Anurag.

"What is this, Dr. Khan? I do not appreciate you digging into my husband's past," she spoke evenly, without commenting on the presence of Sana Sikander

Sheikh in her husband's arms. If he had a past, she could deal with it, but she wasn't going to give the conceited, bigoted man sitting before her the satisfaction of needling her.

"Well, I didn't have to dig at all. I just need to tell you certain things you should know." He sat back, steepled his fingers and contemplated her.

"Dr. Khan, if your theatrics are over, can I leave now? I am kind of done here."

"Not yet," he said, handing her a small stack of odd pieces of paper and photographs that together established her husband's two-year relationship with Sana. And then he gave her Sana's hospital report dated January 6, 1991. He leaned in and said, "Prior to Delhi, your husband was in Kashmir, am I correct? You can check with him which day he left behind Srinagar and Sana Sheikh, alone with a child … his child." He stressed the last few words.

"What are you suggesting, Dr. Khan?" Anandita Devi's voice was low, filled with cold fury.

"I am not suggesting, Ananditaji. I am telling you. Aliya Sheikh is your husband's illegitimate child with Sana Sheikh. The rest … I am sure you can do the math yourself." He sipped the champagne again, pleased that he had chosen to meet her in a public place. Maximum impact. Minimum drama.

Anandita Devi sat still for a few minutes and then got up and left, this time without a word. But she had taken with her the proof he had presented.

36

Aliya peered through the window of the mobile shop that doubled as a service provider and gift shop. The place had a festive feel—decorated with loud posters and bright displays announcing attractive discounts. Due to its proximity to her university campus, it was teeming with student customers.

Twice she had spotted her man, who was a large specimen, seemingly unsuitable for secretive jobs. Yet, he was the clandestine courier service her organization used. If they had a delivery or a pick up, even a message to receive or give, it was done cleanly and without any lingering. In and out.

This courier was beginning to bother her though. She had already given him two opportunities to approach, but he had held back. If he wasn't a courier, then she was undoubtedly under surveillance. *By whom,* she wondered, as her mind played out various options. Maintaining her cover was top priority.

Aliya moved away from the window and mixed in with the crowds. *Better get on with the mission on hand,* she thought. She began ambling towards the store owner by the counter. Round and bespectacled, this guy normally wouldn't have attracted a second look. Nevertheless, his shop had a reputation for questionable dealings locally. It could be the ideal place for a person to purchase four sim cards and two dual-sim phones without the necessary paper trail. She loitered close by, concentrating on cute teddy bear key chains and novelty fridge magnets, until he was free of customers.

Finally, the owner turned to her in a pointed manner. The counter was temporarily empty and Aliya moved quickly, picking up a random red key chain.

"How much for this?" She placed the item in front of him. And then she lifted the plain metal ring hanging by a thick black thread around her neck and turned it in her fingers. The *Rub-el-Hizb* flashed under the store's LED glare. It caught the shop owner's gaze and he turned pale. His eyes darted around the store and then back to Aliya's scrutinizing look. Undoubtedly, he had recognized the symbol. He opened his mouth to speak and then stopped abruptly as his eyes shifted beyond her shoulder.

"Aliya? Where the hell have you been!" Shezii drew up, huffing.

"Why are you here?" She spoke in a low inflamed voice as she stepped away from the counter. The ring was once again hidden under her shirt and the shopkeeper had retreated.

"Did you know your mom was here a while back. She has been looking for you. You didn't go home last night?"

Aliya was walking rapidly away, but Shezii followed

implacably. He let her exit the shop and then blocked her path. "What? You don't want to see your mom?"

Aliya snapped.

"She is *my* mom, okay? And I'll do what I need to do. So get out of my way and stop encroaching upon my life." She jabbed a finger into his chest, "I know guys like you too well. No need for this 'I am the good guy' drama, because it doesn't really matter what I think of you. *You* don't matter to me."

"Hey Aliya, take it easy." Shezii lifted his hands, palms out, and shrugged. "I was just trying to help. Y'know, this anger of yours will burn you. Try focussing it on your problems, not on people, alright? Because right at this moment, I don't feel that you deserve any help." With that he turned and walked away.

Aliya glanced back at the shop. Through the glass pane, she could see the shop owner making a conscious attempt at being busy. He never once glanced in her direction. Damn it! She had managed to scare away and burn an asset, thanks to a nosy suitor. This was the worst possible scenario.

But she knew that this time she had managed to push Shezii away for good. The problem was that she wasn't feeling okay about it anymore. So, with one last glance at him sauntering away, she turned towards her car.

Right now, she had yet another problem at hand. Her mother. What was supposed to be a perfect cover for her as a student was now working against her. Very soon, she would need a neutral site to operate from.

As Aliya walked away, Awais ducked back into the nondescript, dust-covered SUV with tinted windows, parked across the street from the mobile shop. When he had received the contact co-ordinates of a key operative in Delhi, he hadn't expected it to be a young, waif-like girl just out of her teens. But she was sharp no doubt. Through his years of difficult operations executed in crowded markets of Bangladesh, busy subway stations in London and serene parks in France, he had never been spotted by the subject of his surveillance. But she had done it twice, he was sure.

He was supposed to make contact but he had held back for further observation. Firstly, he wanted to verify her and secondly, there was something vaguely familiar about her—something he couldn't put his finger on.

The young man who had come out of the shop with her also didn't quite fit into the scheme of things. They seemed to be arguing about something, like in a lover's spat. *What the hell was she doing? Or was this also a part of her cover?*

37

He watched the girl get behind the wheel of a compact sedan. As she slipped into the flowing traffic, Awais followed. After about 30 minutes, they entered a leafy green locality with large bungalows on either side of the road. Aliya's car drove up to an imposing, wrought-iron gate and disappeared beyond it.

Awais took a picture of the property as he drove past it. As he zoomed into the photo, he froze. Written on a black granite plaque in golden letters was a name he could neither forget nor forgive. That one name was the reason he could never return to India. *Sana Sikander Sheikh*. With clumsy fingers and a fuzzy mind, Awais entered the name in the search bar on his phone. In an instant, the screen flooded with search results on the head of *India Truth*. It seemed his sister was one of the most popular television personalities.

Ignoring the security risk posed by the VIP locality, Awais swung the car around and stopped a little distance from Sana's bungalow. He hunkered down behind the wheel, fighting the urge to flee. He had run away once before. Not this time!

Just then, a Mercedes sedan turned into the lane and stopped in front of the same gate. As it turned in, Awais saw the familiar firm chin and clean-cut Kashmiri profile of his sister. His mind flooded with memories of Sana, of their childhood in Kashmir, the loss of their parents ... of Sana abandoning him for that *kafir*. And the dark days that followed until Allah had plucked him from his misery and saved his soul.

He rubbed his brow with his fingertips to ease the pressure building behind his temples. He needed answers. Most importantly, *what was their key operative doing in Sana's house?*

Awais headed back to the dingy but functional three-storied hotel, the fourth such haven he had occupied since his arrival in the country. Alone in the room, his mind played all manner of twisted games with itself. The hours crawled by. At 6:00 p.m., Awais fished out a black satellite phone and placed the scheduled call to an Egyptian number.

"*Salaam-Alaikum, Siddi,*" Awais greeted respectfully.

"*Wa-Alaikum-Salaam,* my child. Have you made contact with your operative?" Al-Gazzar's voice held a hint of impatience.

"Regarding this key operative for the mission—"

"Yes?"

"I am concerned," Awais spoke hesitantly and decided to veil his concerns a little. "The choice is somewhat unusual. I hope the person is capable of discharging such a heavy responsibility."

"Aah, my Shaheen, ever so vigilant. I expect nothing less. But do not worry. The operative's appearance is deceptive. Have you heard of Black Sand?"

"Of course, *Siddi*. The operative is becoming a legend. As deadly as *Hamad*, the Syrian desert."

"Because that's where Black Sand was trained, by the jihadi elite, after being recruited in Raqqa training camp. Your operative is none other than this rising hero."

Al-Gazzar's pride was apparent. Awais also registered the complete absence of any reference to the age and gender that might give away the identity of the operative, even on a secure line. This is what made Al-Gazzar untouchable. He had wisdom, stealth and cunningness that was beyond ordinary human capabilities. His caution also confirmed that this operative was a high-level asset to the organization.

"But … Black Sand is very much in the public eye. There is a high risk of exposure."

"Oh, you mean because of the current cover story?" Al-Gazzar chuckled sinisterly. "On the contrary, a real family provides the perfect cover. Not only is Black Sand virtually untouchable, there is also the complete freedom to act on will, until it is time."

"The relationship is real?" Awais asked in disbelief.

"Yes. However, both you and Black Sand will soon move to a more secure location. Now, do not worry and keep faith in Allah. He is your only savior."

The line went dead. Awais stared at the phone in his hand and then switched it off, placing it back into the deep recesses of his backpack. *Black Sand*, he thought, *the main operative of their dangerous jihadi mission was his sister's real daughter, his niece*. And she was ready to die with him in the service of Islam and Allah. He felt pained and proud at once.

He sat there, still as a rock, for a very long time. Then he walked up to the window and opened it. He looked up at the yellowish gibbous moon glowing serenely, well above the earthly chaos. It was going to be a full moon night in a couple of days. He sighed deeply, coming to a decision. He loved his Allah. Nothing else mattered.

38

Anandita Devi eyed the small pill bottle sitting in a corner of her work desk. It was running low on its contents, a glaring proof of her aggravated insomnia during the past week. The curtains of her study were drawn tightly shut, and the desk lamp cast a sharp, luminescent circle on her table. She took a deep breath, fighting the urge to pop in a couple of pills, even though it meant another sleepless night. Her doctor had already issued a red alert against them. It was past ten and, with the servants already in their quarters, the house was eerily silent.

This was pretty much the normal scheme of things in her life, with Anurag travelling out of the country almost all the time. His cotton clothing business made him divide most of his time between South African and European markets, with regular trips to oversee his manufacturing facilities in Vietnam. In some ways, she preferred it that way because it made it easier to explain his constant absence from her life.

Yet, Anandita hadn't failed to notice that Anurag's time away from home had increased noticeably after his octogenarian father passed away two years ago. They had since lost all semblance of being a family. Even with all the religious offerings and scientific interventions,

Anandita Devi had failed to beget a child. Anurag had always been a responsible husband to her but he drew the line at duty, and offered little on an emotional front.

With time, she had overcome this personal failing as a woman, while more than making up for it on the professional front. That is, until Dr. Kamran Khan rattled her delicately balanced life, bringing back the dark self-doubt and bitter recrimination in full force. It was making her hate Anurag, knowing full well at the same time that she wasn't being fair. It wasn't his past that bothered her, it was the living, breathing reminder in the form of his young daughter. Unacceptable! She shook herself mentally, determined not to fall into the bottomless pit of self-reproach. No way she was going to let that creep Kamran win, not even if he was making a veiled threat.

She heard a car draw up to their porch, followed by the scurrying of servants. This had to be Anurag returning from his Cape Town trip, though he wasn't expected for another couple of days. Taking this as a positive sign, Anandita rose to receive her husband.

Anurag was already on the couch when she entered the living room. He was slipping his tired feet into a pair of comfy loafers. She sat down next to him with a smile.

"You're still awake? Or did I disturb you?" Anurag said.

"No, not at all. I was in the study. How about some dinner?" she asked, already knowing the answer.

"I ate on the flight. Wouldn't mind a drink though," he said and Anandita quickly dispatched a servant for the job.

"Weren't you supposed to come back day after?"

"Yeah, some of the meetings got cancelled. And I wasn't feeling too well."

"Not well?" She moved closer and felt his forehead.

"No, no, not that way," he said, jerking away, surprised by his wife's uncharacteristic gesture. "Just a bit tired."

Anandita took back her hand, not attempting any more physical contact. Anurag put his feet up and loosened his tie. Anandita Devi eyed him as the servant served the scotch in a crystal tumbler and a slim flute glass of sparkling wine for her. He was undoubtedly an attractive man, even in his late 40s and she couldn't help visualizing him with Sana. *Why had he never mentioned Sana? Was he still affected by their past? How often did they meet up? Did he meet the child as well?* The questions spun around in her head and trapped Anandita in a web of anger and jealousy.

"Anurag, do you ever miss Kashmir?" she asked.

"Kashmir?" He looked at her, surprised. "No, not really. It was so long ago." He sipped the scotch and savoured its smooth glide down the back of his throat.

"Don't you ever wish to go back?"

"No." He swirled the ice cubes around.

"But it must have been tough, leaving everything and everyone behind," she said, scrutinizing his face.

He didn't respond.

"Actually, we've never discussed that part of your life—ever. What happened in Kashmir before you came to Delhi?" she insisted.

"Nothing. It was a time of loss and pain. Must we talk about this now? I am tired you know."

"Can we talk about it a little? You can tell me, if not as a wife, then at least as a friend."

"What's wrong with you, Anandi?" he snapped. "There is nothing for me to tell you. And why this sudden interest in my past? Has your professional life gotten so boring?"

He knew her too well, from the forced familiarity of marriage over the last two decades, to sense that her line of questioning was not merely about innocent curiosity.

Provoked by his unreasonable tone, Anandita felt her fury rise. "My professional life is under threat because of your past!" she snarled.

"What the hell?"

"I am talking about Sana Sikander Sheikh," she shot back.

Anurag downed his drink and slammed the glass on the table, "Can't believe my wife—who I am sure can't remember when we had our last meal together—is digging into my past."

"I wouldn't need to, if you had the good sense to tell me that you had a child with her," she spat.

"Are you out of your fucking mind?" Anurag whispered in shock. "Stop hallucinating! Just because you couldn't have a child ...," his voice trailed off as he realized that he had just crossed the line.

"Anandi—," he began in a softer voice, but she was already storming out. Anurag wondered if he should follow, when the door opened again. Anandita threw a folder in front of him and said, "Here you go. Have fun." Then, with her mind fixated on that small bottle of sleeping pills, she retreated into her study.

Anurag picked up the folder gingerly, his hands shaking a bit.

39

"When can I expect the delivery?" Dr. Kamran Khan typed his question in the dialog box of the chat room and watched the dots move as the response was typed from the other end.

"Third Friday of this month," the message popped up. The use of dates was avoided for tactical reasons, as numbers were more likely to be picked up by the internet spies.

"Any care instructions?" he typed.

"You may need Kashmiri saffron," the response popped up and then the other side went offline.

Dr. Khan closed the dialog box and logged off from his new laptop. The cybercrime department had not yet released his old machine but they had been surprisingly quiet. Which meant they hadn't found anything substantial on it, but he was pretty sure he was under surveillance. He was now being very careful, using only a secure server access provided specially to him by his handlers in Egypt. With a sigh, he removed his specs and rubbed his neck to loosen the tense muscles. He had just received the go signal on the mission. He now had a timeline and even the possible location. Kashmir. But he didn't yet know what the mission was about.

He only knew that he came in at the last step, at the execution stage, for organizing actual resources required for carrying out the mission. Arms and ammunition, transport, safe cover and documents, as and when required, were his responsibility. And his being called in meant the action wasn't far.

He had just hit the sack when his cell phone rang. It was almost midnight. He blinked at his phone and then sat up. Anandita Devi. His brow first knitted and then relaxed as he smiled and answered the phone. This could only be about one thing.

"Tell me, Ananditaji, what's keeping you awake this late?" he said.

"It will be done. As you said," she replied. Her voice was thick and heavy and Dr. Khan wasn't sure whether it was a result of alcohol or crying.

"I am glad you—," but she cut him off before he could finish his sentence.

"This month, during the general secretary election week." She disconnected the call.

Dr. Khan plopped back into his bed, a smile dancing on his lips. The hunt was on and things were finally going his way. All he had to do was execute a few little things neatly, and the second large parcel of money would arrive in his offshore account in Monte Carlo. No questions asked.

But there was something that he didn't know. In this hunt, he was the prey—the one who had left a clear scent of trail in the wind for his predators. And he was slowly being backed into a corner.

40

"The Warning Signs Of Islamic Radicalization," was the internet story of a Canadian woman named Christianne Boudreau, and Shezii was reading it. Bourdreau's son, all of 22 years, had died in Aleppo two years ago, after running away to Syria. This was just one of the numerous stories he had browsed through all morning. He was desperately looking for a sign, any sign. Under some critera, Aliya fit the bill entirely, and then on others, she didn't fit at all. She was intelligent no doubt, but she was also cut off from her mom and socially awkward. She no longer played the violin and hardly appeared without a scarf these days, sticking to dark, deep colors that matched her secretive behavior of late. And his last encounter with her could be easily categorized as aggravated behavior.

Shezii would have been willing to brush aside all this as his obsessive overreaction, if not for Aliya's Kashmiri roots. He knew that he was behaving like a spurned lover, but one observation by Christianne about her son's radicalization was especially troubling. *Sometimes, it's not going to be staring in your face,* she had said.

"What the hell are you doing, Shezii?!" came a voice from behind, startling him. It was Meera, staring intently at his laptop screen.

"Hey Meera." Shezii smiled sadly. She felt like a whiff of fresh cool air on a hot muggy afternoon.

There was no reason for awkwardness between them, otherwise so typical of young couples. But then, they weren't a couple. Not in the strictest sense of the term.

Meera sat down at the edge of his bed and looked into his troubled eyes. "What's up?" she asked in a softer voice.

Shezii looked at the genuine concern on the face of his oldest friend and confessed, "The nightmares are back."

"Oh God, Shezii!" Meera leaned in, her brow creased. She knew the nightmares he was referring to. They were about a large man clad in black fatigues and a mask, holding a shiny dagger that changed into a black, slithering reptile. This man didn't kill him but tried to push the snake down his throat, while Shezii struggled to not open his mouth, not even to scream.

"Yeah. For about a week now. Just like before," he said, beads of perspiration forming on his forehead. It had taken him a long time to get rid of the nightmares.

"Have you told your mom?" Meera knew that Shaziya could offer the strongest support since she had been with her son during the Tel Aviv incident.

"No, she will only get worried. Besides, they aren't as frequent and I am coping alright," Shezii said.

"It's Aliya, isn't it? She is triggering those dreams again. Can't you see it Shezii?"

Shezii sighed again. "I think she's in some kind of trouble and needs help."

"Trouble? What do you mean?" Meera narrowed her eyes.

"I am not able to put my finger on it, but the kind of people she is meeting, the places she is visiting ... none of it is normal for an exchange student from London. Have you seen her lately? She has started covering her hair with a scarf—all the time! And most of all, she has even discontinued the violin classes."

"Hey, hey ... wait a second! Are you telling me that you think Aliya is turning into a radicalized Islamist? If yes, you need to slow down. Are you even hearing yourself, Shezii? This is taking obsession to the next level. You need to stop. Now!" She stared at him, worried for his mental state, and wondered if she should tell his parents.

Then she added in a placatory tone, "Scarves are a fashion statement too, Shezii. And regarding the cancelled music classes, maybe she's busy with course work, you know?"

Meera searched his face, which still looked unconvinced.

"It's much more than that, Meera. Something doesn't fit." He shook his head.

"Don't do this, Shezii. It's not worth getting nightmares over. If you like her, keep the faith," she pleaded, her heart going out to him.

"I know, I am totally messed up. Will you help me, Meera?" He looked at her sadly as she gazed back into his eyes.

"Let's go for a long drive?" She shut off the laptop and moved closer.

"No ...," he shook his head and put his arm around her shoulder affectionately. "Let's just stay home."

The vanilla scent of her hair had a soothing, heady effect on him. She had been in this room with him almost every other day, but today was different. It was like every feature, her eyes, her mouth, her soft skin, all of her presence were in sharp focus, and everything else had faded into the background. Then he softly kissed her forehead and whispered, "Thank you for being there."

There was a sharp knock on the door and they sprang apart. Chand Bibi came in with a tray of sandwiches, cookies and coffee, muttering something about youngsters nowadays not eating enough. But they weren't paying attention as their eyes met in a warm understanding.

41

In the dim lights of the conference room, the officials from the Defense Ministry's acquisition wing were listening raptly to a European technocrat's enthusiastic sales pitch on state of the art night vision devices for Indian battle tanks. Faisal Umer Naqvi and Rajeev Bakshi had been requested by the Defense Secretary to attend in a special advisory position.

Both were impressed by the features of the devices but the presenter's tongue-in-cheek remarks about India's outdated second-generation NVDs were beginning to grate on them. Nor did he miss any opportunity to remind them of the fourth-generation devices that his company was already developing.

Faisal and Rajeev exchanged glances and shrugs. They had each decided to give a thumbs-up for the purchase, but with a strict side note to ensure hard negotiation and exclusive rights to the technology for at least five years.

With the technical presentation over, they both rose and excused themselves from the Q&A session, which would ultimately end with boring discussions on compliance related paperwork.

"Any activities on the ground?" Faisal asked as they stepped out.

Rajeev instantly knew what he was referring to.

"Nothing. Our assets have gone quiet. Dr. Khan is being cautious. One of Major Arya's sources flagged the arrival of a small batch of iridium satellite phones at the airport."

"Isn't that illegal? India allows only Inmarsat satellite service. And even that is restricted to national security agencies and defense services."

"Yes, that's why it's suspicious. Arya is trying to track their IDs. If that happens, Akshara may be able to trace any communication that takes place over the phones."

"Hm. Voice traffic on sat-phones is highly encrypted and their signals bypass the local telecom services," mused Faisal.

Before Rajeev could respond, his cell phone began to vibrate.

"Speak of the devil," he murmured, recognizing Akshara's landline from the Jai Hind command center just two floors below them. He noticed Faisal too was staring at his cell phone's screen.

"I have four missed calls from Major Arya. Something's up." Faisal looked at Rajeev questioningly.

"Let's find out," replied Rajeev and the two men headed for the lifts.

As they entered the command center, they could feel the palpable tension in the air. Arya, Anandan and Akshara were huddled around the table.

"What happened? You guys witness a ghost?" Rajeev raised his eyebrows.

"Worse actually." Major Arya sat back but his shoulders were rigid. "Akshara will brief you."

"It's those illegal satellite phones," Akshara looked around wide-eyed. "I have been tracking their GPS IDs. One of them lit up yesterday."

"Where?" Faisal asked.

"Right here in Chandni Chowk in old Delhi. It had earlier lit up in Paharganj, Jama Masjid and Kashmiri Gate."

"What? Why didn't you report this earlier?" Rajeev asked.

"Because only last night did it open a communication line to someone outside India. This gave me time to intercept the signal."

"Finally! Were you able to find out who was talking and what they discussed?"

Akshara nodded. "I've been decrypting the signal since last night. It's as bad as we expected, I'm afraid. There's a seasoned terrorist leading a mission in India. Someone who was trained at a major ISIS training hub in the Syrian desert. It's also clear this operative—codenamed Black Sand—is very much in the public eye."

"What, you mean a terrorist hiding in plain sight?" Rajeev was incredulous.

Major Arya spoke up, "We dispatched a surveillance team to Chandni Chowk late last night, narrowing the search to a two-kilometer radius from where the signal originated."

"And guess who we spotted?" Anandan placed a photograph in front of Rajeev.

It was of a man, grizzled and innocuous, eating biryani in a crowded restaurant.

"That's Ganibhai. We've been tracking him for a while. His roots are in Kashmir and he acts as a low-level courier between many radical groups active within and outside Kashmir. But we have reasons to believe that he actually plays a bigger role. He is an old-timer and sly as a fox. The only reason he couldn't spot our men was that they were all new." Anandan paused and looked at Major Arya.

"But what's more important is this," Arya placed another candid photograph of Ganibhai exiting a dilapidated hotel. By his side was a broad-shouldered bear of man carrying a large black backpack.

"This man is our concern." He tapped the photo. "This is Ashraf Shaheen, a long-term associate of *Tehrik-e-Islam*. What he's doing with Ganibhai is anybody's guess."

"Did we get him?" Faisal asked, worry writ on his face.

"No." Anandan shook his head slowly. "He was gone by the time we made a positive identification and sent our back-up team. We had to keep it covert. Can't let the media get a whiff of a renowned terrorist organization's presence on Indian soil. At least not until we have actionable intelligence in our hands."

"So are we back to square one?" Rajeev asked, somewhat bitterly.

"Not really," Major Arya spoke. "Thanks to our intelligence exchange program with Israel, we just looked up Ashraf Shaheen's file with Mossad. Apparently, he is an Indian export, right from our own Kashmir. His real name is Awais Sheikh, from Srinagar. We are digging up more info on him."

Rajeev Bakshi pulled the photo closer to him and circled the face of the guy with Ganibhai. Next to it, he scribbled *Ashraf Shaheen aka Awais Sheikh. Origin Kashmir*. He pointed his phone at it, clicked a shot and emailed the image to Jaisinghani.

Then he dialed a number. When the line connected, he said, "Prasanna, please inform the minister that I've sent classified info to his secure email ID. We need him to authorize a red alert across all allied anti-terrorism departments. *Immediately*. I'll be waiting for his response."

He then turned to face his team and said, "I want this guy traced and nabbed. *Now!* Do whatever it takes. I have a few questions only he can answer."

42

The sharp knock jerked Anandita Devi out of her reverie. She looked up to find Krishna Sahu's grinning face peering through the half open door. She nodded and pointed her pen towards the chairs across her table. Sahu immediately took a seat and gazed expectantly at her. On the other hand, Anandita felt edgy and irritable simply looking at him. Though this had been her general state of mind for the past few days. It had taken a lot of mental back and forth before she had summoned this self-declared student leader, who was in reality a borderline goon. Nevertheless, he was the favorite candidate for the upcoming student body elections, with sturdy support from the youth wing of the ruling government.

"How are your preparations for the election coming along?"

"Good, very good indeed, ma'am. The students are charged up."

"Are you going to win?" she said flatly, rifling through random sheaves of paper before her.

"Of course!" He puffed out his chest and gloated, "It is next to impossible to defeat an Akhand Bharat Parishad candidate. ISU has no chance."

"Hm. Isn't ISU funded generously by representatives of minority communities?"

"Yes, but that doesn't matter, ma'am. We have the numbers."

"Still, winning the General Secretary election is a lot of hard work, isn't it? And this year is your only chance."

"Yes, it is."

"So, what would you do if someone tried to sabotage your efforts?" She looked at him directly.

"I ... I don't understand, ma'am." The smug expression had vanished from his face.

"I have just been informed that ISU is using a very rich, very influential student to canvass for them. The candidate has been offering expensive gifts and exclusive parties. Is it really possible you know nothing about it? Even when your voters are turning against you?"

Sahu sprang to his feet, his eyes blazing. "Do you know who this person is?"

"I don't want an anti-government wing like ISU operating on my college campus. I will give you a name ... but only if you assure me that you can do something about it."

"Just give me the name, ma'am, and watch what happens." His tone was hard.

"Aliya Sheikh." She saw a flicker of recognition pass across his face and added. "She is the daughter of Sana Sheikh—the celebrity owner of *India Truth*."

"Aliya Sheikh," he growled, remembering the snooty girl with the violin. That pretty friend of Shezii's, who had given him enough attitude.

"So, how will you handle it? Don't forget, she is very well connected."

"Don't worry, ma'am. I know how to handle this. She is new here and she needs to learn the ways of Madhav Raje College. That's all." His smile was cold as he stood up to leave. "Thanks for the support, ma'am."

"Oh and Sahu, if someone ever asks, I know nothing about it." He acknowledged her warning with a nod.

As the door closed, Anandita Devi sank back in her cushy chair. Then, she clicked the camera icon on her desktop to reactivate the CCTV camera perched high on the wall behind her desk. She had done her part. Now all she could do was wait to see how far the dice rolled.

43

The old refurbished three-storied hotel was actually an old-style apartment building from at least half a century ago. Its rooms had just one cot each with faded bedsheets and a plastic jug filled with tap water on a small side table. But it offered benefits any five-star hotel could not—anonymity and secrecy. The hotel didn't ask for any identification and accepted payment in cash.

This suited Awais Sheikh perfectly and it was way safer than renting. In any case, he wasn't planning to be in Delhi much longer. From the small window in his room, he scanned the crowded street of Chandni Chowk, two floors below. The parapet in front of the window was covered with bird droppings and accumulated feathers. As he started to shut the wooden panes, a couple of pigeons took flight, raising the dust. Awais covered his mouth and sneezed.

He turned and focused on Ganibhai who was sitting on a small plastic stool, his hands clasped primly in his lap.

"What do you think, Ganibhai?"

"Don't know, *janaab*. This is the first time a woman is leading a mission. She is also too young." He shook his head.

"Hmm." Awais nodded but a bigger issue was bothering him.

"But I am sure the high command knows better. *Inshallah*, things will work in our favor."

"*Inshallah*," he responded distractedly.

The only way to proceed was to verify their operative and he decided to get it from the horse's mouth.

"Ganibhai, please alert your ground resources in Kashmir. They should be ready for action. Also, we will be soon moving to the jump site in Delhi, together as a team. Once we do that, all outside communication will be discontinued. We will literally vanish. So, make sure everything is in order at our safe house."

"Yes, *janaab*, I will do that."

"Your home village is near Srinagar, am I correct?"

"About 50 kms from Srinagar, *janaab*. It's called Bongam, close to Shopian." He sounded eager and nostalgic.

"Okay, now go get some good rest tonight, while you can." It was close to 9:00 p.m. and they both preferred to dine alone. "But first, go out to eat something, and stay alert," Awais said.

Ganibhai nodded and left promptly, aware that his dinner trip was more about counter-surveillance measures, to keep an eye out, even when no one was watching.

Left alone in the room, Awais pulled out his Swiss military backpack from under the cot and fished out the black satellite phone from inside it. He then checked his watch. His call to Al-Gazzar in Egypt for follow-up instructions was scheduled for 6:00 p.m. sharp. There were still 15 minutes to go. The call he was about to make was for the ears of 'top clearance' operatives only. And that did not include Ganibhai even though Awais knew he could rely on him.

Ganbhai had the nose of a dog and he could sniff out any surveillance from a mile. He also knew the faces of all key surveillance agents of the Indian secret service and their individual styles. He could spot a suspicious speck in the distance and could see through any fake identity or persona.

Finally, as his mobile hit 9:30 p.m. India time, Awais dialed the country code followed by the number he knew by heart. His call was answered promptly in Egypt.

44

Aliya killed the engine and stepped out of the car. It was 6:30 a.m. on a mild winter morning. The parking lot of Lodhi Gardens was almost empty, with just a few cars belonging to the fitness freaks who jogged there every morning. Dawn was just breaking and the birds were rejoicing, their unanimous chirping filling the atmosphere with a singular, pleasant sound. That was one of the reasons people looking for solace from Delhi's crazy lifestyle escaped to the 90 acres of this fifteenth century garden every morning.

But Aliya was not there for fitness or peace, even though she was dressed in sneakers and a jumpsuit that hugged her slight frame. This was one of her three weekly dead-drop site visits. The other two sites, a shopping mall and her college library, were also public places. Dead-drop meant that there wouldn't be a courier waiting to meet her. It was a foolproof and minimal risk method of transfer, with an option to abort till the last minute. After the incident with Shezii during the last courier drop, she preferred this. For now, things were fairly on track but if there were any special directions or warnings for her from the organization, she would find them here.

Aliya broke into a light jog like a professional marathon runner, her ponytail bobbing rhythmically. She headed towards the square beside the rose garden, to the last bench at the far end of the garden, far from the jogging track and partially hidden behind a bottlebrush tree. Aliya slowed down as she neared the spot and eyed the bench casually, before continuing on her course. It was empty. It was a two-kilometer track, which meant that at her current speed, she would pass the spot again in 15 minutes. She continued jogging. She had to stick to the procedure. No shortcuts.

On her second pass, she spotted a pink flower on the bench. She stopped and squatted, pretending to tie her shoe laces. Then, she rose and moved to the edge of the track and quickly did a few thigh and back stretches, while she scanned the sparse crowd completing their circuits. A couple of dedicated fitness enthusiasts concentrating hard on their breath passed by, followed by a chatty group of aging housewives and a bunch of retired well-to-do businessmen, feverishly debating politics. All was well.

Aliya approached the bench. The fresh rose hadn't been there on her first pass. Plucking flowers in the garden was strictly forbidden and this meant there was a package waiting for her. She had to get to the secluded area behind Bada Gumbad within Lodhi Gardens and look for the trash receptacle marked for her.

She briskly jogged towards the site and, as soon as the track was empty, broke off from the main track onto the grass patch towards her destination. She spotted the garbage bin up front, right next to the green board of the Archaeological Survey of India that announced the area as a world heritage site. But just across the garden patch she also saw a couple strolling, hand in hand, very much in love, probably looking for a spot to make out. They eyed her consciously, clearly uncomfortable with her sudden appearance.

There was no way she could retrieve the package from the bin while they watched. She thought of coming back later but it was too risky. Just then, the couple turned in the opposite direction and started to walk away, giggling. Aliya looked around and quickly approached the bin, hoping that whatever it held for her wasn't too bulky. She cursed herself for leaving her windbreaker in the car. Her body-hugging jumpsuit offered no scope for concealment.

She looked around furtively before bending down to feel inside the bin's mouth. Taped to it was an envelope. Luckily, it was slim and not too heavy. She pried it loose and brought it out. Quickly shoving it inside the front of her jumpsuit, she zipped it up higher. She turned and plugged in her headphones and then put her hands in her pocket, adapting the stance of a casual stroller.

Just as she started to walk away, a male voice called out to her. She froze and turned slowly. It was the same couple. The girl had fallen back but the tense looking boyfriend was approaching her purposefully. He had a suspicious look on his face. *Had he seen her getting the envelope out?* Aliya stiffened, working out various scenarios in her head. She could not afford to draw the attention of the law just because some bloke was feeling overly responsible towards society on that particular morning.

"Excuse me!" He gestured for her to stop.

Aliya stopped. He had seen her face. Running was not an option. At best, she would convince him and at worst, she would have to neutralize him. The girl too would have to be collateral damage. Removing her headphones, she glanced around. There was nobody on the tracks now and the next pass of the group of strollers would probably be at least 12 minutes later. She had enough time.

"Excuse me, could you please tell me if there is a metro station nearby?" the worried guy asked.

"Huh?"

"My girlfriend needs to get back home quick. Metro is the fastest," he explained.

"Oh, I think JLN Metro Station is the closest." Aliya gave him quick instructions and jogged away without responding to their thankful goodbyes. She didn't stop until she was in her car. She wiped the sweat off her forehead and opened the envelope. It had an address and the name and contact number of a man. The address in Saket was new to her but she was aware this was the secret jump-site she would have to move to by the end of next week.

The man she knew well. In fact, the name surprised her and she smiled to herself. So, this was the man who would be providing them tactical and logistical support, including the guns and explosives. This meant that things were now moving fast. And with each passing day she was getting closer to her target. She could sense the hard work of the past few years coming to a culmination.

A little distance from her car, a nondescript man in casual shirt and pants chucked the paper cup with half-drunk tea in a bin and started to walk away. He had a phone stuck to his ear. "Everything is on track," he spoke tersely and disconnected the call.

45

The normally well-organized desk of the Defense Minister Arjun Jaisinghani was now cluttered with files and documents awaiting his perusal. With the red alert declared for all allied anti-terrorism departments, the reports were flooding in. They were all urgent and important. But that wasn't the reason he felt edgy. The real reason was lying in front of him, on top of all the documents. A photograph of a man identified as Ashraf Shaheen aka Awais Sheikh, by Team Jai Hind. He eyed it one more time and glanced through the copy of a file on the man in question, provided by the world's most renowned secret service, the Mossad. There was no doubt that this was Ashraf Shaheen, a known member of the dreaded terrorist outfit *Tehrik-e-Islam*. Unfortunately, he was also the younger brother of Sana Sikander Sheikh, a well-wishing renowned celebrity, whom the minister considered a sister. Additional background checks had confirmed this fact beyond doubt.

Sana deserved to hear this from him, even though he had no control over Awais Sheikh's ultimate fate. After a short deliberation, he had decided that this was best done in as straightforward a manner as possible. So, he had invited her immediately to his office.

A short double-tap knock broke his reverie. Seeing Sana, he quickly turned the A-4 sized photograph face down and inhaled deeply before calling out, "Come, come."

Sana didn't say anything as she entered but her creased forehead revealed her state of mind. It wasn't normal to be urgently called to the office of the Defense Minister, by the man himself. She took the seat in front of him without a word.

"How are you, Sana?" The minister smiled uncomfortably.

"What's this about, Arjunji?" She searched his face.

"I have something to tell you, Sana."

"Yes?"

The minister slowly turned the photograph over and pushed it across the table towards her.

"Who is ...," Sana started, but then her voice was lost as she slowly pulled the photo towards her. Her eyes changed first, from faint recognition to wide with shocked disbelief.

"Is he dead?" She looked up sharply, her expression a mix of pain and hurt.

He shook his head slowly. "He is very much alive and possibly in Delhi now. He is working with *Tehrik-e-Islam*." The minister didn't say any more, leaving Sana to deduce the rest.

Silence engulfed them as Sana grappled with the news. All these years of waiting for her brother, fearing the worst and hoping for the best, had finally come to this end. She stared at the photograph for the longest time. *Her brother was a terrorist?*

"Sana?" Arjun Jaisinghani finally called out softly. Not because he was getting impatient but because he was worried. Apart from the personal loss, this news had professional and legal implications for Sana.

She looked up and said, "You know what, all these years, my brother died many times in my imagination. And I never stopped grieving for him. It felt brave and good, but now ... it feels like it was a waste." She looked away. Her eyes were dry but the hollowness in them had a haunting quality. "It's like ... like facing pitch black darkness. The one you experience after a bright light has been suddenly extinguished."

"Sana, this isn't on you. You are not responsible."

"Then why does life feel like a series of personal losses?" she whispered.

"What your life is depends upon whether you want to focus on what's shredding you to pieces or what's keeping you together."

"I have to tell Aliya," she spoke suddenly, as if stepping out of a trance.

"No, Sana," he advised cautiously. "Aliya is going through a rebel phase, just like any other young adult. I don't think you should further upset her already troubled psyche. The current circumstances of Awais might just tip her off the edge. Besides, you need to first weigh all your options, on all possible fronts."

Sana did not respond. There were legal aspects to be considered. If word got out about her relationship with a terrorist, she would be definitely looped in for questioning. And that was the not-so-bad scenario. The worst case would be for her to be accused of conspiring with a terrorist.

"This is a copy of his file." He handed her a slim folder. "As of now, I am keeping this on a 'need to know' basis. Which means, until we track him down, no one apart from me and my special team will know of his identity. But you do know that I will have no further control on things, once we get him."

"I understand." Her tone was guarded. "You said that he is in Delhi. Do you think he will go back to Kashmir?" Her hands were white as porcelain, tightly clasping the file.

"Don't know, Sana. All I know is that he is a terrorist out on a mission." The minister stared at the photograph as he spoke. He knew what her sharp mind was thinking. But he couldn't divulge more to her, even if he wanted to. He had already crossed a line by sharing a classified file on a known terrorist with Sana, who was a media personality.

For now, he sat back and watched Sana slowly turn the pages of the file on her brother. The minister decided not to disturb her, fervently hoping that she would find some closure in those pages. He had a feeling that this was the one and only death ritual she would get to perform.

46

The atmosphere was electric. It was election day at Madhav Raje University and large groups of students roamed its campus and corridors, wearing T-shirts that proclaimed their allegiance to the General Secretary they were supporting. There were only two in the race—the favorite, Krishna Sahu of Akhand Bharat Parishad, a popular student front and the other, a relatively unknown name representing Indian Students Union.

Shezii and Meera were ambling towards the canteen when Shezii's phone began to ring. It was a vaguely familiar number and he picked it up.

"Hello, Shezii *bhai*?" The voice was overtly friendly.

"Is that Krishna ... Krishna Sahu?" Shezii asked.

"Yes, yes."

"What's up, buddy? You must be super busy today. How are things looking for you?"

"Shezii *bhai*, that's exactly what I wanted to talk about. More specifically, about your lady friend."

"My lady friend?" Shezii looked quizzically at Meera, who was now curiously listening in. She knew that if Krishna Sahu had called, he must have an agenda. And that it wasn't going to be either pleasant or normal.

"Sheikh *sahiba*, remember?" Sahu said bitterly.

"You are talking about Aliya? What about her?" Shezii's grip on the phone got tighter, his manner no longer easy. Meera shifted restlessly next to him.

"You tell her to stay out of my way, Shezii *bhai*. She is a friend of yours so I am making this call as a courtesy. Otherwise, I have easier ways to fix girls like her." Sahu's words had lost all semblance of friendliness as he ground out the ultimatum.

"What? What do you mean, fix her? What has she done?" Shezii spoke frantically.

"Tell her, she is messing with the wrong guy, Shezii *bhai*."

"Wait ... Leave Aliya alone. I am in college now. I'm coming over to meet you. You leave Aliya alone, do you he—," he spoke hurriedly only to hear the beeping tone. The call had already been disconnected.

Shezii turned to Meera and said, "Hey, sorry but I have to rush off for a bit. Looks like Aliya is in trouble."

Meera nodded tersely. The ease with which Shezii prioritized Aliya over them hurt, but she was also proud of the decisive way in which he stood up to help someone in trouble.

At the car park, Aliya locked her car and entered the campus, only so that she would be seen as part of the crowd on the pretext of exchanging library books. She decided to take the roundabout route to the library via the canteen to avoid the bustling crowd on the main campus. The path that passed the canteen was also teeming with students, but at least the groups were smaller and scattered. She slowed in her tracks as she spotted Krishna

Sahu at a distance. She remembered him because she herself had tagged him as a pesky troublemaker, right at the beginning. Not an obstacle exactly, but a stumbling block at best. Right now, he was surrounded by a group of senior students who fancied themselves on par with Black Cat Commandoes. In reality, they looked more like inflated bean bags, unfit and untrained in any security skill. Before she could look away, their eyes met and she could sense a hostile vibe. Krishna Sahu was looking directly at her. She continued on her path, deliberately ignoring him. She wanted no unnecessary attention but now that he had seen her, she couldn't change her path or retreat. She sensed trouble brewing as he said something to his group and the formation around him changed. They were now standing in a semi-arc flanking him, openly confrontational.

"Wait, Sheikh *sahiba*," Krishna Sahu called out as she drew closer.

Aliya looked at him questioningly, as she slowed down without stopping. But then he quickly moved into her direct path.

"What do you want?" she said in a calm, low voice, eyeing the aggressive posture of the group behind him.

"What I want? She is acting innocent now." He laughed cruelly and gestured towards his cronies. "I want you out of this college. No wait. I want you out of this country," he snarled.

"And I want to remind you that neither this college nor this country belongs to a dumb, bigoted ass like you," she replied coolly.

"Watch your mouth, you whore," Sahu thundered.

Heads began turning their way at the noise of an altercation brewing.

"Don't shout," she spoke slowly, dropping her backpack to the ground and strategically positioning herself for what was going to happen next. She was calm, while Sahu was frothing at the mouth in anger. "You think mad dogs like you, suffering from religious rabies, can scare me away?" she said.

And then it happened, just as she had thought. With a howl of rage, Sahu lunged at her, his hand clenched in a fist. But he wasn't prepared for what Aliya was. She ducked his punch, lifted her right knee and connected squarely with his groin. As he doubled over with a painful scream, her left knee knocked him forcefully on the jaw. In a final flourish, she turned sideways, bringing her heel down hard on the back of his knee. Sahu crumpled to the ground. His henchman stared in slack-jawed shock. Their leader had just been beaten by *a girl*.

Aliya hadn't planned for a public scene and if an expert had been watching, her moves would be attributed to Krav Maga, a close combat technique developed by Israeli Defense Forces and copied to perfection by the merciless Palestinian rebel groups. Around them, a crowd had their phones raised, capturing the moment. Murmurs of confusion were giving way to catcalls and encouraging shouts. Aliya picked up her backpack and walked towards the crowd. She didn't notice the small guy who hung back near Sahu's group. He moved slowly at first and then sped up behind Aliya, with a small Rampuri knife which made a clicking sound when opened.

Aliya turned, but not fast enough. The knife would have sliced right through her face if it weren't for the arm that shielded her. Aliya found herself staring into Shezii's face. His forearm had taken the brunt of the rusted knife and the amateur lunge, but it had cut him no doubt. He was bleeding. He moved towards the guy who was still holding the knife but now shivering at the sight of blood. In a fit of rage, Shezii slapped the attacker with the back of his hand. The impact was so hard that in an instant, the guy was cowering on the ground.

Krishna Sahu was slowly recovering, still on the ground. "You bitch, I will kill you," he screamed in hateful anger but his voice drowned in the din that erupted in the next moment. The crowd had swollen to a few hundred by now. Agitated members from both campus groups, ABP and ISU were waiting for a sign. And then Sahu did what would turn the scene into an unstoppable religious tug-of-war, between the equally divided factions. He made the battle cry. The Hindu majority Akhand Bharat Parishad and the Muslim minority driven Indian Students Union were on each other within seconds. The clash quickly started to escalate into a riot-like situation, with no sign of being contained anytime soon.

A group of neutral students pulled both Aliya and Shezii aside. Meera was among them, in a flood of tears. Someone suggested that Shezii be taken to the dispensary for first-aid. The cut was small but bleeding profusely and

Meera was desperately trying to staunch the flow with a wad of napkins someone had handed to her.

Shezii smiled at her. "Hey, don't worry, it looks worse than it is."

Aliya assessed the crowd for more possible threats to her. Things were fast spinning out of control. This exposure had already risked her mission. She had to get out of there quickly. Amid the chaos, Aliya looked at Shezii's wound. He had saved her today but this wasn't the time or place for expressing gratitude. *Besides, emotions made people weak and vulnerable. And it wasn't as if she had asked for his help*. The wound was a mere laceration and would heal in three to four days at the most. It could have been worse. But the knife used by his assailant had been rusted.

She spoke to him directly, "Don't worry about the wound, it will heal. But make sure you get a tetanus shot soon."

Before she left, however, she looked straight into his eyes and said, "And I am warning you again. For your own sake, stay away from my life."

With that, she pushed through the group of students and vanished.

But not before she was photographed leaving the scene by Nikki Rajpal. Things were going as orchestrated. Nikki had everything recorded on her camera. She fished out her cell phone and punched in the number.

The voice asked from the other end, "How did it go?"

She answered with a sly smile, "It's just getting started. The news channels will be here in a matter of minutes. Police too is already on the way. Madhav Raje University is a war zone now. And *you* are a genius, Dr. Kamran Khan."

47

A group of journalists had decided to lay siege to the office of the vice-chancellor of Madhav Raje University, waiting for a comment on how things had escalated to such an extent. Were the perpetrators of the crime, identified as the members of Akhand Bharat Parishad, being supported by the management? The skirmish had broken out more than an hour ago but it was continuing to flare as more and more students were joining in. It was a matter of their religious identity and no one wanted to back off. The elections now stood indefinitely postponed.

Anandita Devi had virtually locked herself in the office, refusing to comment, relying upon her staff for all updates in real time. She stared helplessly at one of the several videos of mob violence on her campus, already going viral on social media. The University's emblem was clearly visible on the entrance of the canteen in the background. This was a permanent dent to her career. In the world of education, she would always be labelled as an incompetent manager who had allowed riots on her campus. But hurting her even more were the images of injured youngsters, bleeding, limping, running scared. And she was responsible for all this. *If only she hadn't allowed that cunning Dr. Khan to get into her head.*

She rubbed her temples, trying to ease the throbbing pain.

The secretary rushed into Anandita Devi's office and stood guiltily in front of her. She was the bearer of more bad news and wasn't sure how to deliver it.

"What is it now, Martha?"

"Ma'am, the police squad has arrived at our gates."

"What? Did *we* call them?"

"No ma'am, officially we did not. But the news channels are covering the incident now. Somebody must have informed them."

"Goddamn it," she cursed under her breath.

"Ma'am, I think it's best if you take charge of the situation quickly now."

Anandita Devi looked at her and nodded silently, and that was the cue for the secretary to leave. She switched on the TV in her office and it took her only a few minutes of browsing through the channels to realize how hopelessly out of control the situation was. The media was not only questioning her capability as a leader but also holding her responsible for abetting riots on her campus. Right now, if she kept quiet, she was a sitting duck. She had to take charge. But first she needed to fix what was broken within her. She dialed her husband.

"Hello?" a mildly surprised Anurag answered.

"Anurag, I am sorry," she said in a strained voice.

"What's happening, Anandi? I was about to call you. Are you okay?" he asked softly, muting the sound of the news channel reporting the Madhav Raje campus incident. Anandita Devi spoke for the next few minutes, words pouring out of her like a dam had been broken. She spoke uninhibited, telling him everything about Dr. Khan's proposal, her visceral hatred towards Sana and her illegitimate daughter, and her current predicament. After she stopped, Anurag didn't speak for a few seconds.

And then he said, "You know what, Anandi? Your best quality is that you always know what to do."

"No, Anurag, this time I don't know what to do." She was exasperated.

"Of course you do. Ask yourself and you will have the answer."

"You think I should tell the police everything? Including Dr. Khan's threat to blackmail me?" she said, unsure.

"I think that would be a wise thing to do."

"But what about Sana?" She knew that no matter what, a scandal was still a scandal. Both Sana and Anandita Devi were public personalities and her husband was an established businessman with considerable goodwill. All three of them had a lot at stake.

"Now is not the time to worry about that, Anandi. And listen, I will be back in Delhi before dinner. Wait up for me."

"Yes, I will." Anandita Devi disconnected the call and looked at her computer's screen. She had made up her mind. She opened a file and started typing a press statement. Soon, she buzzed in her secretary.

"Here's my official statement to the media. I am accepting full responsibility for the failure of law and order on the campus. Tell them this was the work of certain miscreants who wanted to disrupt the campus elections today."

The secretary nodded and promptly took the typed and signed note from her to make multiple copies. She was about to turn and go out when her boss called out again.

"And Martha, this statement is for the media. Please also inform the Senior Inspector of the local police station within our area that I would like to visit them tomorrow to give my official statement, in person."

Martha smiled and with a polite nod, she exited the office of Anandita Devi, softly closing the door behind her.

48

At the residence of Dr. Kamran Khan, the television was tuned to a popular news channel covering the religious riots that had flared up on the campus of Madhav Raje University. The footage of Aliya with Krishna Sahu was of no use to Dr. Khan, despite Anandita Devi's ingenious move to involve Sahu. Unexpectedly, instead of becoming Sahu's victim, Aliya had knocked him to the ground. But the screaming death threat that Sahu had issued to her, in full view of Nikki's cameras, was something that could prove to be of good use. As expected, *India Truth* wasn't covering the news on the ground, choosing to explore other benign angles of the story, such as high stress levels in students due to pressures of academic performance, leading to emotional outbursts. Basically, they were covering anything that didn't involve Aliya Sheikh's name.

Nikki smiled triumphantly at Dr. Khan as she raised her glass of sparkling wine. From across the table, Dr. Khan responded with "Cheers!" and winked at her indulgently. Then their collective gaze settled on the third person present at the celebratory dinner table. Najeeb Ahmad—the man who did not exist on any record or papers, living in a parallel world of crime, emerging only to execute dangerous jobs for the likes of Dr. Kamran Khan. His life was full of privileges and luxuries, afforded by the complete lack of morality and fear. Law was for minions and he was above it all.

Right then, Najeeb Ahmad was eyeing the pair sitting in front of him curiously. He raised his glass of light pink milk flavored with Rooh Afzah. He didn't drink or smoke, and specifically despised people who swore by Islam and yet broke most of its tenets each day. People like Kamran Khan. This was the first time Najeeb had met him in the presence of a third person, that too a woman.

"So, what's the job for me?" Najeeb's dark liquid eyes, which held a hint of kohl in them, were fixed on Dr. Khan. He was itching to get on with the action. To him, Dr. Khan was just a good client who always paid well and upfront.

"Aliya Sheikh. Madhav Raje University." Dr. Khan thumbed at the TV screen. And then he placed a candid shot of Aliya in front of him. He had no idea how Nikki had gotten her hands on it. Probably from one of the media coverages because, as far as social media went, Aliya Sheikh did not exist.

"And you have to do it on campus, so that everyone thinks it's either Krishna Sahu or one of his cronies," Nikki added enthusiastically, as if ordering a pizza.

"She is a Muslim," Najeeb stated as his eyes bored into Dr. Khan's, completely ignoring Nikki.

"Yes, but if it makes you feel any better, she has the blood of a Kashmiri Pandit mixed in her." He smiled slyly.

"And is that the reason you want her dead?" Najeeb ran his hands across his heavily gelled dark hair, plastered to the skull.

"No. Her death is a *shahadat*, a sacrifice for a bigger cause. I want to wake up our brethren from their slumber of false security. None of us are safe anymore in this country. We are all easy game ... targeted by maniacs like Krishna Sahu."

"Dr. Khan, this will cost you double if you want it done on campus. And I am not interested in your reasons." Najeeb Ahmad's eyes were cold.

"Very well!" Dr. Khan spoke after a brief pause and walked over to the adjoining room. Within minutes he returned with a sleek briefcase. "Here it is. The price was always of your asking."

"She will be at the vice-chancellor's office the day after, for an inquiry into the incident," Nikki said, but Najeeb Ahmad's icy stare discouraged her from speaking any further.

"Remember the rules. No more calls to me. At least not until things cool off," warned Najeeb.

Najeeb Ahmad then lifted the sleek briefcase as if it were weightless and prowled away like a lithe predator with the prey in its mouth.

Dr. Khan settled back into his chair and Nikki was on his lap in no time. As he was busying himself with the zipper of her little black dress, he was distracted by the buzzing of his phone. It was an email alert from his bank in Monte Carlo. The money had come in—an unimaginable amount of money, actually. And only some part of it would electronically travel to dark, unheard of places of the third world economies. And in exchange, he would have the means to please his jihadi masters. It was a very lucrative venture. He smiled as he felt the high of power, money and a willing woman all within his grasp. He could rule the world if he wished.

49

Tracy knocked on the door to Sana's office precisely at 6:30 p.m. and walked in with a steaming mug of coffee. It was a custom on every late evening that her boss planned to spend in the office.

"Good evening, ma'am." Tracy placed the coffee on the table.

"Thanks, Tracy," Sana murmured absentmindedly, concentrating on the screen.

"About that visitor—shall I send him in now?"

"What visitor?" Sana peered up at her.

"The one I informed you about, an hour ago."

"He has been waiting for an hour?" She sat up, startled.

"Actually, more than that. He didn't have an appointment and he didn't give me a name. So I thought it must not be important," Tracy added apologetically.

"It's okay, Tracy. Must be somebody looking for a favor. You can leave now. I will call him in once I finish."

Tracy left promptly and Sana went back to the report she was filing on ISIS's infiltration of the Indian subcontinent and its radicalizing effect on the youth. When she looked up from her screen again, it was closing in on 7:30 p.m. She gasped, suddenly remembering the visitor. She wondered if he was still there.

She stepped out into the deserted office corridor and noticed a lone person sitting comfortably on one of the reception lounge chairs, engrossed in his tablet. He was well dressed and his posture was authoritative. He didn't look like the kind of man who would need to ask for any favors. She walked briskly towards him, ready with an extended hand to welcome him, when he looked up at her. Sana froze and her hand dropped slowly. Even after decades, she would know that face in an instant, anywhere.

"Sana," Anurag Kaul whispered, his voice tight with emotion as he stood up, making no attempt to move towards her.

She approached him unsteadily, her numb mind refusing to offer any reaction. "Anurag?" she spoke softly, blown by the sudden appearance of the two men that mattered the most to her in her life. First her brother and now Anurag. The timing of it all had an ominous ring to it.

She looked around and simply said, "Come, let's talk in my office." Anurag followed quietly.

Once in her office, they sat quietly across each other, until Sana could no longer bear the suspense of it all. They both knew each other's whereabouts but had never tried to reach out. It was best to leave the things of the past untouched, just like you wouldn't scratch a healing wound. Anurag was now a highly successful businessman and happily married, so his sudden appearance was worrisome. *Why was he here after all these years? Was this about Aliya?*

"Why didn't you tell me you were coming?" she finally spoke. In all the reactions she had reserved for when she faced Anurag again, practical coldness was something she hadn't considered.

"I thought it best if I drew the least attention."

"You are a well-known businessman."

"But unlike you, I am not on TV every other day." He smiled, "You did well for yourself Sana." He looked around the office.

"I worked very hard." She shrugged. "And it's all thanks to you. If you hadn't left me all those years ago, I wouldn't have reached here."

"The time and situations were very different then, Sana. I never wanted to leave you behind. But it's okay if you don't understand." His eyes were sad. "All I can say is that I am very sorry about what happened. But I did come back to Srinagar after a few months. Your house was locked and nobody had any idea where you had gone." He paused to sigh, "Then mom fell sick and passed away. Things weren't the same after that."

Sana did not respond but she felt a lump rise in her throat, as a deep sense of loss and unfairness hit her with full force. She could have had a life with Anurag after all, but it was all a wasted dream now.

"Why have you come now, Anurag?" She wiped away the stray tear and braced herself.

"It's about Aliya. Why didn't you reach out to me, Sana?"

"What about Aliya? She is my daughter and none of your concern." Sana wasn't ready to share her daughter. She also knew she had to protect Aliya.

"Sana, my wife Anandita knows about Aliya and that I am her father."

"What?" Sana stared at him in disbelief.

"Yes, in fact she was blackmailed into creating the recent unpleasant situation at the Madhav Raje campus."

"By whom?" she asked in a low voice. She knew that challenging Anurag's claim as Aliya's father was not only futile but pointless.

"Dr. Kamran Khan. I have no idea how he knew when I myself had no clue. It seems that he had documented evidence." He sounded defeated.

"I will kill that bastard," she snarled in anger, quickly connecting the dots about the banished Nikki Rajpal and her joining Dr. Khan's AIM. She would have to investigate.

"This is not the time to lose your cool, Sana. I came to tell you that Anandita will have to report this to the police during the investigation. And you know what this means."

"I can't let that happen, Anurag," Sana panicked. "I cannot drag Aliya into a controversy. I haven't been a good mother to her. She doesn't deserve this," Sana said, knowing that it wasn't the public scandal she was worried about, but the emotional trauma it would cause Aliya.

"Sana, be strong. We have to do the right thing." He got up and placed a reassuring hand on her shoulder.

"From what I know, she is a lovely girl, and if she is half as strong as you, she will not only understand, she will appreciate what you did with your life." There was a certain fondness in Anurag's voice, laced with pride and nostalgia.

"Anurag ... I don't know." She hesitated and then held his hand resting on her shoulder.

"Don't worry, Sana. Tell her that I was the one who ran. I will come over to apologize to her when she's ready. You will know where to find me." His tone had a finality to it and they could both feel a closure.

"I am sorry you had to wait for so long today." Sana got up and they held hands for a few moments.

"I wish I could have waited for you that day in Srinagar, Sana. I must go now." He looked into her eyes, resisting an urge to hug her.

"Will I see you again?" she asked, her guard down.

"Like this, maybe never. But Delhi is not so large that we won't bump into each other sometime." He smiled.

Sana nodded in tacit understanding. In this life, they both had traversed a long distance, away from each other. And their paths were so diverse that their crossing now was as unlikely as witnessing a falling star on a cloudy night. She sighed as she watched Anurag walk away across the corridor and vanish out of her sight.

50

The gamer's lounge at Delhi Golf Club was fairly occupied even during early morning hours, especially this weekend. Dr. Kamran Khan watched a few eager golfers happily devour their breakfast, excited to tee off soon at their favorite 18-hole championship golf course. He recognized a couple of them as professionals, either there for a warm-up game or to oblige a group of friends.

Dr. Khan always played alone as he liked to concentrate on his game. He loved golf because the game wasn't based on brute show of strength. Instead, it was minimalistic and exacting. He often mentioned to the uninitiated that golf isn't just about putting the ball in a hole; it required sharp judgment of terrain, wind factors and even how the ball is going to react once the golf club found the sweet spot on the ball. And to win, one has to play as few strokes as possible to putt the ball. This suited his operational style of calculated prediction and shrewdness.

Normally, he was cheerful on his golfing mornings, but today the manager had regretfully informed him that his regular caddie, Dashrath Singh was running late. This meant he would either have to drop his golfing plans for the day or carry his golf bag himself. He simply hated the golf carts as they disturbed his game by their mere presence. And of course, nothing could replace Singh's insight about the Lodhi golf course's challenges and obstacles. Most players admitted that as a caddie, he invariably improved their game.

Dr. Khan downed his banana smoothie and was contemplating leaving, when he spotted the manager scurrying in his direction.

"Has Singh arrived now?" Dr. Khan asked hopefully.

"No sir, but I have organized a replacement if you wish," the manager offered eagerly.

"Hmm." He had nothing planned for the rest of the morning and even Nikki wasn't in town. Dr. Khan thought for a brief moment before nodding his consent. The caddie may not be as good but if he could shut up and keep up with him on the course, then at least he would get his game of golf. The new caddie was waiting outside with his golf bag.

Looking forward to the game, Dr. Khan stepped out and inhaled the cool air carrying the dewy whiff of freshly cut grass. As he spotted his caddie, the first thing that hit him was his slender frame. The caddie was dressed in the club uniform at least two sizes too large for him and had a cap pulled down on his face. He looked more like a hip-hop dancer. *Damn, they are getting teenagers as caddies,* Dr. Khan cursed under his breath. Without bothering with conversation, he irritably selected his teeing club from the golf bag. He had all the time this morning to go for the entire 18-hole game, he thought sadistically. Let's see if this caddie can keep up.

But an hour into the game, much to his surprise, the caddie was still keeping up. He spoke little and was efficient. Moreover, he walked ramrod straight, without a hunch, which a weight such as the golf bag would have normally caused to anyone. Dr. Khan was slowly beginning to like him. After putting the seventh hole, he looked closely at the caddie for the first time. The boy was almost beautiful, with pale skin and a slender nose. Only his hands were strong and the veins on them bulged as he hoisted the bag. They were the hands of a professional weightlifter.

As they proceeded towards the more secluded area of the course, Dr. Khan relaxed and his natural game began to emerge. He loved playing in this part of the golf course, where the ancient tombs of the Lodhi Kings were in sight. To him, they were the markers of a grandiose time, when Islamic kingdoms ruled the land. He was concentrating on placing the ball on the tee when he was startled by the sound of his own name.

"Dr. Kamran Khan." The caddie had called out his name and was now staring at him. The golf bag was on the ground next to him. He removed his cap and looked straight into his eyes.

Dr. Khan slowly stood upright and his face blanched as he recognized the face. The caddie wasn't a boy. It was a girl with her hair tied in a top knot. And she was not just any girl, but one with a very familiar face. Aliya moved closer to quietly show him the *Rub-el-Hizb* ring on a thread around her neck. Nothing else needed to be said.

Dr. Khan finally understood what had really happened with Krishna Sahu at their college.

She handed him a piece of paper and said, "We need those supplies to reach the safe house by day after latest and the other firearms and ammunitions should also reach soon, along with at least three more sat-phones. We will have a go-signal next week. Make sure the travel arrangements to Kashmir are made and our base there is ready for us. All locations and other directions are in there." She pointed at the paper in his hands. "Don't lose it."

"Yes," he mumbled.

"You do know that you are under strict surveillance, even here." She looked around cautiously. "That man, a game ahead of you," she nodded imperceptibly at a golfer at some distance, concentrating on his game, "he watches you every time you are here."

Dr. Khan knew this regular golfer of the past six months as Ranjan Pathak, a retired bureaucrat who had a bad joke for every situation. *He was spying on me*, he thought. Imagining that he could be under watch was one thing but actually seeing it happen was something else.

"Don't look so shocked. You are marked because of your political actions and your party. Not because of us. And about the game, you will have to cut it short. A caddie can't return without the golfer, and I am not inclined to finish this game with you. So come with me and sign me out formally. Make sure you give a damn good excuse for not finishing the game, because that man is going to cross-check." And then, just like a true caddie, she put the cap on, hoisted the golf bag and started to walk back.

Dr. Khan had barely managed to comprehend what she had said. He could feel his blood rushing in his ears as the enormity of his error slowly dawned on him. He had ordered a hit on none other than Aliya Sheikh, the main operative of the organization from whom he had taken a lot of money. He could not even begin to imagine their wrath if they found out. They were very dangerous, and they were as easy with lives as they were with money. They could give and take as they wished. Dr. Khan shivered in the morning chill, as cold sweat traced his spine.

After signing out his so-called caddie, he rushed straight to his car, declining the manager's polite offer for more breakfast. The moment he was in the car, he dialed Najeeb Ahmad, but the phone service promptly informed him that the number he was calling did not exist. And then he remembered Najeeb's rule. *No more phone calls,* he had warned. Dr. Khan had no clue where Najeeb Ahmad was. And Najeeb's incommunicado status wasn't going to change until much after he had executed Aliya. Dr. Khan broke into another cold sweat.

Then he noticed Ranjan Pathak at the other end of the parking lot, getting into his car. Only this time, Dr. Khan knew that Pathak's timing wasn't coincidental. He waved as their eyes met and Dr. Khan waved back enthusiastically, put his car in drive and moved out of the parking. He thought of calling Nikki but stopped short.

What was he going to tell her? He couldn't reveal to her why he wanted to call off the hit on Aliya. Not without signing a death warrant for both of them.

Suddenly, things had taken a dangerous turn. A perfect storm had erupted on the calm, sunny day of Dr. Kamran Khan's life. This isn't going to end well, he thought.

51

The investigating committee's members eyed Aliya, as if she was the one on trial. They were all present in one of the largest lecture halls on campus, which in her opinion was overkill. It was clearly an attempt to make the process seem more serious and authoritative than it really was, because the total number of attendees for this university-level closed-door inquest into the campus clash incident was less than a dozen, including Aliya. She had contemplated missing the procedure, but in the end had decided to attend. Her absence would have raised unnecessary alarms and she didn't need that at this point in time. In any case, she was the supposed victim. She just had to make a statement and get out. So she had decided to sit it out on a bench in front of the investigating committee, which at best could only ruminate upon the events on the day of the campus riots.

"Did you know Krishna Sahu before this?" The head of the committee, an aged yet stern looking woman continued with her line of questioning.

"No. I was first introduced to him on Madhav Raje's campus."

"Did he ever threaten you on campus before?"

"No." Aliya didn't want to complicate matters. The simpler it came across, the better it was.

"On the day the riots broke out, what did he say to you?"

"He was very angry with me. He told me that I should leave this college and this country."

"You said he was angry. Any specific reason why he was angry with you?"

"I have no idea why he was angry with me," Aliya responded.

"Did you hit him?"

"Yes, I did."

"And then what happened?"

"He fell to the ground and I started to leave. But one of his friends came to attack me from behind with a knife. Someone saved me by intervening."

"Was that someone Shahzaib Umer Naqvi, a student of our college?"

"Yes."

"And that's when the groups started to clash?"

"Yes."

With that, the head of the committee peered at the other members from under her glasses and nodded. Then she looked back at Aliya, "Okay Ms. Sheikh, you may go now. But please make yourself available if we need you again."

Aliya nodded and exited the hall. She had no intention of making herself available to any of them. Because, soon she would be vanishing into thin air. As she walked through the campus, a strange feeling gripped her. An inexplicable sense of loss and hollowness. For mysterious reasons, and despite her aversion to anything normal in her life, she had come to like this place. And now she knew with certainty that she won't be ever coming back here.

As thoughts about Shezii plagued her, something inside of her felt raw and sensitive. What she had seen in his eyes was something very precious. It was a variety of love which, if gone haywire, could destroy things, upset lives and end them in unimaginable ways. Yet, it was so pure and rare that she had to protect it, and she could do that only by keeping herself away from him. If he came to know of her reality, it would kill his love. He could never understand why she did what she did.

As she crossed the main campus, she saw the pathway that led to the wooded area behind the campus, where she had first gone with Shezii. That one time she had played the violin only for him, although she wouldn't admit it to him. She was drawn to the path and she glanced at her watch. There was still plenty of time. She decided to allow herself this rare luxury of visiting that place one last time.

In a soldier's life, there are rules that are never to be broken, no matter on whose side the soldier fights. One such rule was to never, ever look back. In that one brief moment of weakness, Aliya had overlooked this rule, along with the man who had been shadowing her for some time now. He had fallen back briefly when she had stopped to contemplate her detour, but as she took the path to the wooded area, he followed her at a safe distance. The man had a triumphant smile on his face, like a gambler who had unexpectedly won a large game. He knew there was only one way in and out of that place.

Halfway on the path, Aliya belatedly realized that she had committed the cardinal sin of breaking the rule. She had let her guard down and she had stopped paying attention, even if it was for the briefest time. And now she was in an isolated place with someone who was steadily stalking her at a safe distance, waiting to strike. She had sensed a presence as she had taken the last turn leading to the clearing by the pond. It had been almost instinctive—maybe it was the faint sound of leaves under his feet or simply the change in the air caused by his movements, but she knew. She continued at an unhurried pace, not wanting to provoke him into grabbing her from behind. Plus, she didn't want her adversary to know that she knew, not until she had a chance to asses him. And that was possible only once they reached the clearing where he would have no option but to expose himself.

She stepped out into the clearing and after a few steps, turned to face the path from which she had emerged. Her stalker should be coming out of the same path within minutes, unless he had changed his track or gone back. Both possibilities were unlikely, as this was the only path in and out and she had not given him any reasonable doubt to retreat.

She stood her ground, with her feet apart, waiting. As expected, the man emerged out of the bushy trail and stopped in his tracks. They stood in a stand-off, the sound of wind rustling the dry leaves as their only company. He hadn't expected her to be ready for him, so this was an advantage for Aliya, although a weak one as she was unarmed and the guy was at least double her size. She assessed him quickly, noticing that he wasn't attempting to bring out a gun. This meant he would need to get close to hurt her—that was an advantage she could use.

He stepped ahead menacingly and pulled out an automatic knife. She recognized it as a Benchmade hunting model with a scimitar blade. *Dangerous and totally illegal*. But perfect for stabbing or slicing the jugular. Aliya didn't move, quietly working out her options. She knew she could easily outrun the man but that wasn't a real option. She had to know who he was and why he had followed her. This wasn't a loose end she could leave untied.

Then he charged, the knife at an angle to slice through her abdomen. A good move to incapacitate an amateur, but not Aliya. In a fraction of a second, she judged the move and jumped backwards as the knife sliced through the air. He paused to notice that she wasn't running or screaming. He readied for the next attack, this time grabbing her by the collar to ensure that she stayed within the knife's range. Aliya was about to outmaneuver him, when he stopped. He stared at her neck and something shifted in his eyes.

He let go of her collar, roughly pulling the ring from her neck. He stared mesmerized, as it glinted on his palm and whispered, "The *Rub-el-Hizb* symbol, how do you have it?" Najeeb Ahmad looked at her with the strangest expression. Then he pulled out his cell phone and started to dial a number, distracted and inattentive.

He knows, she thought and the split-second decision was made. He had forced her hand. The answers could wait but she couldn't allow the phone call to go through. Without a sound, the Black Sand made her move, blinding and lethal.

52

Sana had exhausted the entire list of possible phone numbers before she had finally called Shezii. He too had no idea where Aliya was, but had promised to make enquiries. She had arrived back home early in the evening and asked the servants about when they had last seen Aliya. And to her shock, none of them had seen her in two days. But that was the kind of schedule Aliya always kept, erratic and odd. Her interaction with the servants was limited to calling for room service, as if she were in a hotel.

Normally Sana would have waited for some more time before pressing the panic button, but in the current circumstances, with Dr. Kamran Khan's involvement and Awais's return, her instincts were screaming red alert.

She got up decidedly to recce the house once again. This time systematically, room by room. Everything seemed to be in order, including Aliya's room. It was cluttered with study books and other knick-knacks and looked as if she had just stepped out of it in a hurry. Sana's eyes fell on a bright pink sequined purse and a pair of flashy oversized sunglasses. They weren't in Aliya's style at all, but that didn't mean anything.

She returned to the main hall and gulped a shot of vodka in the hope of some warmth. The empty house felt chilly and she hated it. But it seemed like fate wanted to punish her by leaving her alone, again and again. Exasperated, she even considered calling Jaisinghani. Exasperated by her thoughts, she even considered calling Jaisinghani, but restrained herself. *Was she overreacting?*

As she mused over the possibilities, a servant entered the main hall, followed by Shezii and Meera. They both looked worried. Sana dismissed the servant and asked them to sit. A usually private person, Sana now felt relief wash over her at the prospect of company.

"Sorry for dropping in unannounced, ma'am, but we thought maybe we could help," Shezii said.

"No, no, that's perfectly fine. In fact, I am glad you guys could come. Aliya is such a private person, I have no idea about her college life," she spoke with a tinge of guilt and regret.

Shezii shot a quick, knowing glance towards an uneasy Meera before he spoke again.

"Actually, we checked at the college. Aliya was last seen attending a meeting with the investigating committee, day before yesterday, late in the morning. But nobody saw her leave the campus. Even the security at parking couldn't confirm anything."

"She didn't take her car. It's still in the driveway," Sana added worriedly.

"Yeah, we noticed," Shezii answered. "Have you checked her room? Maybe something there will tell us where she went."

"I've checked already. Do you guys want to have a look?"

The three of them got up and Sana led the way to her daughter's bedroom on the first floor of the bungalow.

They found nothing amiss as they gingerly moved around the room as if it was a crime scene, while Sana stood at the threshold and watched them hopefully. After a while, Shezii looked at Meera and shook his head. There was nothing of relevance.

Just as he turned to leave, his eye discerned a slip of paper resting under a chunky bracelet amid the clutter on the dressing table. He picked up the piece of paper. It was a hand-written note. Shezii looked at it in confusion and held it out to Sana.

"Is this from Aliya?" He stared at her as she moved closer and took the paper from him.

Sana read the note and then staggered back, collapsing onto the bed, her face ashen. The note simply said, *I am going back to Kashmir, to fix the mistake I made.* It wasn't signed but Sana knew that handwriting.

"Are you okay, Mrs. Sheikh? Is that from Aliya?" Shezii asked, sitting down next to her.

"No." Her eyes were unfocused as her mind raced and her breathing shallowed.

"Tell us, Mrs. Sheikh," Shezii persisted.

"That note is from my brother," she whispered.

"You mean Aliya is in Kashmir with your brother … her uncle?"

"I haven't seen or heard from my brother in 17 years."

"But this note ...?" Shezii let the question trail.

"Aliya is in danger." Sana shot a panicky glance at both of them in turn, her eyes glistening. And then she responded to the obvious question in their eyes.

"Because my brother, Awais Sheikh, works for *Tehrik-e-Islam*. He is a terrorist." Her tone was bitter and broken, but matter of fact. She slowly redialled Arjun Jaisinghani and exited the room. She had to protect Aliya at any cost.

Shezii and Meera were about to follow Sana out when Meera's cell phone buzzed, startling them both. She had left her number with many of the students, with an urgent request to call back if they spotted Aliya. Meera listened intently for a few seconds before disconnecting and looked up worriedly at Shezii. Outside, they could hear Sana's faint voice speaking agitatedly on the phone.

She moved closer to Shezii and spoke tersely, "A man's dead body has been found in the wooded area behind our campus."

A deathly silence followed as none of them spoke. They both knew that area. And, they also knew of the only other person who was aware of that place.

Shezii's face was set in grim determination. He hadn't reacted to any of the news and this troubled Meera. She knew that it was impossible to change his mind once he had come to a decision. She also knew that right then, he had already decided.

53

"Project Death Valley," Akshara scanned the worried faces of her teammates at the Jai Hind Command Center, "we now know for sure." Dr. Kamran Khan's link with *Tehrik-e-Islam* and their mission in India had been finally established.

"Two days ago, Dr. Kamran Khan received his final instructions about a project named Death Valley through another website, catering to the European market, that sells special designer *abayas* and expensive *attars*. And it's an easy guess from our earlier interceptions that the valley refers to Kashmir."

"Could you get any specifics out of it?" Rajeev Bakshi asked.

"The decrypted messages mention something about the money being sent and requisition of specific arms."

"You mean they actually asked for firearms online? Such audacity!" Major Arya was livid.

"Actually, they used a fairly simple code. Like referring to the item by the name 13039sh," Akshara answered and looked for a response. For few seconds there was silence and then a flash of understanding passed across Faisal's face.

"Damn! That's bold and cheeky. They literally asked for the item by its HS code. If you reverse that alphanumeric code it will read HS93031. That's the international trade code for muzzle-loading and other hunting and target-shooting firearms." He shook his head in disbelief.

"Exactly, Mr. Faisal. But there were other codes, which I couldn't figure out and I believe they could refer to explosive devices. Also, there were specific instructions for the redistribution of money. They are planning something big in Kashmir. Not just a suicide mission, but something to cause maximum damage." Akshara looked at them worriedly.

"That explains the heavy activity in Dr. Khan's offshore account in Monte Carlo. Just yesterday, more than a million dollars have been transferred to trading companies in Ukraine, Indonesia and Vietnam." Rajeev tossed a file on the table. "All of them are shell companies, meant for providing cover and re-routing funds for illicit trade and organized crime worldwide. And that's just 25 percent of what Dr. Khan received in his account, from one such company in Bulgaria."

"Okay, I think it's time to pull in his chain." Major Arya looked at Rajeev Bakshi, awaiting a green signal.

"Hm, we still need a legitimate cover for bringing him in. He is a public personality, revered by the minority community. There will be riots, even if they are staged by him, if we bring him on POTA or terrorism charges. He will effectively play the victim card." Rajeev Bakshi hated to throw a wet blanket on Major Arya's enthusiasm, when he himself wanted to drag Dr. Khan in and give him the third degree worthy of a criminal like him.

"Don't worry, Rajeev," Anandan smiled victoriously. "You can bring him in lock, stock and barrel. Here's a copy of the FIR filed by the vice-chancellor of Madhav Raje University, Mrs. Anandita Devi, with the local police station, alleging that Dr. Kamran Khan coerced her to take certain actions that led to the campus violence. In short, it's a charge of blackmailing, leveled against him by a high-profile society member. Good enough to call for a proper inquiry."

Rajeev Bakshi picked up the First Information Report and smiled for the first time in days. Then he looked directly at Major Arya. "I guess this works. Let's move, Major Arya. It's time to get that son of a bitch."

As the team scattered, Rajeev Bakshi sat back in his chair. The case was finally making headway. He curbed the urge to dial the minister right away as there was already a briefing session scheduled with him in the evening.

His thoughts veered towards Meera, the only silver lining in the dark clouds of his life. Sometimes, when he thought of how unsafe the world was due to people like Dr. Khan, he worried about her. He never wanted a hate-ridden, scared existence for Meera and continually resisted the parental urge to warn her about how risky the shopping mall was, or about the security threats at airports and the vulnerability of being at any crowded place such as a metro station.

All it took was one misguided human who was convinced that it was him and his Allah against the whole world. He presses the detonator and ends his own life along with that of so many others—an abrupt and grisly end. He could not. Rajeev Bakshi could not tell his daughter that they were all a target. *At any given place or time.*

54

The windowless room had no heating, turning the iron chair bone-chillingly cold to the touch. More so when its occupant was dressed in the bare basics of a white kurta-pyjama. Dr. Kamran Khan shifted uncomfortably in the hard, cold chair, assessing the two men wordlessly staring at him. He knew he was in trouble when they had plucked him from the breakfast table of his centrally-heated house the same morning and placed him in a holding cell in the basement of an unmarked building. They had not offered any explanation. Which was okay; what bothered him was the fact that they had been in plain clothes. Uniform he could have handled, but the lack of it spelled trouble because he had no idea who his adversaries were or what their agenda was. He had been waiting handcuffed in the bare cell for over two hours before the grim men walked in and settled down without even casting a glance at him. He knew with surety that this wasn't the department of police, because these men moved like they knew what they were doing.

Finally, unable to bear the tension, Dr. Khan jangled his handcuffed hand against the chair's arm and asked pointedly, "Why am I here? And is this necessary?" He looked at his handcuffed wrists.

The men seated in front of him exchanged a long, silent glance. And then Rajeev Bakshi nodded imperceptibly at Major Ram Arya.

"No, not necessary. But sometimes it's earned," Major Arya sounded cool, even as his eyes bore into Dr. Khan's. The interrogation, to be led by Major Arya, had officially begun.

"Why am I here?" Dr. Khan asked again, with as much authority as he could muster. He knew this was going to be a long drawn out match of patience and grit. He didn't want to lose ground early on in the game.

"You tell me." Major Arya placed his leather-gloved hands on the table and leaned in.

"I have nothing to tell you, and you won't be able to hold me down here for too long."

"We know enough to keep you here forever."

"Really? So am I under arrest?" He scoffed, "On what charges? I hope not because of a delusional woman's baseless allegation." Dr. Khan's defiance was more about the panic he was experiencing than the untouchable status he was used to. He was desperate to make the phone call that he knew they owed him as his basic right under detention.

"Dr. Khan, you don't have much time. So please start talking now."

"I need to call my lawyer." He ignored Major Arya and instead looked at Rajeev who was sitting back in his chair with his arms crossed, exuding definite authority. But the man didn't even bat an eyelid.

"You know, you are being stupid." Major Arya shook his head. "But it's okay, if you want to play it that way." He then placed a few photos in front of him. They were of the *Tehrik-e-Islam* operatives, clicked in the streets of old Delhi.

"Who are they?" Dr. Khan's face blanched at the evidence even though he shook his head to feign ignorance. Ganibhai and Ashraf Shaheen were not faces anyone would forget in a hurry.

"No? Well then smile, Dr. Khan, we are about to make you famous." The Major hadn't missed the shift in Dr. Khan's mood.

"You need to release me. Now!"

"Yes, of course we will," Major Arya said with exaggerated politeness. "Tonight you will be our guest and tomorrow morning these pictures will be the main story in the media. With special thanks from the Bureau to Dr. Kamran Khan, the great social worker and leader of AIM, for providing us the leads against the *Tehrik-e-Islam* operation in Delhi and Kashmir. The nation will salute you for your patriotism." Major Arya smiled congenially.

"No, you can't do that," Dr. Khan whispered slowly as he processed the implications. *Tehrik-e-Islam* would hunt him to the ends of the world and kill him, without a doubt.

"We will do exactly that, Dr. Khan. Or, you could talk to us and choose not to die. You will live, even if in jail."

"You have nothing on me. I want my lawyer and then I will sue you and whichever organization you represent for dragging in an innocent and respectable citizen for an interrogation without any reasonable ground, just because I am a Muslim." Dr. Khan knew he was clutching on to the last straw.

"Reasonable gound?" the Major smirked. "Looks like you wish to play hard ball. We have all of your online communication with *Tehrik-e-Islam*. And we can make it public easily. Sadly, the victim card won't work for you this time."

Dr. Khan remained silent.

"Still want to call your lawyer?"

"What do you want?" Dr. Khan spoke curtly.

"You can start by telling us everything. The execution plan, identities of the operatives, their locations and most importantly, their target." Major Arya wanted to get him talking fast, now that he had finally seen a chink in Dr. Khan's armour.

"And what do you think will happen to me if I talk to you?"

"You will be under our protection."

"In jail?" he smirked.

"Alive," the Major emphasized.

"Even if I choose to talk, most of the information you are seeking is way above my pay grade." He paused to weigh both the men before continuing, "But I have a valuable piece of information which I am willing to trade."

"You are in no position to negotiate, Dr. Khan," Major Arya leaned in and growled, using every bit of restraint he had because all he wanted to do was smash the terrorist's face in.

"But you will negotiate. Because this is about identifying the key operative of a mission that is about to cause great damage to your country. And the clock is ticking."

"Oh *my* country, is it?" The Major first smiled and then snarled. "You snake, I can beat the shit out of you if I need to." He banged his fist hard, shaking the entire table with a metallic thud.

"You can't make me talk." Dr. Khan eyed him coolly.

"You will talk. Eventually."

"For me, this is the end of the rope already." Dr. Khan shook his head and smiled wryly. "I am going to die anyway. The only way you can make me talk is by giving me a chance to live. Safe and away from here. In return, I will give you the identity of the key operative who is heading the project. Ever heard of *Rub-el-Hizb* and the Black Sand?"

Major Arya sat back and folded his arms. His heart was racing at the prospect of a major breakthrough in the case, but he wasn't going to let this be known to his captive who was just beginning to open up. He looked at Rajeev Bakshi sitting absolutely still next to him.

Rajeev Bakshi shifted and stepped into the game. "How do we know your information is correct?"

"I will give you the location of the team's safe house in Delhi before they go dark for the mission."

"What do you need from us?"

"A new identity, new passport and safe exit from India with none of your men following me. And no messing with my overseas bank accounts. I will simply cease to exist for you guys."

Rajeev Bakshi nodded and turned the little blank notebook in front of him in Dr. Khan's direction and offered him a pen from his breast pocket. Then he said, "Write it all down. Every little thing you know."

A look of concern passed over Major Arya's face; the interrogation was taking a turn he didn't like. He knew that giving such a pass to a scumbag like Dr. Khan was not only unwarranted but dangerous. It was also not approved by the department yet and most likely, would never be. He could see his boss getting himself into a tight spot. But he also knew that time was a crucial element now. They could ultimately crack Dr. Khan, but the time lost in the process could mean lives lost. And they couldn't take that chance.

"You think I am stupid? Not unless I have your commitment in writing." Dr. Khan sat back in his chair.

"You know these things don't work like that. You have to trust me now. Or you could simply choose to die." Rajeev shrugged. He knew how desperately Dr. Khan wanted to live, even though he was willing to let thousands of people die at the hands of the jihadi monsters he was feeding as pets in his own backyard.

Dr. Khan stared at him for a very long time before slowly pulling the notebook towards him. Then he scribbled furiously in it for a few minutes. Finally, he turned the notebook towards Rajeev Bakshi and sat back.

Rajeev Bakshi glanced at the booklet and then quickly snapped it shut. His face was ashen and his brow furrowed. He looked at Dr. Khan and whispered, "This better be true."

"It is. One hundred percent," Dr. Khan smiled smugly.

Rajeev looked at Major Arya and said, "Debrief him properly for the next 48 hours. Report back to me every hour over the phone. I have something to attend to urgently."

He stepped out of the room, leaving its other occupants bewildered although for different reasons. The highly sensitive nature of the information he had received demanded top clearance before the next steps could be taken.

He dialed Prasanna to set up a meeting, off the record, with the official head of Project Jai Hind.

55

Rajeev Bakshi would have preferred to type out and file a formal report for a case as grave as the one on hand currently, but for now he was at the minister's office for an off-record meeting.

Rajeev crisply reported the interrogation of Dr. Khan to the minister verbatim. Then he handed over Dr. Khan's notes to the minister. Arjun Jaisinghani turned the pages of the little notebook back and forth a few times and then placed it back on the table. He sat in quiet contemplation for a few minutes, staring at the notebook as if it was a bomb about to blow at any moment. Then he got up and opened the blinds of the French window behind his desk and the room was flooded with the soft, natural light of late afternoon. The window looked out over wide green lawns bordered by rose bushes in full bloom. A gardener was pruning the bushes, diligently and lovingly. Jaisinghani envied the man his straightforward, guile-free duty. Suddenly, he felt tired. *How long and how far can we fight?*

The appearance of Aliya Sheikh's name as the lead operative had complicated things. This was a matter to be tackled discreetly as they couldn't afford to have the department blundering around.

It was quite obvious that the wheels were already turning and that *Tehrik-e-Islam*'s plan was in action. But what was he going to tell Sana? *That after her brother, it was now her daughter who has joined a terrorist faction?* The prospect was dark and the irony of it all was too painful. He wished it were some other faceless name that had come up and not Aliya Sheikh's—for which he could have simply issued an extermination order.

"Are you sure about this information, Rajeev?" he asked finally.

"Sir, I don't think Dr. Khan is in a position to lie. He knows he will never see daylight if he tries to mislead us."

"If Dr. Khan works for *Tehrik-e-Islam*, he knows of their extreme ways with defectors. For a radical Islamist, he has had a rather quick change of mind, don't you think?"

"This has got to do with the generous release clauses he is trying to bargain for—a new identity, a free pass out of India and access to his bank accounts with no interference from the Indian secret service in the future. As for him being a radical Islamist, I think he is more an opportunist who peddled his religion to the highest bidder."

"Hm, and he really thinks he can negotiate with *us*?"

"Yes."

"What about the target?"

"We can only find that out by raiding the safe house Dr. Khan told us about. We will most likely find more clues there. On the downside, if we do that, *Tehrik-e-Islam* will know that we are on to them and things will escalate quickly. They may change their target, go into hiding or, in the worst case scenario, they may hasten their hit. So we will need to act real fast. I am awaiting a go-ahead from you."

"You have your go-ahead, Rajeev. I will get the formal order signed in an hour. Proceed with utmost caution."

"Yes, sir." Rajeev sat up alert, ready to leave and then hesitated. "What about Dr. Khan's demands?" he asked dubiously.

"We owe nothing to a traitor like him. Escort him respectfully to his home and make sure people notice you doing so. Let his masters handle him."

Rajeev Bakshi smiled and nodded in understanding.

"One more thing, Rajeev." The minister raised a hand slightly, gesturing for him to sit back down. "You are aware that in this case a lot of people we know personally are involved, including Sana and even your daughter and Faisal's boy."

"Yes, sir," Rajeev responded crisply.

"I want to personally speak to all those who have been in touch with Aliya at any time in this case, including the children. Please arrange this as soon as you can. Things will move very fast once we raid the safe house and I don't want any last-minute surprises because of Aliya's association with any of you. It's better if all things are on the table beforehand. My residential office would be best suited for this meeting I think."

"I understand, sir. I will get it lined up right away."

"And Rajeev, who is the best field operative on your current team?" the minister asked as Rajeev was getting out of his chair.

"Major Ram Arya, undoubtedly," Rajeev responded without any hesitation.

"Can we rely on him?"

"Yes, sir. He is a decorated officer with a series of successful covert operations to his credit. I am aware of instances in the past where he had refused to accept a medal or citation, simply for the sake of keeping his identity undercover."

"Okay. Please send me his updated file."

With an affirmative nod, Rajeev Bakshi rose from his seat and walked out.

The idea of bringing Meera in for a matter as sinister as global Islamic terrorism was making his stomach turn. His daughter's proximity to Aliya over the past year was something that had been nagging his mind ever since Aliya Sheikh's name had come up during the interrogation.

But he was a soldier at heart. The possibility of losing was not going to stop him from fighting. He decided to make a series of quick calls to line up the meeting, starting with his daughter Meera.

56

Meera watched helplessly as Shezii rang Aliya's number for the umpteenth time only to hear that the mobile connection was no longer in service. She couldn't help but scream in her own head, *Hold yourself together Shezii! She is unravelling you.* But she couldn't bring herself to say it out loud. They hadn't spoken to each other since they had returned from Aliya's house. He hadn't even answered Chand Bibi's insistent knocking on the door of his room. Luckily, the Naqvis were not home.

Meera could sense that Shezii was deliberately locking her out. With a misplaced sense of protectiveness, he had decided that the further she was from him the safer she would be. But he was wrong. Terribly wrong. And her heart was aching with a pain she had never known before.

Finally, Shezii stopped pacing and looked at her thoughtfully.

"Meera, I think you should go home now," he spoke firmly, without meeting her eyes.

"What are you planning?" she asked.

"I am about to make some very bad choices. The kind that might put me in a messy place." He finally smiled but his eyes were sad. "And there is no way I am dragging you down with me."

"But why? Why are you shutting me out?" She searched his eyes desperately. "You love her more than anything, don't you? You love her so much that you are willing to throw away everything."

Reflexively, Shezii moved close to her and hugged her tightly. She was tense and rigid in his arms and they both sensed it.

"I have to go to Kashmir," he murmured. "Meera … my nightmares come from a childhood scarred by the madness of Islamic jihad. You have no idea what it's like to be apologetic about one's own identity. That extremist won because he made me believe that the blood on his hands was smeared on mine too. If I don't do anything now, he will win again. And I can't let that happen. I can't lose another person to a pointless war."

Meera disentangled herself from Shezii's confessional embrace and sat them both down on the bed. He could barely look at her.

"Listen to yourself, Shezii. You really think going to Kashmir in search of Aliya will help? And even if you do manage to find her, what are you going to say to her? Don't you understand that she has already made her choice?" Meera knew that she had lost the battle already, but she wasn't going to give up yet. If this needed her to go right till the end, then she was ready.

"No, Meera, I don't know if that choice was hers." He shook his head. "I only know that Aliya needs me."

"What about that dead guy on the grounds behind the college?" she asked vehemently.

"There could be any number of possibilities. Maybe Aliya is in trouble and needs help."

"Come on, Shezii ... how can you help her? What experience do you have in dealing with terrorists? What will you do if there are more of them with Aliya? You know nothing about Kashmir either. Are you going there to die?" Meera was panicking now.

"Sometimes, we must do what we need to do, even if we know it's going to bring us closer to our own end."

"Oh Shezii!" Suddenly, she collapsed next to him as she finally, totally, came to terms with her unreciprocated love. The kind of love that grips a person completely until it reaches a stage where pain begins to feed it—till love itself remains to be nothing but pain.

Meera looked up at Shezii, "I guess you already have your thumb on a self-destruct trigger. So, what's your plan? Should we pack a torch and some sandwiches?"

"You aren't coming anywhere with me, Meera." He shook his head resolutely. "And first, I need to meet your dad. Tracking Aliya also means tracking the terrorist faction Awais Sheikh is working with. And I think your dad can help."

"What the hell!" Meera was incredulous. "You want to discuss your plans to track down a known terrorist with the head of the country's anti-terrorism department? Whatever makes you think he will entertain your mad fantasies, or that you even qualify for such a job? Do you even know the kind of rigorous training and years of experience required to make it to his team?"

"Something tells me that if I meet him, he will have a different opinion. In fact, he would see me as an asset."

Just as Meera was starting to protest, her phone rang and she stared at the screen. She then looked up at Shezii, confused. It was her dad calling.

"Dad?" she answered in a guarded manner.

"Meera, where are you?" Rajeev sounded urgent.

"I am at Shezii's, dad. What happened?"

"Is Shezii with you?"

"Yes."

"Good. I want both of you to reach an address I am messaging you. Don't drive yourself and don't take public transport. My office car will reach you guys in 20 minutes with an escort. And tell Shezii, I have called his parents and they are reaching here soon. We will be waiting for you." With that he disconnected the call. Meera's phone pinged with a location pin the next instant. She checked and found it to be on a road filled with high-end political abodes.

She looked at Shezii and spoke softly, "Dad wants both of us to come right away. He is at Defense Minister Arjun Jaisinghani's residence. Faisal uncle and aunty are also reaching."

Shezii got up quietly and started packing his laptop to take along with him. He then coolly glanced at his watch. It was 7:30 p.m. He knew this was going to be one long and tedious night. And he was about to take the first step in his dangerous journey to Aliya. Oddly, he felt ready.

57

The old grandfather clock's grim-sounding gong declared the tenth hour of the night, intruding solemnly into the stunned and uncomfortable silence of the room. The successful and polished media baron, the invincible Sana Sheikh, looked unkempt and unraveled. The Naqvi couple sat together with Shaziya clutching onto her husband's hand, disbelief etched on their faces. Shezii perched on the armrest with an air of detachment. Meera occupied a tense spot on the couch beside him.

The minister had broken the news to all of them as gently as he could, making his expectations clear. Rajeev Bakshi was now briefing him about the safe house. Major Arya's team had moved fast, reaching the location within 45 minutes of the orders being issued. But it hadn't been fast enough. By the time they reached, the place had been cleaned out. It looked as if it had been hastily abandoned by its occupants but even the team's meticulous search had failed to provide any clues. There were no fingerprints or personal items to be found; the old building had no CCTV installed and the only watchman was an aging uninterested man with a tired soul. He had informed them in a shaky voice that he hadn't noticed any suspicious activity.

Bakshi's stoic face hid his rising concern over the situation. He gazed at the anxious faces around him and returned to the minister, who sat in deep contemplation, his hands steepled in front of his face.

Sana broke the silence.

"How do you know for sure that Aliya's involved in all this? You didn't find anything at that place." Her tone was flat and bitter.

Rajeev replied softly, "Sana, I understand how you feel, but we do have a substantial lead. Besides, Dr. Khan also identified the man who was found murdered behind Madhav Raje University. It seems Dr. Khan paid him to assassinate Aliya within the university complex."

"So, you are saying that my daughter not only works for a terrorist outfit but is also a cold-blooded murderer?"

Rajeev bristled under her gaze but remained silent.

"Sana, please!" Arjun Jaisinghani intervened. "This is not just about us. This is bigger than us. Innocent lives are at stake and we need you to work with us. Now, please tell us if you've noticed anything odd about Aliya in recent months."

He sounded both desperate and placatory, torn between his need to watch out for someone he cared about and his duty towards the multitudes at risk.

"Nothing much. She had always been aloof and now she has been missing for more than two days. Nobody seems to be bothered about that." She looked away, denial in her eyes. This must be a misunderstanding which would clear itself in due time, she believed.

"Anything else?" The minister looked around.

"May I, sir?" Shezii offered and continued at the nod. "I think Aliya must have been facing some kind of trouble. Meera and I noticed someone following her car from the college, all the way out to the outskirts of Delhi. We too followed her, actually. We were worried." He glanced at Meera, who shifted nervously in her seat.

"What happened then?" the minister asked.

"Nothing. By the time we caught up with her, the man had vanished. When I tried to warn her about it, she told me to mind my own business. When I told her that I was worried about her, she demanded that I stay away."

"Was this the man following her?" Rajeev Bakshi put up a photo of Awais Sheikh for Shezii.

"No, sir, this man looks of Indian origin. That man was distinctly Middle Eastern and even built like one."

"This means there are more operatives than we know of." The minister shook his head. "Anything else that you noticed about her?"

"She has changed quite a bit lately."

"Tell us more. Even the smallest possible detail may be helpful," Rajeev said.

"She stopped attending lectures and even discontinued the violin classes she used to conduct on weekends."

"She conducted music classes at college?" Sana was first surprised and then immediately lapsed into an embarrassed silence. This was her own daughter they were discussing and with every passing minute, she was turning into a stranger for Sana.

"Yes, ma'am." Shezii nodded uncomfortably and continued, "I can't be entirely sure, but I felt as if she was being very guarded about something." He looked towards Meera for help.

"She started dressing differently too, more modestly I mean, in darker shades of non-revealing clothes. Prior to that, I had never seen her wear scarves," Meera added cautiously.

Rajeev scribbled in his notebook as tense silence followed.

"I can help look for her." Shezii's sudden declaration made everyone sit up.

"How? You know about her location? Did she give you any clues about where she is going and what she plans to do?" Rajeev's eyes were narrowed. Meera opened her mouth to say something and then held herself back.

"No, she didn't. But we all know that she is going to Kashmir." Shezii scanned the faces around the room.

"Yes, and we are setting up an experienced anti-terrorism squad to go to Kashmir right as we speak."

"I want to go to Kashmir. I can help look for her." This time around it was the conviction in Shezii's tone that grabbed everyone's attention.

"*You* want to go to Kashmir? To look for *Aliya*?" Rajeev repeated the words slowly, his eyes boring into Shezii's.

"Yes."

"Do you realize that she is part of an international terrorist faction, which is planning a terrorist strike on India? With all your romantic ideology about patriotism and nationalism, you would be dead even before you begin. This is not a video game where you get second and third refills at life. The bullets and bombs here are real and they kill in real life not in some virtual reality. In that world, you don't get to come back from dead." Rajeev was already fuming at the preposterous suggestion.

Tears were flowing freely from Shaziya's eyes as she sat silent but sobbing. Her worst fears were manifesting themselves—the demons of that ugly night in Tel Aviv had not left her son alone, not even for a second. Those demons had been lurking in the shadows, waiting to jump at him, while she believed that they were gone for good.

"Wait a second, Rajeev," the minister intervened, "Let's hear him out."

"Sir, all I am saying is that there will be a difference in me finding her. If I find her, maybe I can convince her to come back. But that's not possible if the anti-terrorism squad finds her." Shezii challenged the unsure faces around him.

"Hmm." The minister slowly nodded.

"But we can't allow that to happen. We can't send a young novice out there. We might as well feed him to the wolves," Rajeev was vehement and Meera was nodding in agreement.

"Rajeev Uncle, I just wanted to inform you. I will go anyway, with or without any support."

"In that case, Shezii, you will be forcing me to put you under house-arrest. Faisal, my friend, unfortunately I will need to charge your son with obstructing an ongoing investigation." He looked at Faisal, who barely managed to nod in agreement as he too battled with the ghosts of his past.

"Hold on." The minister raised a hand, "We are not here to start arresting each other. I have another solution, which is a little bold and dangerous if not as foolhardy as what has been suggested by the young man here." He paused to peer at the group and then addressed Rajeev, "How about using Shezii as a cover for our stealth team?"

"I don't understand, sir." Rajeev was still rattled.

"Shezii can go to Kashmir, followed closely by your team. He will have the first contact with locals who will be more open and trusting towards a youth who is one of them than they will ever be towards your ATS team, Rajeev. He will be able to generate leads faster for you."

A silence ensued as both Shezii and Faisal tensed at being referred to as *one of them*, even though they knew it wasn't spoken with any malice. Some of Arjun Jaisinghani's closest friends were Muslims who practiced Islam faithfully. But the father-son duo also knew the bitter truth. Islam was their religion and it was being monopolized and manipulated by those few fanatic extremists who wanted to paint it in a single dimension of hatred and anger. Instead of being apologetic about its waywardness, the need of the hour was to save Islam, in its peaceful form. It was a tough ask, but somebody had to do it.

"But sir, this is far too dangerous. Not only for Shezii but also for my team."

"Rajeev, we need to act fast. Our enemy already has a lead on us and we need to catch up quick. I agree, there is a risk involved but if it's about saving thousands of lives then I am willing to take it. Because I do believe Shezii's presence will help in making quick breakthroughs. I also know without a doubt that this will go down in the history of the department as the most unusual and radical decision ever taken—involving a civilian." He paused to check and was satisfied to see agreement taking over Rajeev combative expressions. He continued, "Now, please get me your team's details. Let's quickly chalk out a strategy plan for them."

"Dad, if Shezii is going then I am going too. A couple on an adventure trip will surely look more believable than a sole guy. I will be his cover."

Rajeev looked incredulously at his daughter even as Shezii's verbal protests faded into the background. It took him a few seconds to react, which was long by his secret service standards. But then his demeanor softened and his eyes cleared. He knew *his* daughter wouldn't back off now. Besides, he was a soldier and if he could agree to put someone else's son into danger then he wasn't going to shy away from doing the same with his own daughter. He nodded slowly and spoke, "Okay Meera, I trust you will be careful."

"Are you sure about this, Rajeev?" For once the minister was hesitant.

"Yes, sir!" Rajeev smiled at his daughter and responded without hesitation. "I will revert tomorrow morning with the operation plan. We will get started right away."

"God help us all," the minister sighed. His mind was distracted as he passively observed the occupants of the room slowly file out with murmured greetings of good night, which it certainly wasn't going to be. He had a long night ahead of him, to be spent in the company of heavy, 'for his eyes only' intelligence reports and liasoning with the heads of at least three international secret services located in three different time zones.

Rajeev was the last to get up and the minister could sense there was some unfinished business.

"Anything else, Rajeev?" he finally provided the cue for his department head to speak.

"Sir, I only hope we aren't making a mistake in sending Shezii in. These are hardened terrorists we are talking about."

"Agreed, there is a risk but I think he can help. From what I understand, he knows Aliya better than even her own mother. Plus, the kids won't be having any direct contact with the *Tehrik-e-Islam* operatives. And you know what to do as soon as we have anything on her."

"But if she is fully turned over to the other side, he stands no chance."

"Well, the boy does have the combined appeal of chocolates and potatoes. It's very difficult to not like him. All we need to do is find a little chink in Aliya's armour and I think Shezii can do it for us. Besides, we will have a team closely shadowing him. I am worried about Meera though."

"Don't worry, sir, she is a strong girl. And we will pull them out of Kashmir as soon as we have a clear lead." With that Rajeev got up to leave, knowing that there was nothing more to discuss.

But Jaisinghani called out after him as if in an afterthought, "By the way, Rajeev, I need to meet with your lead officer first thing tomorrow. What did you say his name was?"

"Major Ram Arya. He will be there, sir," Rajeev answered crisply and moved out. He knew that the minister read all files the same day that they arrived on his desk. And, as instructed, Major Arya's file had been sent to the minister's desk two days ago. The minister had never before intervened in the operational aspects of Project Jai Hind.

First, allowing a young civilian to be a part of an ATS operation in hostile territory and then demanding to meet an officer under operation. Two off-beat actions, very close together was no coincidence. Something was definitely not falling into place. Maybe he wasn't yet seeing all the pieces of the puzzle. Eventually, they will have to fall into place. *Eventually*, he sighed.

58

Aliya's hands felt stiff from gripping the steering of the SUV and she felt her exhaustion from the long drive in her neck. It was almost 6:00 a.m. and the sun was struggling against the winter morning. They had left Delhi post-midnight and were fast approaching the small town of Bafliaz. She had been driving fast and non-stop because once in Kashmir, she would have to forego the wheel. A lady driver was bound to attract unnecessary attention from the locals as well as the army, as no tourists in their right senses would self-drive in Kashmir.

A last minute tip-off about the ATS team's planned raid on their hideout had made her decide to leave Delhi at the earliest. They had been on the road ever since. Although the six hours that she had driven continuously was nothing in comparison to her personal best, which was the 13 hours non-stop from Bulgaria to Nusaybin, a restless Turkish city bordering Syria.

She had managed to stay off the radar during the last few years simply by avoiding public transport hubs, which were under maximum CCTV coverage. Facial recognition software nowadays was surprisingly accurate and she couldn't have taken a chance. But right now, all she needed was a break.

She glanced at Ganibhai, an aging man with the disposition of a hawk. His eyes, though bleary, were alert and fixed on the road ahead.

"Should I drive? I have driven on Mughal Road many times before." He spoke without looking at her, confident in the knowledge that negotiating Mughal Road in the heart of Kashmir was not for those unfamiliar with the terrain.

"We will be taking a break soon. You can take the wheel after that." Aliya hadn't missed the patronizing tone of her comrade.

She glanced at the sole passenger in the back seat through the rearview mirror. Celebrated among the jihadi ranks and in *Tehrik-e-Islam* as one of the deadliest and most ruthless operatives was a man of above average height and a sinewy built. With a thin mouth and the oily eyes of a snake, Essam-al-Maghrabi was dreaded even by the terrorists. Not because of what he could do, but because he thoroughly enjoyed what he did. The story that regularly made the rounds among the jihadi world was of the one time when he had ripped off the jugular of a soldier of the Israeli Defense Force. Without a knife, with his teeth alone. But to Aliya, his most offensive attribute was the cloying oily scent of sandalwood he wore all the time. It gave her a headache.

In short, Essam-al-Maghrabi was a big gun and second-in-command in *Tehrik-e-Islam* and he had landed at the safe house unannounced. Why was he present in her operation? Did the high command not trust her completely? Or was he sent as a back-up? Was there a change in plans? Just as she was about to look away, Maghrabi turned his head and locked eyes with her in the mirror and smiled a slow, sly smile. A smile that said, *I know what you are up to* and forced her to look away quickly.

She could see the settlement of the small town of Bafliaz in the distance. They were to take the picturesque and less travelled Mughal Road from here all the way till Shopian. This way, they could avoid the crowded NH44 to Srinagar and the possible *nakabandis,* in case an alert had been sounded. Spotting a secluded tea stall up ahead, Aliya stopped the vehicle and traded places with Ganibhai before they approached it. The tea shop was manned by a young Kashmiri boy whose handsome features seemed confused. His first customers of the day were dressed like locals but didn't look like they belonged. But then he happily busied himself with preparing fresh milky tea and omelet-bread for them.

Aliya and Ganibhai stood huddled inside the small tea stall in front of a dying bonfire while Maghrabi chose to stay in the car. Better, thought Aliya, as there was something about his countenance which made him stand out. Almost like an evil spirit.

"Shopian is less than 100 kilometers now. What's our next stop?" Ganibhai asked.

"We will stay in Bongam for a day before moving further. That's your village isn't it?" Aliya held the glass in both her hands and sipped the sweet tea.

"You knew," Ganibhai raised an eyebrow. "We will have to drive a further 50 kilometers once we reach Shopian to get to Bongam."

"Yeah, I know. Our supplies are supposed to reach Bongam tomorrow. Our second team will also meet us there. After that, we will avoid any main roads and stay quiet." The supplies were a crucial consignment of communication devices, arms and ammo being organized by Dr. Khan.

"What's the plan?" This was the longest that he had been kept in the dark about a mission's details.

The sudden disappearance of his comrade, Ashraf *bhai* already had him edgy. Ashraf had gone incommunicado just hours before their meeting at the safe house in Delhi. Then, their safe house had been compromised. Alarm bells were ringing in Ganibhai's head. He didn't have a good feeling about any of it.

"We humans don't make plans, Allah decides for us." Aliya stared at the smoldering embers among the white ash of the now almost dead fire. "Keep faith in him."

"Do you think it was him?" Ganibhai blurted.

"Who?"

"Ashraf Shaheen. You think he tipped them off about our location?"

"We shall know with time." Aliya shrugged.

"Too many things have gone wrong for it to be just a coincidence. Should we proceed with our plan?"

"Everything is on track, as long as our target does not change his plans," Aliya whispered.

Ganibhai took the plate of omelet-bread from the teenager with a false smile. "Do you know that more than five hundred years ago, Akbar travelled through this same Mughal Road to win over Kashmir?"

"I know. Also that his son Jehangir died on the same road, not much later." Aliya concentrated on dipping a piece of buttery bread in her tea.

Ganibhai smiled and started to say something when the distant whirring of a heavy engine distracted Aliya. A bulky, olive-green truck was slowly coming their way. Instinctively, Aliya eyed Maghrabi who was sitting alert now.

"That's a military truck on rounds," she spoke under her breath and Ganibhai stiffened. "Don't look in their direction ... their presence is common for locals." She caught Maghrabi's eyes and shook her head slightly. He immediately sank back into the seat like a tired, sleepy passenger, while the truck continued its approach. Aliya wasn't sure if an alert had been sounded about them, but she didn't want to draw the attention of the BSF by moving now.

The truck continued to move in their direction and then slowly prowled past the tea stall like a predator. Just as they were about to let go of their bated breath, the truck came to an abrupt halt a few meters from them. Ganibhai and Aliya exchanged a furtive glance as there was no movement from the truck for a few seconds. Then, a lone BSF-Kashmir soldier jumped off the truck and started walking towards them. His gait was purposeful and Aliya was furiously working out their options. There weren't that many. He was an armed soldier with possibly a truck full of similar back-up.

The soldier came to the counter and carefully scanned the occupants of the tea stall. Ganibhai slurped his tea and Aliya looked up from her plate of omelet to openly gaze at the soldier with wide eyes. She smiled as if she were smitten by this military hero. The young soldier, clearly not used to female attention, nodded at her awkwardly and then asked for a pack of Parle-G biscuits and a bottle of water at the tea stall.

"Is something wrong with him?" the soldier asked them suddenly, nodding towards their car with the sleepy passenger in it.

"My brother is unwell. We are taking him to the government dispensary in the next village," Aliya spoke without hesitation.

"Now? The doctor won't be in so early." The soldier shook his head and eyed them strangely. "Your brother doesn't look so good. We are headed towards the base. Why don't you follow our truck? We can have the military doctor look at your brother."

"We are waiting for my aunt to join us. She will be here soon," Aliya answered, trying to mask the impatience in her voice.

"Let me have a look at him," he said and turned towards the car. Aliya tensed and Ganibhai's hands gripped the pistol in his pocket.

Just then the tea stall boy called out with a sheepish grin and extended a plate towards the soldier, "Sir, I made you an omelet."

The soldier turned back and laughed heartily. "Will you make omelets for all of us?" He pointed towards the truck and then politely declined the boy's food.

When he started to pay for the water and biscuits, the boy shyly refused to accept the money. The military truck honked for his attention. The soldier playfully tousled the teenaged boy's hair and tossed one final look at Aliya, "Actually the military base is closer than the dispensary." Then he turned and jogged away. The truck was soon gone, disappearing into the town. Aliya and Ganibhai slowly let go of the breath they had been holding.

"So, you think you can handle 85 kilometers non-stop to Shopian?" Aliya asked Ganibhai, who had just finished paying for their food.

Ganibhai nodded wordlessly. For better or for worse, they had just saved their plans from getting totally derailed. All he knew was that at this stage of their journey, they had no option but to keep going.

59

"This is a mistake!" Masood Raza, the de facto national defense advisor, shook his head vehemently. In the many years of their strong partnership, this was the first time Arjun Jaisinghani was ignoring his warnings. Raza's deep international network of diplomats was the reason for his impeccable track record of valuable tip-offs and insights pertaining to security issues of the country. So, if Masood Raza said that a stone was going to float, it usually did.

"What do you think we should rather do? Let them win?" Jaisinghani smiled.

"It's a dreadful cliché under the circumstances, but sometimes you lose a battle if you want to win the war."

"We have already discussed this, Masood. You know I can't go back on my word to those leaders of Kashmir who wish to open a dialogue with the government. They are bringing the public mandate to the table. I can't just not go."

"Fine, so bring them to *your* table in Delhi."

"You know it's not the same. The problems of Kashmir can only be sorted on their soil."

"Come on Arjun, if this is about earning brownie points with media then it might prove quite expensive."

"You know this isn't about the media. It's about giving the average Kashmiri some faith in our government. One step at a time."

"It may be so. But now, with the Rashtriya Sewa Samiti also joining you for the meeting, this will become a mega media event. Imagine the headlines announcing that the Defense Minister of India plans to meet the separatist leaders of Kashmir for a discussion, along with the head of the largest Hindu organization of India. It will be dubbed as an act of appeasement." Exasperated, Masood Raza turned to the third occupant of the conference table and said, "At least you should be able to see reason in what I am saying, Rajwat *bhai*."

Sohan Rajwat, chief of the nationalist social service organization, Rashtriya Sewa Samiti, was a man of measured words. The scion of a long line of freedom-fighters, he had a steadfastness bordering on obstinacy in his genes. He was touted as a reformist of some sort and the future face of Hinduism. In his early thirties, Sohan Rajwat was nothing like an average *neta*. This worked in his favor while connecting with the youth of the nation. And in his modern, social media savvy avatar he appealed even to the urban youngsters. He had a finger on the pulse of both the statistical data and the emotional mood of the nation. For now, he shifted slightly in his chair to acknowledge Raza's plea but took his time responding.

"I look at it the other way around, Raza *bhai*. If we go with Arjunji, we will be seen as a progressive, tolerant and open-minded public service organization with only the country's best interests at its heart. I am sick and tired of the pro-Hindutva narrative being thrown at us. Nobody recognizes the good work we do for the common good, irrespective of religion."

"Besides, having the Rashtriya Sewa Samiti and the separatist Muslim leaders on the same table in Srinagar will provide a sense of inclusion to the Kashmiris. I think we can expect good results out of it." The Defense minister's tone had a conclusive quality to it.

"Possibly," Raza shrugged, "but have you considered the number of things that could go wrong? Apart from the huge security risk, that is." He wasn't backing off yet.

"My dear friend, if it's our lives you fear for, then don't." Jaisinghani walked over to his friend and placed his hand on his tense shoulder. "Sometimes, winning hearts is more complicated than winning a battle."

"Then I guess the only thing that is left for me to do is pray that Rajeev Bakshi and his team do a darned good job."

"Oh! That reminds me, I have to be in an operations related meeting with a Jai Hind team member." The Minister eyed his watch.

"Operations? Since when did you start sitting in on operations related meetings, Arjun?" Masood Raza stared at his friend.

"Ever since our country came under threat." He smiled sadly and turned towards Sohan Rajwat, "So Rajwatji, shall I take this as confirmed."

"Yes of course, Arjunji. And I should also be leaving now." Sohan Rajwat politely shook hands with both the men and exited the conference room and was immediately surrounded by his plain clothes security detail.

Arjun Jaisinghani warmly shook hands with both the gentlemen, seeing them off. He then instructed his personal secretary, "Prasanna, please include Mr. Sohan Rajwat in our Kashmir itinerary for this week. And make sure that this is kept under wraps until we appear for the official press briefing in Srinagar on Friday."

Masood Raza moved towards the door, wordlessly shaking his head in response to the minister's final instruction to his personal secretary. For his part, the minister fully understood his friend's concern but changing the plans now would also be construed as an act of cowardice. Whether taking the game to the next level by bringing in the Rashtriya Sewa Samiti was going to work in their favor or blow up in their faces remained to seen. He internally winced at his own blowing up analogy and picked up Major Ram Arya's file. *Once again*.

60

Major Ram Arya was a soldier at his core and his default posture was attentive and alert. That's how he had been waiting in the corridor outside the Defense Minister's office for the last 15 minutes. He had chosen the corridor with an open view of the garden over the stuffy VIP waiting lounge. The outdoors always helped him think better. Right now, he was trying to work out the various possible angles regarding his meeting with the head of the defense services of the nation.

Major Arya's thoughts were interrupted by sudden activity in the corridor. As he turned, it took him only seconds to recall the name of Rashtriya Sewa Samiti's chief, Sohan Rajwat. He smiled and nodded at Major Arya who responded but was immediately distracted by his name being called out. He took a deep breath and marched into the office.

"Welcome, Major Arya. Thank you so much for coming at such short notice." Arjun Jaisinghani stood up and extended a hand.

"Sir, when the head of the defense services of the country wants to meet me, in the middle of a critical ongoing mission, then I believe it has to be of crucial relevance." The Major shook the hand but continued to stand.

"Please sit," he gestured at a conference chair, smiling at the Major's opening move. The minister was already liking the man. "I can see you have been wondering about the agenda for this meeting."

There was no response proffered by Major Arya, as he took the seat silently.

"When does your team leave for Kashmir?"

"We are scheduled to depart tonight."

"Be very careful, Major. Kashmir is now a place where the locals are willing to die for the militants."

"Yet I believe you are scheduled to hold peace talks there with separatists. You still hope for peace in the valley?"

"Kashmir has seen five generations of conflict, Major Arya. What do you think a mother will do if her son, though errant, is being shot at? Won't she step in front of the bullet?"

"Sir, our concern right now is a global jihad that has reached our own backyard. So if we could please discuss the purpose of this visit now? I need to get back to the Project Jai Hind headquarters at the earliest."

"Hm, actually, Major Arya, this meeting is to discuss Aliya Sheikh," the minister leaned in, his voice somber.

"What about her, sir?"

"Have you sounded a state-wide alert for her?"

"Not yet. You must be aware of the involvement of two young civilians in the mission. We need to give them a headstart. But it will be done soon."

"What are your orders about Aliya?" Jaisinghani countered.

"She is the prime target. If not captured alive for interrogation, the prime target is to be eliminated in a manner as suited. There is no third option."

"What if I were to instruct you that Aliya Sheikh should only be captured alive?"

"Then I would have to ask you, sir, why do you take such a soft stance on someone who is targeting our nation? Why do we let them kill as we stand by to watch innocents die and then deliberate over fairness and justice?"

"That is not the point."

"Then what is, sir? Is it about politics or are your reasons personal?"

Major Arya sat rigid in his seat, his voice icy. He was already at a stage where professional niceties ended and the gloves came off.

"I thought you might say that." The minister stood up slowly and said, "Come, let's take a walk outside."

For the next 35 minutes, the Defense Minister's staff were on stand-by, reduced to merely looking out at the garden and waiting, hoping for their boss to return to more urgent matters. But he maintained a leisurely pace as he strolled the vast expanse of the garden along with the military man. All they could surmise was that the two men were engrossed in an intense discussion, which could not be interrupted.

Finally, the staff heaved a sigh of relief when the two men shook hands firmly at the far end of the garden. And then, the military man marched off towards the exit area. Then the usual day resumed, where casual visitors were denied meetings, urgent calls were placed and important files hurriedly rushed to the official desk.

Only Prasanna, the middle-aged personal secretary to the Defense Minister stood quietly at the window, gazing at the green expanse of the lawn. The minister never took casual walks in the garden with visitors. *What was the team leader of Project Jai Hind doing at the minister's office on the eve of his departure on a sensitive mission*? This was definitely unusual.

61

Shezii dumped his backpack on the ground and deeply inhaled the pine-scented mountain air. The combination of a slightly warm early afternoon sun and the chilled air felt refreshing. Even though summer was just around the corner, the trees surrounding Srinagar International Airport were yet bare, giving the otherwise pretty and welcoming garden island in front of the arrival area a sparse look. It was the middle of the week and the arriving guests were few and the place was quiet. Yet, Shezii could sense a certain tense urgency. Maybe he was imagining it, but the soldiers stationed in pairs at regular intervals definitely appeared alert and ready for action. He also knew that this was going to be a regular sight in Kashmir.

"Are they picking us up?" Meera stepped in next to him and murmured, wearing an excited tourist's look on her face.

"Nobody is picking us up. We're simple tourists, remember? We're hiring a car."

It was just a front of course. The team had allocated a Mahindra Thar with a driver for them. It was one of the non-negotiable conditions to letting them embark upon this journey.

"There it is," he spotted the approaching Mahindra Thar.

Behind the wheel sat war veteran Captain Bana Singh, dressed in civilian clothes and a thick Kashmiri cap. He stepped out, nodded wordlessly at the duo and put their luggage in the SUV. Shezii got in the back with Meera.

Within minutes it was apparent that the vehicle was hard on suspension but was sturdy and powerful, just like its driver. Shezii eyed him in awe. Retired Captain Bana Singh of Jammu & Kashmir Light Infantry had been a part of Operation Vijay during the Kargil conflict. He was now skillfully maneuvering the Thar at a steady pace, his alert eyes darting constantly in all directions. They drove wordlessly for the next 30 minutes until they arrived at their first destination. Sana Sheikh's house in Barzulla.

They had expected to find a large, imposing house. But instead, it was a small and nondescript single-storied wooden structure wedged between a dilapidated concrete building and a shop selling traditional Kashmiri clothing. Also, contrary to their plans of blending in, they were standing out like a sore thumb as people from the houses and shops across the street eyed them curiously. An ancient looking octogenarian lady from the shop next door moved closer and stared at them. The house had not had visitors for almost two decades. Captain Singh ignored the old lady and pulled out the key to the house and together they ascended the four steps to the door. Shezii turned the key in the old heavy lock. It clicked open with surprising ease and he pushed the wooden door inwards.

He had no idea what to look for, but his instincts had been drawing him to this house right from the beginning. Now, he could sense that thin ray of hope disappearing. The house felt cold, forlorn and unvisited. There were no signs of human habitation. Deep within, Shezii had been hoping to find Awais Sheikh there. But now, this was the end of the road for him. Without any clues it was going to be difficult to justify their stay in Kashmir. And going back meant going away from Aliya. It meant leaving her alone.

Captain Bana Singh came bounding down the creaking staircase and declared "Nothing upstairs either. We will get you checked into a hotel for tonight. Tomorrow, you take the first flight back to Delhi." Before Shezii could respond, he was already exiting the house. Meera and the Captain waited in the car while Shezii locked up and pocketed the key. As he neared the vehicle, his eyes met those of the inquisitive old lady standing by. He nodded and smiled but she did not respond, only continued to stare hard at him.

He turned to enter the car and stopped, feeling the sharp tap of a walking stick on his shoulder.

"Are you related to Sana?" Her voice was phlegmy with age.

"No, I am a friend."

"You are too young to be her friend. Don't lie." She glared.

"Actually, I am a friend of her daughter's."

The lady nodded thoughtfully.

"You wanted to say something to me, ma'am?" he spoke haltingly, unsure about his choice of words.

She shook her head, her eyes fuzzy with memories. Shezii waited.

"Listen, if you meet Sana, tell her that Awais had come looking for her."

Shezii stared. "Awais Sheikh was here? When?"

"Just two days ago … Poor boy looked very upset. He asked me for the key to the house, but I didn't have it. I told him Sana left years ago and that she lives in Dilli somewhere."

Shezii stepped closer to her. Casting a glance around, he quietly pulled out a photograph, "Is he the one who came?"

"I told you it was him! I don't need a picture to recognize him." She batted away his hand. "I have seen these kids grow up in front of my eyes."

"Did he say where he was going?" Shezii asked tentatively.

The old lady was lost to him for a few moments as if busy collecting her thoughts. "Ma'am?" he prodded gently.

"Sopore … Yes, I think he mentioned Sopore. He was going to see a friend there." Her cataract-ridden eyes lit up briefly, as if celebrating a rare win over her treacherously unreliable memory.

"Sopore, in Baramulla?" Shezii knew enough through regular media updates about the area surging with militancy.

"Yes," she nodded slowly, "but don't go there."

"Why?"

"What?" The old lady blinked twice and stared at Shezii.

"Why shouldn't I go there?"

The old lady clicked her tongue. "What are you talking about, young man? Step aside. I don't have all day to spend with you!"

Shezii frowned. "You just said I should not go to Sopore. Why?"

"Sopore … Sopore," the woman mumbled and then slowly retreated into the shop.

Sopore! Shezii grabbed on to that one clue and left.

62

The sun was barely up when the Mahindra Thar exited the gates of Srinagar's Lalit Hotel, carrying its tense passengers and their driver. Within minutes it passed the main road, where it picked up a tail. A battered Tata Qualis, carrying the most sterling counter-terrorism team headed by Major Ram Arya, followed Shezii and Meera at a measured distance.

Meera shivered as even with the windows up, the morning chill seeped into the vehicle. She zipped up her jacket further to cover her neck and leaned towards the driver, "How long will it take, Captain?" Receiving no response, she raised her eyebrows at Shezii, who smiled back at her. They had been driving for barely 15 minutes.

"Under normal conditions, not more than an hour or so, but you never know how the road is going to be," Shezii told her, his eyes scrutinizing Meera who sat uneasily hugging herself. He was beginning to wonder if he had made a mistake in dragging Meera into this mess.

Sighing, she fished out her phone and busied herself in video-graphing the beautiful vistas.

The ride was uneventful apart from the two occasions when they were stopped, once by an Army barricade, which was handled by the Captain smoothly and a second time by the Jammu & Kashmir Police to warn them about a protest and clashes between Army jawans and locals in a village up ahead. They were right, Shezii thought, that without the official back-up it would have been impossible for them to travel in Kashmir beyond the tourist destinations.

After nearly two hours, they arrived in the main market area of the village named Segipora in Sopore. Captain Singh brought the vehicle to a halt near a small shanty selling tea and hot fried snacks.

"So, this is it," said the Captain. "You have five hours, starting now. Remember, don't go around flashing his photo. You will never know if you were talking to his fellow militant. Be discreet. Be back on time." With that, Captain Bana Singh glanced at his watch and settled down on one of the benches at the food stall and ordered *rajma-chawal*. At a distance, Major Arya and his team scattered themselves strategically to cover Shezii and Meera, while keeping a vigil.

For the next two hours, Shezii and Meera played the happy tourist couple while scouting the Segipora village. They tried kahwa and Meera even purchased expensive saffron from a young vendor, knowing full well that it wasn't original. Also a Kashmiri woolen cap that looked a little goofy on her. The locals were friendly but guarded; the people of Segipora village and Sopore in general had a hard time trusting the outsiders. Such was their history with terror and tragedy, and of being crushed in a war between the militants and the armed forces.

By the end of the second hour, the couple returned to their vehicle. The Captain was pretending to take a nap in the driver's seat. They climbed into the back and it was Shezii who spoke first.

"I guess Bakshi sir was right. This isn't as easy as I thought. I am sorry for wasting everybody's time." His tone had more of defeat than regret in it. Captain Bana Singh sat up alert and did not respond. Shezii pegged this as suppressed anger and was about to speak again when the Captain silently raised his finger towards the road branching off from the main market. On it was a dull, silver hatchback, probably a Wagon-R, bumping away quickly, leaving a spray of mulchy melted snow in its wake. It had Delhi number plates.

The Captain shot a glance towards Major Arya who was standing across the street holding a cup of kahwa, and received a quick nod in response. Captain Bana Singh put the SUV in gear and took off in the direction of the Wagaon-R slowly getting away. Behind them, Major Arya quickly hopped into the already moving Qualis.

"Are we following that car?" Shezii was on the edge of his seat.

"Delhi number plates are worth checking out. You might just meet your quarry soon."

"What do we need to do?" Shezii asked urgently.

"We will follow them as far as possible and then we will fall back. You will proceed to take a closer look to confirm if it's Aliya and Ashraf Shaheen. And I am reminding you again that if you spot any of the two, do not attempt to approach them. Call us using the walkie-talkie I gave you."

Shezii nodded as the Mahindra Thar continued to bounce on the potholed dirt road, maintaining a safe distance from the Wagon-R while keeping it in sight. The small hatchback started to slow down on a narrow path that had low mud houses with small courtyards in the front. Two people stepped out of the car and entered a house with a grey tiled roof and unfinished plaster work. They were carrying hefty gunny sacks. Neither of them was Aliya or Awais.

"Let's move out," the Captain whispered. "And remember, you are only on a lookout. Do not make contact."

63

Captain Bana Singh skirted the direct route and disappeared down an alley. Shezii hoisted the backpack on his shoulder and held Meera's hand. Together, they started walking towards the targeted house, in the casual manner of exploring tourists. The expensive Nikon DSLR camera hanging on Meera's neck was an added accessory for the benefit of their cover. As they neared the house, they slowed down. They knew they would only get one pass in front of the house without attracting attention. Even with novice surveillance tactics, Shezii knew he had to find a way to stop in front of the house. And then he saw the reason. He squeezed Meera's hand and smilingly pointed at a stunted apple tree in the courtyard of the house, bearing early fruits. They were now in front of the house and Meera took to clicking pictures of the tree while making the appropriate sounds of awe and excitement. Shezii tried to steal surreptitious glances at the quiet house but it was dark beyond the open door.

Just then, one of the men who had arrived in the car emerged and held Shezii's gaze directly. Unlike most local Kashmiris who chose to keep themselves warm, he was dressed only in a thick grey Pathani suit.

"What do you want?" His voice was gritty and his posture was definitely territorial.

"Just clicking some pictures of your tree," Shezii answered cheerfully.

"Go away." The man was now clearly hostile.

"You from Delhi?" Shezii asked, gesturing at the Wagon-R.

The man's face hardened but he did not respond, instead he stepped forward into the street and carefully surveyed both directions, his eyes coming to stop at the Mahindra Thar parked at the far end of the road.

Shezii knew that in asking that question, he had ventured into the forbidden area, against all professional advice. He tensed, deciding his next move while Meera now stood still with the camera.

"You followed us here, didn't you?" the man growled and lurched at Shezii, pulling him by his jacket into the courtyard of the house. Shezii judged the man's strength as only average, being driven more by anger and adrenaline. He knew he could put the man to the ground in a second. Meera let out a little cry and tried to intervene, but the man flung her aside. Shezii struggled free from his grasp. The brute brought his right fist in an upper cut, but Shezii dodged and, in a simple maneuver, pinned the guy's hand behind his back. Putting everything he had into it, he landed a knee in his opponent's solar plexus. The man grunted and went down.

Alerted by the ruckus, two more men rushed out from the house and stood menacingly, their feet apart. One of them held a gun that was slowly rising in their direction. This was it, Shezii thought and slowly let go of the man's arm. He eyed his backpack lying on the floor, which held the walkie-talkie. Back-up was out of question. Meera shrank in fear and he protectively pushed her behind.

"What's going on?" boomed an authoritative voice. A tall burly man was now standing calmly at the door of the house, his arms crossed. Shezii's eyes lit up in recognition as Awais Sheikh commanded, "Bring them in."

64

They were dumped together on the floor, their hands and feet cuffed in black nylon cable, tied with a swiftness which revealed their captors' regular experience in taking hostages. Meera tried to sit up and groaned as the cable chaffed against her wrist. Shezii looked up and met the eyes of Awais Sheikh who was sitting on a wooden chair, peering down at the pair curiously, like a predator deciding whether to eat or play with its food.

"You are that guy who followed Aliya from the college." Awais Sheikh narrowed his eyes when Shezii finally spoke.

"Where is Aliya?"

"Have you two come alone?" Awais ignored the question.

"I need to know where Aliya is," Shezii repeated.

Awais looked at one of his comrades and gestured towards the door. The man nodded and quickly left to look around for possible back-up.

"Where. Is. Aliya!" Shezii demanded a third time through clenched teeth.

Awais let out a mirthless laugh. "There is no Aliya left for you to find."

"How can you do this to her? She is your own niece!" Shezii blurted out in anger.

Awais paused and then spoke, looking deep into Shezii's eyes, "In fact, I am doing this only because she is my niece. *My only family*." He then pulled out a knife from his pocket and started cutting the ties binding their hands and feet.

65

Captain Bana Singh immediately spotted the man briskly approaching his car, his body language urgent and purposeful. He was the same man who had interacted with Shezii in front of the house. The 15 minutes since Shezii and Meera had entered the house had been tense for the entire team. They were about to swing into action any moment now.

The Captain immediately pressed the button on his walkie-talkie and whispered, "Hostile approaching. Unarmed."

"Looks like he wants to talk. Hear him out. If the situation escalates, we will move in quickly," Major Ram Arya responded.

The man in the Pathani suit came to a stop in front of Captain Bana Singh.

"Come with me. Quietly. And don't act smart."

He cast a suspicious glance around before moving away. Wordlessly, the Captain followed the man into the house.

He froze when he saw Shezii and Meera seated comfortably, sipping tea. Ashraf Shaheen, the notorious operative of *Tehrik-e-Islam*, sat beside them.

Nobody spoke while the Captain was thoroughly searched and his weapon and walkie-talkie confiscated. Once he was clean, he was given a seat.

"I believe you work with the army."

"Retired," the Captain answered, sitting down.

"So, when did the Indian army start sending kids to a war such as this? No more real men remaining on your side?"

"And what does a terrorist like you know about being a man?" the Captain smirked.

In a flash, Awais was onto him, gripping his throat while his cronies stood stiff with guns in their outstretched hands.

As if on cue, Major Ram Arya stormed into the house with two officers of the squad, their guns pointing at Awais.

"Step back," Major Arya commanded.

Awais shot a corrosive glance at the Captain and let go of him with a shove. Four men now stood in the room with guns pointed at each other.

"Welcome, Major Arya." Awais smiled, "Ganibhai was correct, that you were the one leading the team. Have always heard a lot about you."

"Good, then you also know I am here to arrest you." He shifted uneasily, trying to notice any signs pointing to suicide attempts from the terrorists. In his experience, they preferred death to arrest. And with Shezii and Meera present in the small room, a shoot-out would without a doubt lead to civilian collateral damage.

"Arresting me will only bring you to a dead end, Major."

"Well, we will still get a prized *Tehrik-e-Islam* operative. I am sure with some persistence you will spit out all the secrets of your mission." This time the Major smiled a winning smile. This was an important breakthrough in their operation.

"If only, Major ... if only I was still working for them." Something shifted in his voice.

"What do you mean?"

"Lower your gun, Major and then we can talk," Awais said, gesturing at his men to back off.

66

Major Arya accepted the cup of black tea from one of Awais's men in an unspoken temporary truce. They all sat huddled around a small *angithi* with red smoldering coal, while two of the Major's men stood guard outside. Trust, he knew, was one of the key reasons for failure in such operations.

"First things first, Major, you need to send these kids back." Awais began. "This is not their place."

Shezii started to speak but the Major held out a hand to shut him up and said, "Let me first hear your story, Ashraf Shaheen. And if you lie, I will know."

"My real name is Awais Sheikh. It was only when I arrived in Delhi that I first came to know."

"What?"

"That Aliya is my sister's daughter. I couldn't believe that my path would cross my sister's in such a manner. I didn't know what to do."

"Hmm … and then?"

"The jihadis drove me apart from my family when I was young. I see they've done the same with my niece. I suddenly understood how it was one of the most important tactics used in the training process by our

Islamic masters." He sighed, "But I can't do it anymore; not to myself, or to Sana or to my young niece. I wanted to warn her, to take her away with me. To make her understand the futility of it all. I tried to contact her, but when I was about to reach the safe house in Delhi, I got the news that Maghrabi was already there."

"Maghrabi? You mean Essam-al-Maghrabi?" Major Arya asked slowly. This was definitely bad news.

Awais tilted his head and continued, "I knew then, something was wrong. Maghrabi has always been a lone wolf; he operates alone. His comrades listen to him but they often still die. He is an animal."

"So, you ran?"

"You have no idea how they operate, Major." He shook his head, "Al-Gazzar doesn't do anything without a motive. If Maghrabi is here, it means I am of no use to Al-Gazzar. Aliya only *thinks* that she is leading the mission. I did not meet her at the safe house and instead came here, because I knew that I can help save her only from the outside. If they come to know of my relationship with Aliya and that I am trying to convert her, they would kill us both. But then it's possible that they know it already."

"Do you know where they are now?"

"To the best of my knowledge, somewhere in Shopian."

"Can you contact any of them?"

"The designated date of the strike is just two days away. This is a silent period with no communication with the outside world. They have gone into hiding and only the leader would have known the location beforehand."

"No trusted informers who can give away their location now? I am sure you have a deep network in the area." Major Arya knew there had to be some courier, some informant in place, for contingencies.

"None who would not then trade my own location back to Maghrabi for a profit."

"Am I right in thinking they plan to attack the Defense Minister during his meet with the local leaders?"

Awais nodded, "My part in the operation was only to activate the sleeper-cells and co-ordinate ground activities. Aliya was the one to lead. I have her sat-phone frequency, but if I call now, Maghrabi will get suspicious."

"And this could land Aliya in danger." The whole picture was taking shape clearly in Major Arya's mind but he had yet to determine how useful Awais Sheikh was going to be. He was reminded of the specific instructions he had been given. Aliya had to be captured alive. She could not die.

Shezii, who had been quietly hearing the conversation between the two stalwarts, finally spoke.

"I have a plan, Major Arya, and it will work perfectly. If you can please hear me out."

Awais and Major Arya both turned in his direction and stared at him disbelievingly.

67

By the end of Shezii's narration, Major Ram Arya was pacing restlessly in the small room. "You know, your plan would make an excellent Bollywood sequence. But in real life, things don't work like that. There are hundreds of things that can go wrong."

"But sir, we are at a dead end!"

"No, we are not. We know they are in Shopian. We will narrow our search there with Awais here to help us."

"What if they spot him and go into hiding? Worse, what if Aliya gets into trouble with Maghrabi because of him? We have to draw them out to us and this is our best bet," Shezii was desperate.

Support came from an unexpected quarter. Awais said, "I think the boy is making some sense. I know how Maghrabi's mind functions. He likes having the leverage of hostages, in case things don't go as planned. If I tell him that I was delayed picking up two hostages, he will not only believe me, but he may even agree to give me the location for delivery."

"What if they are on a suicide bombing mission? Hostages won't matter then."

"Suicide missions and Maghrabi?" Awais shook his head. "Out of the question. He only sends other people to their death."

"Sir," Meera intervened and the room went silent. "I think he will be drawn into it once he knows that one of the hostages is the daughter of the head of India's anti-terrorism squad." She had a point. No hostage was more valuable in the world of terrorism.

"This is a huge risk," Major Arya sighed. "I'll need to get clearance."

"You only need to get clearance to dangle the bait in front of Maghrabi. There is no need to actually deliver the kids to them. Once we have the location, I will lead the way and your team can cover me. We will have them trapped." Awais's eyes were twinkling with clarity.

Major Arya studied Awais's face. "You understand that once we nab Maghrabi and take Aliya into custody, you're not getting away free?"

"I have come full circle, Major *sahab*. It all ends for me here, in this valley. I intend to surrender." Awais smiled.

68

Dusk was fading into darkness and the group decided to stay put in Segipora for the night. Major Arya had called for back-up and it was due to arrive the next morning. He then left along with Captain Bana Singh to take care of a few things. Two of the Major's men were holed up in the Qualis, while Awais's comrades left to organize dinner.

Meera looked at her phone and noticed she had full signal. She eyed the screen thoughtfully, then keyed in a name and hit call. This was the first time she was making an outgoing call since her arrival in Kashmir.

The line connected at the first ring.

"Meera, where are you guys? Any news of Aliya?"

"Sana ma'am, we are in Kashmir." Meera paused and then added, "With Mr. Awais Sheikh. He is helping us find Aliya. Would you like to speak to your brother?"

There was a long silence on the other end followed by a choked "Yes!"

Meera walked up to Awais and held out the phone for him. He looked up questioningly and she said softly, "Sana Sikander Sheikh."

Awais stared at the phone as if it was an alien object and then looked up at Meera, "I have nothing to say to her."

Meera stood awkwardly for a few moments and then brought the phone to her ears and spoke hastily, "Ma'am, I will have to call you back."

She disconnected the line and looked at a frowning Shezii. Just then Major Arya walked in and stood staring at everyone.

"Is everything okay?" He had sensed the heavy atmosphere, but upon receiving no response he continued, "We have a go signal from the department. We swing into action tomorrow, first thing in the morning."

Awais got up and nodded at the Major, and then disappeared into the poorly lit recesses of the house.

69

Nikki dragged herself out of the bed, fighting an extreme hangover. With a groan, she rushed to the bathroom and threw up violently. Too much to drink, too little to eat and almost no sleep was all finally catching up. Her mouth was constantly bitter and no matter what she did for it, her skin looked blotchy. Ever since Dr. Khan had started staying aloof, she had had a sense of coming untethered. He rarely took her calls and whenever he did, he sounded preoccupied and was always too busy to meet her.

She knew that he was breaking up with her and her mood swung from extreme rage to bleak despair. Every morning she promised herself that she was going to clean up her act, but by the end of the day she had the perfect reason to have that one drink. And then, she could never bring herself to stop.

Deciding to get some food into her system, Nikki filled a cup with cold milk and along with a piece of buttered toast, settled in front of her large TV, which was already tuned to *India Truth,* an old habit she was yet to ditch. And then her eyes went wide while her still fuzzy brain tried to focus on the TV screen.

The news flashing on the screen was about a death under mysterious circumstances. Nikki rubbed her eyes and turned up the volume. Dr. Kamran Khan, the popular leader of the minorities and head of Aware Indian Muslim Party had been found dead in his posh apartment that morning. Nikki's head reeled as she heard more. The circumstances of his death were not established and the body was being sent for a post-mortem analysis. Though the cause of death had been confirmed by forensics as an unidentified fast-acting poison, they were yet to determine if he had committed suicide or if it was a case of cold-blooded murder, reported the animated news anchor. However, the absence of Dr. Khan's cell phone and laptop from the crime scene pointed towards foul play. From the state of rigor mortis, time of death had been between midnight and 2:00 in the morning. *Between midnight and 2:00 a.m.?* Nikki's face turned white.

She searched frantically for her phone, which she knew was on silent mode. Her panic was growing with every passing minute. She had gotten into the habit of making drunken threatening calls to Dr. Khan, way past midnight. *Had she called him last night too?* She thought of the vile messages she often left on his phone and her heart sank. Finally, she spotted her phone peeking out from behind a cushion. She snatched it and immediately went to the outgoing call list. To her relief, no outgoing calls to Dr. Khan were listed last night. In the next instant she noticed that her call list was showing three missed calls from Dr. Khan's personal mobile, between midnight and 1:00 a.m. There was also a text message from him at 1:30 a.m.

Nikki sank back into the couch and with trembling fingers, touched the screen to open the message. *They are going to kill me. I need help, but no one is willing to listen. Not even the government. Help me, Nikki. PLEASE.*

She read Dr. Khan's final text message to her again, and then again. On the TV screen, the officer in charge of the case was appealing that if anyone had any information about Dr. Khan's mysterious death, they should call the police helpline immediately.

Nikki sat staring at the message, her thumb paused over the text for a very long time. Finally, with a deep breath, she looked up and saw the empty bottle of vodka lying on her dining table.

And then, her thumb hit the delete button.

70

Fed by the fast-melting Himalayan snow, the Rambi Ara river was getting livelier by the day. But the river's gurgling happy sound was not able to improve Aliya's mood that evening. She abhorred dusks, instead preferring the dark of nightfall. At least the dark had a finality to it, unlike the dusk, which held a sense of impending doom … a sense of fast approaching darkness.

She and her group of six operatives had holed up in a long abandoned timber mill, near a small village named Gagran in the Shopian district. They were all fatigued from the long drive and the palpable nervous tension building up before an operation. A dense coniferous jungle of pine and fir separated the timber mill from the village and the nearest habitation was more than 2 kilometers of walking distance away. Things were proceeding as planned, but Maghrabi's presence was beginning to grate against her nerves. With him around, she felt a constant need to look over her shoulder. He had made it amply clear that he didn't like being led by a woman. He was like a compressed spring ready to recoil and she only wondered, *What was he waiting for?*

She had a plan and she had worked very hard to reach where she was in the *Tehrik-e-Islam* order. Now only one last thing remained to be proven, before she could escalate to the top-most ranks. Al-Gazzar needed to know if she could strike against her own roots, her own country. And this operation was her ultimate test. She could not afford to let this primitive buffoon upset her plans now.

Suddenly, a gust of mountain breeze caught her scarf lightly and she was reminded of that cold, windy day in college and the brisk walk to the car with Shezii. She had loved the warmth of his car. As an operative, she had often braced extreme weather conditions and had returned from near death experiences more than once, but no warmth had ever felt so comforting. With a deep breath, she brushed aside such thoughts and turned to go back. And that's when she spotted Maghrabi. He was squatting on a large boulder at the far end of the clearing on the river bank. He was on his satellite phone.

They were already in the silent phase of the operation. *Who was he calling? And what was the purpose?* She wasn't going to allow him to flout the rules so easily. Not on her watch and certainly not under her leadership.

71

That Essam-al-Maghrabi was a cruel man reflected strangely in his smile. It was cruel in a way that could make children stop crying or curdle the blood of any human in an instant. Right then, that demonic smile was playing on his lips.

"Do not worry, big brother, I am taking charge here," Maghrabi spoke in a low growl.

"May *Allah* be with you, *biradar* … with you there I have nothing to worry about. We will bring Hind to its knees. And only then will it learn to respect its *Musalmans,*" Al-Gazzar's voice was tinny but clear over the sat-phone. He sounded heady with pride and confidence.

"Have you spoken to our allies? We need funds. Our *fauj* needs to be taken care of and it requires more arms and ammunition. Tell them if they want to pet a lion, then they must be ready to feed it."

"I have already spoken to the *hukumaran* of Islamabad, the money is on its way. Now, I wait to see Hind burn."

"That is very good. Soon, every *kafir* Hindustani will see what it means to deny Islam. The current *hukumat* of Hind will have to forget about the word Hindu."

Maghrabi let out a short laugh and the birds resting in the nearby trees flew away in a ruckus of scared chirping.

"The rest of the job will be completed by the opposing political parties of Hind, who are awaiting such a situation. But they are weak. Just like that Kamran Khan. And for that, he had to die," Al-Gazzar spat out the words hatefully. "Let the war begin and only we will emerge as the new rulers."

Just then, Maghrabi spotted Aliya coming towards him and his jaw clenched. He wanted to twist her neck and wrench it away from her spine. But she was a part of the team and he still had no clear instructions about her from his great leader Al-Gazzar. Even a man like Maghrabi had to fear someone. And Al-Gazzar was omnipresent. One could fight anything that could be defeated with strength and skill, but Al-Gazzar was a system, a powerful system that chewed and ingested people and left no trace.

"What to do with this girl, Aliya?" he asked impatiently. "We don't need her anymore. Should I *release* her?"

"Has Ashraf Shaheen contacted yet?" The voice had grown cold.

"Not yet."

"Then wait, my lion … wait till he calls. Because he will. For sure. *Allah Hafiz* for now."

Maghrabi disconnected the call and jumped off the boulder. He stood defiantly holding the sat-phone.

"Who were you talking to?" Aliya challenged. There was no way she could win a fight against a predator like him if she gave even an inch of ground.

"Your men are tired and hungry, why don't you go take care of them." The derision in his voice was apparent and Aliya bristled.

"You know that you are jeopardizing the mission by breaking the rules," she said, ignoring his remark.

"The only rules Maghrabi follows are the rules of Allah," he growled back.

"The rules for this mission are laid down by our leader himself. In this mortal life, he is the only one for us after Allah. And he won't be happy to hear you say that," she baited him.

"We shall see," he merely smirked.

"Get back to the barn. Now. We have to go over our plans for the day after." With that, she turned and started to walk back. Maghrabi had sounded like trouble and she wasn't carrying her weapon. She had tactically chosen to bring their stand-off to a sterile end. She knew she had to take care of Maghrabi. *Soon*. Or else, he was going to kill her without a doubt. Aliya had seen it in his eyes.

72

Sana Sheikh checked her cell phone's lit-up screen and disconnected the call. It was her secretary, calling for the fourth time that morning. Sana had virtually stopped visiting the office. Between seeking updates from various agencies and the Defense Minister's office on an hourly basis, she barely managed to oversee the essential operations of *India Truth,* whose TRPs were nosediving. But nothing else mattered right now except her daughter.

While Rajeev Bakshi sat with his arms folded, his posture withdrawn and non-committal, Arjun Jaisinghani was leaning on the table, his hands clasped in front of him. Faisal Umer Naqvi looked ill at ease, his face strained with worry.

"You know they are in Shopian, Rajeev, why can't your team just storm the goddamn place?" Sana was frantic.

"It's not that easy. The militant network there is extensive. They will know the second we set foot in Shopian. We can't afford for them to go into hiding any deeper," Rajeev said.

"But I am not sure about Shezii and Meera being in the middle of all this." Faisal looked at Rajeev Bakshi.

"It was Shezii's idea, Faisal. We wanted to bring them back right away," Rajeev grimaced.

"You know what they are capable of. See what they did to Dr. Kamran Khan. And now they are targeting you, Arjunji." Sana was panicking.

"Once we get the location for the drop, a helicopter will bring the kids straight back to Delhi. Only Major Arya and his team will go to the rendezvous point, along with Ashraf Shaheen." The Defense Minister looked around the table and belatedly regretted the use of Awais's terrorist name. He was met by Sana's stoic eyes.

"Sir, I too will be leaving for Srinagar tonight," Rajeev said.

"Don't you think you can play out your role better here at the project command center?"

"It's best if I supervise the security aspects personally. This is a high-risk scenario. Especially now, with Mr. Sohan Rajwat's presence, it's no longer a quiet political meet. It's going to be a bigger event with full media attention. The whole nation will be watching."

"Hmm ... I hope your reasons aren't emotional, Rajeev. You do know that you have an extremely capable team operating in Kashmir."

"I know Meera and Shezii are in safe hands, sir." He smiled, "My responsibility now is your safety."

"Good then," the minister flashed a quick smile, "I hope Prasanna has shared our travel itinerary with you already. We are reaching Srinagar tomorrow evening."

"I know, in separate travel arrangements." Rajeev nodded.

"Yeah, it means more work for you." The minister pursed his lips.

"Travel arrangements from Delhi to Srinagar are not an issue because we are keeping Mr. Sohan Rajwat's plan to participate in the talks undisclosed until he reaches Srinagar. But I would have preferred if you both had travelled together to the meet's venue in Srinagar, the day after. It's easier to secure one route and one convoy."

"I had suggested it, Rajeev, but the Rashtriya Sewa Samiti insisted on a separate convoy for their leader. I guess they want to send a message about their leader attending in an independent capacity. I don't think even Rajwatji had any say in this matter," the minister shrugged.

"This does pose a security risk. But don't worry, it will be handled." Rajeev Bakshi responded crisply.

Satisfied, the minister turned to the worried faces of Sana and Faisal, "Friends, we are going to bring those kids back. I promise." Then he added, looking into Sana's eyes, "Including Aliya."

The group broke up and they went their separate ways. Rajeev decided to return to the command center and leave directly from there.

Arjun Jaisinghani barely slept that night as he considered the upcoming visit to Kashmir and the gravity of his promise to Sana. He knew this was going to be a tightrope walk for him, on both political and bureaucratic fronts.

"Are your guns ready for tomorrow?!"

Aliya received a chorus of "Yes!" from the five battle-ready faces. Three belonged to young Kashmiri locals named Munir, Yaseen and Farooq who had lost family members to army firing. Majid was older and part of the sleeper-cell activated in Delhi by Ganibhai. He wasn't very talkative, but twice Aliya had seen him whispering with Maghrabi and immediately stopping when he noticed her. Ganibhai was the last. This would be his first active field operation.

"Remember, you are on this journey for Allah. You will not tire and you will not stop until you achieve what you have set out for." She sensed Maghrabi's mean eyes weighing her ability as a leader.

"Munir and Yaseen will reach Gandhi Bhawan Center at Kashmir University's main campus in Hazratbal by 6:00 a.m. along with the weapons and grenades. They will take cover as kitchen staff. Arrangements have been made to hide the weapons at a secure location in the same building. You both will await our signal to come into action. Is that clear?"

The young men nodded. Being locals, they would have no problem blending in. Besides, the canteen manager was a distant cousin of Munir.

"I will be a part of the media convoy covering the event. The event starts at 10:30 a.m. and I will be seated in the media enclosure latest by 9:30 a.m." She examined their faces and then continued.

"Exactly at 10:15 a.m., I will excuse myself and meet Munir and Yaseen behind the building where there is no camera surveillance. We will wait till Majid gives us confirmation of the minister's arrival in the hall." She looked at Majid and he nodded in assent.

"As soon as the meeting begins, we three will storm the event hall. I will target Arjun Jaisinghani and the separatist leader Gafoor Mallik, while Munir and Yaseen will provide cover fire against the minister's security. Our guns are light and effective, so take advantage of it. Move fast and do not waste time engaging unnecessarily with the general public. A stampede of nearly 300 people can make our escape difficult. Remember, speed is key to the success of this mission and we can't afford to get trapped. Am I clear?" She paused, but the silent attention was her cue to go on.

She then turned to the other group, "Maghrabi, along with Farooq and Ganibhai, will be acting as our exit team. Ganibhai will be waiting for us in the vehicle at the gate while Maghrabi, Farooq and Majid will tackle the security outside the venue with cover fire. Is that clear?" Her tone and eyes challenged Maghrabi directly.

"Yes, apart from one thing," he grinned maniacally, "Why not just take the AK47 and open fire? Once our target is shot dead, kill everyone else too. Dead bodies can't cause a stampede."

"Because this is not a battle, this is a targeted hit. My gun has a range of more than 200 feet and I am sure about my aim. I just need two quick shots. Moreover, this is my mission and my rules will apply."

"And you know what I think about your rules," Maghrabi openly scoffed. Ganibhai shot a worried glance at Aliya. Even he could sense the building tension. This wasn't good if they were going to rely upon each other as a team. The mission's success and their lives depended upon their flawless co-ordination.

Just when Aliya was about to retort, her sat-phone's tinny ring tone reverberated in the cavernous space of the barn. It was kept on the wooden crates stacked at a little distance from Maghrabi. Both he and Aliya turned towards it, surprised at first. Their eyes met quickly and then, before Aliya could reach out for it, Maghrabi grabbed the phone and answered it with a knowing smile.

"This is Ashraf Shaheen," the voice identified itself.

"Aha! Shaheen, my good fortune to have finally heard from you, brother." The sarcasm in Maghrabi's voice was as apparent as its fake jovial manner. Aliya was listening carefully to every word he was uttering, trying to confirm if it was the same Ashraf Shaheen calling who had been absconding ever since the Delhi safe house meeting. Wrestling with Maghrabi for the sat-phone in front of the entire team could have gone either way.

"I am in Kashmir." The response was delayed but clear.

"That I know, but what made you think of us now?" Maghrabi's tone had taken a raw edge. "Remember, you are the one who ran away."

"I want to speak to the leader," Awais said, half wondering if something had happened to Aliya already.

"You are speaking to one, my brother. Tell me."

"I said I want to speak to the leader."

"That isn't going to happen. You know this is the silent phase of the operation. Have you forgotten the rules already?"

"I have good reason to speak to the leader," Awais spoke into the sat-phone. He couldn't help but shift in his seat as he looked at Major Arya, who nodded as a signal to proceed.

"You have to talk to me," Maghrabi growled impatiently.

Aliya was about to pounce on Maghrabi when she felt a restraining hand on her shoulder. It was Ganibhai, shaking his head slowly.

"I have hostages," Awais finally said.

"Hostages?"

"Yes. Two youngsters."

"If we want hostages, we can take plenty on our own," he smirked. "Besides, why should you be trusted?"

"These are not just any hostages. I have Shahzaib Umer Naqvi *urf* Shezii, who is the son of a top government official and the other is Meera Bakshi, daughter of Rajeev Bakshi, the head of the counter-terrorism department."

Maghrabi was silent for a beat.

"These hostages will prove very useful." Awais emphasized, "Especially in our exit strategy. You must inform the leader that I have been working for our cause all this while." Awais was making a point to not let it be known that he knew of Maghrabi's presence.

"What do you want?" Maghrabi relented.

"I want to bring the hostages to you. I can't keep them here any longer. The armed forces and the local police both are on high vigil. Please tell me where to bring them in Shopian?"

There was another silence on the other end but Awais had no way of knowing that Maghrabi was smiling. A cunning, foxy smile. Then he said, "Of course, brother." He recited the location co-ordinates for the benefit of Awais.

Aliya's eyes were screwed in concentration as she tried to figure out Maghrabi's play. Ganibhai mentally checked the co-ordinates recited by the new self-appointed leader, and his brow creased.

"Meera Bakshi and Shahzaib Umer Naqvi," Maghrabi guffawed, "They will be joining us soon as hostages." He then added in a chilling tone, "At the end of it all, I will personally enjoy killing them."

Aliya froze as the name hit her. *Shahzaib Umer Naqvi? Shezii? Here, in the middle of all this?* And for the first time, she felt panic rising within her. Her face stayed blank but small beads of sweat formed on her forehead.

74

The night was still, its silence echoing in the gentle sway of pine trees and the steady gurgles of the river. Ganibhai was almost dozing off against the butt of his rifle when he was jolted awake by the sudden faraway cry of a wild animal. His eyes scanned the barn. Finding everything in order, he picked up a thermos, poured sweet, milky tea into a large plastic mug and sipped. A tap to his wristwatch lit up its digital face. It was 2:00 a.m. Four more hours to go before his watch ended.

As his eyes readjusted to the gloom, he sensed movement beyond the barn. He set aside the mug, got up and padded to the door. Gripping the rifle tightly, he peered out of the barn. Maghrabi was walking towards the river with a satellite phone in hand. Ganibhai cast one quick glance across the barn and its sleeping occupants, and then quickly slipped out after Maghrabi.

Ganibhai had the advantage of being dressed in black yet he quietly tip-toed from one patch of sand and mud to another. By the time he caught up, Maghrabi had parked himself on a boulder and was dialing.

"*Salaam-Alaikum Qayid,* the call from the *kafir* has come already," Maghrabi started without any preamble.

There was mirthless laughter at the other end. "*Wa-Alaikum-Salaam* brother, didn't I tell you."

"He says he has got hostages for us. What am I supposed to do with him?"

"How much does Black Sand know about him?"

"Right now, I have no idea. She is preparing for the mission as instructed by you. The target is that peace-loving minister of Hind."

"Bring them all in. We shall see what Black Sand has to say." Al-Gazzar paused and added as an afterthought, "Maghrabi, brother, just make sure that the cat is not dragging in a dead rat."

"I understand. I will take care of it. What about the mission?"

"Ah! I have good news. Our target has become bigger. You are going to enjoy this mission," Al-Gazzar said meaningfully.

Al-Gazzar then spoke for a long time with only monosyllabic responses from Maghrabi. When he was done talking, Maghrabi spoke coldly, "This will put the fear of Allah in the hearts of every *kafir* in Hind. And they will know that we mean business. Once they see what we can do, there will be no more protests. They will give in to our power."

"You are correct, my brother. You know what you have to do. *Allah Hafiz*, may you be in his protection."

"*Shukran* and *Allah Hafiz*, I will now prepare for the new mission."

The call was disconnected. Maghrabi started walking back. Ganibhai let go of the breath he had been holding and shrunk back into the dark shadows of the boulder. Maghrabi half-turned and cast a careful glance at the dark behind him. Ganibhai tightened the grip on his rifle. Then suddenly, Maghrabi resumed walking and disappeared into the barn.

Ganibhai sat still but his mind raced with questions. Why was Maghrabi on the phone at this point in their mission? What new mission was he planning? Who were these hostages? And why was Black Sand, their leader, in the dark while Maghrabi did all this?

75

The morning dawned in Segipora, heavy with possibilities. Major Arya and Awais huddled around the *angithi*. Today was the day they would come face to face with *Tehrik-e-Islam*.

A squad had arrived to pick up Shezii and Meera and escort them back to Delhi. The team's departure for the location was just an hour away and they were in the last stages of checks. Shezii was suddenly filled with compassion for the man who was now ready to risk his life for his family.

He stood up and shook hands with Awais. "Thank you very much for doing this."

"I am not doing this for anyone else. I am doing this for myself. You both must get home safely," he gripped Shezii's hand. "And try to forget about Aliya. People who walk this path are changed forever. If you look for her, you will only find her fading shadow. And you won't be able to recognize it, even if you try your best."

From a distance, Major Arya studied Awais's strained face. He wondered if the man was having second thoughts about being used as bait. As Awais stepped away from the children, the Major walked up to him.

"Is everything okay, Awais?"

"Yes. I am fine."

"Good. If things go as planned, we will have them in our custody by afternoon."

Awais did not respond.

"Something you want to tell me?"

"No, it's nothing."

"You know we won't let you die," the Major offered.

"I am not afraid to die."

"Then?"

"It's Maghrabi. He agreed too quickly to meet me. No questions asked. This is very unlike him. I am afraid that I am missing something."

"Is it because you couldn't speak with Aliya?"

"No—," Awais started but was cut off by the shrill ring of the Major's secure phone.

It was Akshara from the command post in Delhi. Major Arya answered and put the phone on speaker.

"Yes Akshara, is the location verified?"

"Actually, I have a critical update for you," came the worried response.

"Tell me."

"The location co-ordinates you sent to me are supposed to be of some out of business bat-manufacturing facility, right?"

"Yes."

"Major, it's an empty piece of land. No factory there."

"Are you sure?"

"I checked, and then double checked the satellite images," Akshara emphasized. "There is nothing there."

"Got it. Will connect soon." He disconnected the call.

Shezii and Meera exchanged worried glances.

"Do you think Maghrabi could make a mistake while giving the co-ordinates?" the Major asked Awais.

"No, it's not a mistake. He wants to meet me. He is playing us, only I am not able to understand his game."

That's when Awais's sat-phone rang. He stared at the number and knew that the series belonged to *Tehrik-e-Islam*. He lifted his finger to his lips and then answered the call on speakerphone. The entire room had gone still.

"Brother, are you ready for your journey?" Maghrabi's tone was conversational, as if checking on a favorite relative.

"Yes, I will see you soon."

"With the hostages?"

"Yes, of course."

"Good," he smirked, "Then you must reach the given location and send me a video of yourself with the boy and girl. I will send you the directions to the final location then."

The line disconnected and Awais went pale. "He is on to us. He knows," he whispered.

"Not necessarily. He just doesn't trust you yet. Maybe he wants to play it safe," Major Arya cautioned.

"But this means we can't go through with the plan. He wants to ensure Shezii and Meera are with me."

"Actually, this changes nothing," Shezii spoke before the Major could respond.

"What the hell do you mean?" Major Arya retorted.

"We reach the location, send our video from there and then we leave. Just like we were to leave from here now ... Only a little later."

Shezii looked at the blank faces around him. "I am sure your team can easily extract us from there, can't it, Major sir?"

Major Ram Arya did not speak. He sat back and stared at the kerosene lamp burning brightly in their midst. This young man always had a simple solution to complex situations. Because just like the terrorists, he wasn't afraid to die. *Maybe the boy did want to die,* thought Major Arya. But it was his job to keep everyone alive, including Aliya.

76

Major Arya paced the muddy courtyard, clutching the phone tightly to his ears. "But sir, we don't know Maghrabi's endgame yet. I hope you realize what great risk you are putting them into. Especially Meera."

"Major Arya, I know you will take care of them. Besides, we are now too close to the strike day." Rajeev Bakshi continued, "I can't risk the operation just because we are not ready to take the next step."

"Taking the next step might put Shezii and Meera in the hands of *Tehrik-e-Islam*."

"And your job is to not let that happen, Major." Rajeev's tone was decisive. "You will personally lead the shadow team. I am right now organizing additional back-up for you. A chopper will be on stand-by at the Awantipur Air Force station in Pulwama."

"Yes, sir," the Major replied and then hesitated. "But what if this is Maghrabi's trap?"

"You know his profile, Major. He *is* trying to trap you. So let him think he has the upper hand. But as soon as you get your next location, you send away Shezii and Meera and proceed with Awais to their hideout. The back-up team will follow you closely." Rajeev paused, sensing his overpowering intensity and then added, "Don't worry Major, you will get them."

"Yes, sir."

"Good luck, Major. You better get going. The clock is ticking."

The call ended but Major Arya could sense the pre-operation high beginning to hit him. The fact that he had not reported the contents of his meeting with the minister to Rajeev Bakshi was bothering him. Major Ram Arya believed that protocols and well-defined operating procedures kept people alive on the battlefield. Yet he had broken the rule, even if it was for the first time.

Besides, he hadn't yet heard from the person he was supposed to hear from. The situation was escalating fast and he was still in the dark. The stakes were high and he could not afford to lose.

77

The two-car convoy had been bouncing along on the wild dirt track for almost an hour when Major Arya glanced at the GPS monitor and gestured at the driver to slow down. They were barely 50 kilometers south of Srinagar but having passed the last habitation almost 40 minutes ago, it seemed like they were in the middle of nowhere. Behind them, the four-wheel drive SUV came to a halt and Captain Bana Singh hopped out. He held up a hand for Shezii, Meera and Awais to stay put in the vehicle and walked over to Major Arya. They were parked on the mouth of a narrow path branching out from the main track leading into the denser part of Hirpora Wildlife Sanctuary. The track was surrounded by tall deodars and chinars on both sides, as far as one could see. It was obvious that the only way to traverse this protected jungle of Hirpora Sanctuary was on foot. The mid-afternoon sun was already weak and there was residual frost on the edges of the track from the light snowfall earlier in the week. Captain Singh rubbed his hands and blew into them as he huddled with the Major and three other team officers.

"It's going to be on foot from here," Major Arya spoke in a low voice, as if not wanting to disturb the jungle.

"According to Akshara, the location is less than three kilometers in that direction." He pointed towards the path ahead, and whispered again, "Keep a close eye on Awais."

"We will, Major. How far behind are the extraction and back-up teams?" Captain Bana Singh asked. He was to accompany the group as Awais's comrade. Once the contact with Maghrabi was established, he was to lead Shezii and Meera away while the others proceeded to the terrorists' hideout.

"Less than three hundred yards behind, at all times. Keep the secure line open." Major Arya turned to inspect the occupants of the vehicle parked behind them.

Shezii shot him a brave smile. Meera shivered. No words were suitable in the current situation and they all knew it. Last to alight from the vehicle, Awais silently followed the group to the jungle trail without looking in the Major's direction. He knew these woods like the back of his hand and felt a sense of finality in the homecoming.

Bracing themselves against the forest chill, they walked silently, their feet rhythmically crunching on the dried foliage and leaves. Awais led the trek expertly, as deeper into the jungle, the path began to vanish and was replaced by dense shrubs and vines, which at times required cutting through. Twice Captain Singh commanded Awais to slow down. Meera tripped and Shezii held her hand protectively to lead her on. The rarified, glacial air was fast exhausting her. In a couple of kilometers, her breathing was labored.

"I need a break," Meera finally whispered hoarsely and leaned against a high boulder.

"We are very close now." Captain Bana Singh looked around suspiciously. "We must keep going."

"Just give her five minutes," Shezii said urgently.

"Keep your breath steady and cover your neck and nose. This chill is dangerous if it gets to your lungs." Awais's eyes were scrutinizing Meera who had turned markedly pale.

"I am fine. Just give me a minute," she held up a hand defensively.

Captain Bana Singh was about to respond when there was movement behind the thick growth of vegetation at a little distance. Someone was moving there. The group went still. *Maghrabi!* thought the Captain. He slowly reached for his gun. Awais saw the move and whispered, "Hold on."

A large bearded ram with blazing, yellow eyes and great spiral horns emerged from the thicket. The thick hairy beard extending from its chin to its neck and its calm manner gave it the wise look of an old man. Then the elk raised its head, as if smelling something in the air and bounded off.

"That's the Pir Panjal Markhor. Only a handful of them left in the region now," Awais spoke reverently.

"I am glad it wasn't a bear," Captain Singh replied, holstering his weapon.

"This is not the season for them. A couple of months from now, you will quite certainly encounter them in this area," Awais said.

The Captain's walkie-talkie beeped just then. It was Major Arya, "Captain, I see that you have stopped. All okay?"

"Yes, all good, Major. We are very close to the location now."

"Good then. Connect back once you hit the location. We are right behind."

The call was disconnected and everything went quiet. *For a bit too long.* Awais turned towards Captain Bana Singh and froze.

The Captain's eyes were wide and blood was seeping through the fingers of his hand, which was pressed against his neck. Awais's eyes darted in all directions, looking for the sharp shooter. His worst fear was confirmed when, in the next second another silent bullet hit Captain Bana Singh right above his heart and he started to collapse, the front of his shirt fast turning crimson. Awais rushed towards the dying man for his gun and the walkie-talkie still in his hands. But he was too late. A masked man appeared out of nowhere and stood between the Captain and Awais. His gun was pointed at Awais and the hatred in his eyes told him that the man wouldn't hesitate to shoot.

Awais raised his hands and turned slowly to find Shezii and Meera in a similar ambush. Only Shezii had been pushed to the ground by his captor and a large blue bruise on his forehead was visible even from a distance. Meera was heaving heavily while another masked man had pinned her hands behind her and held a gun to her temple. This was a typical Maghrabi ambush. In less than a couple of minutes, things had gone horribly out of their hands.

Awais wasn't going to give up easily. He judged the masked man behind him to be of average height, someone he could tackle easily if the guy wasn't holding a gun at him. Awais decided to take the chance and started to turn towards his captor. But then, sudden darkness swam in front of his eyes as he felt the impact of the heavy rifle butt on his skull, followed by a blinding pain. He started to collapse as his knees buckled. Finally, he hit the cold damp ground like a falling log. His last conscious memory was of utter helplessness and nausea, before everything blacked out.

78

The Lalit Hotel's prestigious Durbar Hall had been temporarily closed to the public. The luxurious venue, normally reserved for high-profile events hosted by the elites of Srinagar wore a disheveled look. The thick velvet curtains were drawn shut and the furniture had been hurriedly pushed to the dark corners to create space for a makeshift communication center where Akshara and her team were frantically assessing every piece of information and leads available to them through the data pouring in from the international secret service agencies and anti-terrorism wings of the partnering nations. They were avoiding each other's eyes and only spoke to provide terse updates. The atmosphere was rigid with tension, which seemed further enhanced as their words echoed in the expanse of the 2000 square foot hall with less than ten people in it. But for now, it was Project Jai Hind's command center in Srinagar.

An ashen-faced Rajeev Bakshi sat with Major Arya at a nearby desk.

"I should have paid more attention to Awais's warning," the Major huffed. "I didn't even get a chance to close the gap. If only I had been with the group—"

Major Arya stopped mid-sentence. He had been the first to reach Captain Singh, who was still breathing then. The Major had literally felt the warmth seep out of the Captain's body within minutes. "We need to fix this," he snapped, unable to bear the lack of action.

"Major!" Akshara rushed towards them. "There is unusual activity over sat-phones in this area." She jabbed at the screen of the tablet she was holding. "These sat-phones are of the same series as those we tracked in Delhi."

"*Tehrik-e-Islam*?"

Akshara nodded.

"Can you triangulate the location?"

"We've done it. We have the general area within a two-kilometer radius."

"Good. Send me the co-ordinates right away. We will mobilize immediately."

Akshara nodded and rushed back to her station.

"Major, this time, take a larger team. I am personally looking into the security of the leaders arriving tomorrow. You are in charge of extracting Shezii and Meera. Also Awais, if he hasn't gone hostile. We must hunt down and annihilate this *Tehrik-e-Islam* unit from our soil. *Each of them*. We only have time until the event because that's when they will plan to strike. Successful or not, after the hit, they will want to vanish. Hostages will be of no use to Maghrabi then. And you know what happens to redundant hostages," Rajeev looked directly into the Major's eyes.

"Yes, sir," the Major said, getting up. "I will get back to you shortly with a plan."

Crossing through a labyrinth of corridors, the Major walked out eventually onto an open terrace. In the late afternoon chill, he pulled out his phone and hit call on a pre-fed number. "Sir, I haven't received the call yet. Should I proceed as planned?" the Major spoke into the phone and listened intently to the response for a few seconds. Then he disconnected the call without a word and stared out at the placid Dal Lake. Far off, a *shikara* floated in a silhouette against the setting sun. The lake looked reassuringly calm, as if time didn't exist in its dimension. With one last look, Major Ram Arya turned and quickly disappeared into the hotel.

79

Shezii woke up with a start, gasping for air. His eyes felt as if they had been glued together. His brain swam with erratic visions. Slowly, he took in the cavernous mill around him. Meera lay bruised and unconscious but was breathing evenly. They were shackled together, to a pair of iron anchors built into a large cement structure. Shezii assessed himself quickly. They had beaten him up but there were no bleeding wounds or cuts. He knew he would limp if he tried to walk now, but at least they hadn't shot him. It meant they still needed them alive. He sensed Meera stirring next to him. Shezii turned towards her and sat up after a few painful maneuvers.

"Hey," he whispered.

She moaned in reply, sitting up groggily. "Ugh, where are the Captain and Awais?" she asked hoarsely. They had treated her better for now, but she was a *kafir* woman trapped among the Islamic jihadis. Shezii's blood froze at the thought of what could happen.

"Shh, quiet." He looked around cautiously.

Before Shezii could reply, their attention was drawn to a commotion at the far entrance. A man on the floor was being kicked around by a group of jihadis. Two men and a lithe woman stood back watching. The woman was dressed in a black jumpsuit and something about her form seemed familiar to Shezii. Shezii's heart skipped a beat as she turned. It was unmistakably Aliya striding towards him. A dark mask covered the lower portion of her face and her eyes were empty. Shezii huffed involuntarily, fighting the wave of pain shooting through his head.

Awais's torturer kicked him again, laughed maniacally and followed Aliya while dragging Awais along. They dumped him on the floor next to Meera, who flinched at the sight of him bloodied and panting. Shezii was overcome with a sense of déjà vu, a strange feeling of being in the same place before. Long ago.

A tall man stepped up, smiling congenially yet with undisguised meanness. He looked down at Awais pitifully, "Tell me again, *brother*, why should I trust you?"

"I brought you the hostages, as promised," his words were laboured.

"So she is the daughter of their chief?" He prowled over to Meera who shrank into herself. In a sudden move, he grabbed a handful of her hair and pulled her up. Meera yelped in pain as tears wet her cheeks.

"Let go of her, you bastard!" Shezii screamed at Maghrabi, who let go of Meera and turned on him.

In the next instant, he had Shezii's throat in a death grip. He felt his head go hot and full of blood and with the rushing blood surfaced dark memories. And the blinding recognition of that oily sandalwood scent. It was the creeping odour of his frightful evening in Tel Aviv, which was etched in his memory.

Shezii looked into Maghrabi's eyes and knew. This man had tormented his family. This man had imprinted his mind with a lifetime of nightmares. This man had murdered Rotem and bombed a club full of people on vacation. Shezii's hazy vision fell on the knife hanging at Maghrabi's waist. All he had to do was to reach out, but his hands were busy prying Maghrabi's hands off his neck. Suppressing the urge to fight for his breath, to claw at the choking grip, Shezii went for the dagger. Maghrabi was too focused on the boy's bulging veins and bloodshot eyes. Shezii's fingers touched metal but fate intervened in the form of Awais.

"Essam, my brother!" Awais called out. "You should pay attention to the mission. The army might be getting closer." He hacked and coughed up a mouthful of blood on the floor.

Maghrabi dropped Shezii, who fell back devastated and gasping for breath.

"So, you do know about the army's plans?" Maghrabi chewed out the words.

"Nothing more than what you do, brother."

"Lying will only bring you death."

"I am working for *Tehrik-e-Islam*. *Inshallah,* I will give my life only for Islam."

"That you will," Maghrabi spoke thoughtfully, "But is that why Hindustani army officers were following you in the jungle?" He arched an eyebrow.

"I told you. I did not know we were being followed," Awais answered evenly through the pain, mustering all his will and dignity.

"Oh! You did not know?" Maghrabi smirked and casually strolled towards Aliya who had stood unmoving right through his showdown. "How about the Black Sand? Don't tell me you know nothing about her?"

"I do not understand, brother," Awais swallowed hard.

Maghrabi chuckled and turned towards Aliya, "How about you, Black Sand?"

"If you are done with your antics, let the men return to their practice. Tomorrow is an important day," Aliya responded coolly.

"Why don't *you* help me be done with it, Black Sand?" he sneered. "Here," he pulled out his gun and held it out for her. "Please ... end this traitor's worthless life. Send him to his maker."

80

Aliya stared at the gun glinting in Maghrabi's outstretched hand and then looked at Awais. She had known who he was even before she had returned from London. He was high enough in the ranks of *Tehrik-e-Islam* but it was only when he was flagged as a fellow operative in Project Death Valley alongside her that she had dug into his background. Now, she had to choose—loyalty to her jihadi masters or to spill her own blood.

Shezii tried to get up, alarmed by the turn of events, but could only manage to clank his chains. Meera drew in a sharp breath. They knew the game Maghrabi was playing. A game he knew he couldn't lose.

Awais stared at her with the defiance of a martyr. Moments ticked by but his face was fearless and his eyes shone with an unknown emotion. Then he nodded imperceptibly. Aliya shifted. She grabbed the gun from Maghrabi's open palm. Without a word, she changed her stance and raised the gun towards Awais.

Awais gazed at her as time slowed to a stop. A beatific smile played on his lips. Without warning, his body began to shake. Blood rushed to his face as he breathed in gasps. Then, he slowly keeled over in the grip of a seizure. Aliya lowered the gun with a frown and everyone stared uncomprehending. Maghrabi stalked over to Awais who lay face down breathing in fits. He kicked the body over. Awais was choking and frothing at mouth. He clawed at his own throat as if an invisible force was choking him. Then as abruptly as it had all started, he went still. Maghrabi kicked the dead man and spat, "Cyanide! You coward, you couldn't face the gun."

Aliya's mind was spiralling into chaos. But outwardly, she kept her mask on.

But her emotions were reflected by Shezii as he screamed, "You fucking bastard. Unshackle me now and I will kill you!"

"You two beautiful birds," Maghrabi said with fake sweetness, "Now what do I do with you?" He looked greedily at Shezii and then Meera.

Tapping his brow thoughtfully, he asked, "Shall we have some fun? Oh but our leader says we must practice for tomorrow, an important day. Don't worry. We'll play tomorrow for sure." He walked towards the door. Laying a hand on Ganibhai's shoulder, he ordered, "Take care of the body." Taking this as their cue, the other men got down to the business of dragging away Awais's body as if he were a dead animal. Meera sobbed inconsolably.

For the first time, Aliya looked at Shezii. Her eyes were ablaze with emotion—anger and hatred. Shezii knew that Aliya was hating *him* for getting into this situation where his life hung by a thread. For putting *her* in this situation. Ganibhai stood watching her from a corner.

81

Meera sobbed quietly, trying to find a comfortable position to sit in. Her shackled legs were bound backwards in a manner that did not allow her to sit up. Her skin was beginning to chaff and burn with frost bite. The harsh, biting cold winds, howling through the cavernous timber mill were numbing.

"I am sorry, Meera, so very sorry." Shezii looked at her and then quickly looked away.

"My feet are numb," she was trying to keep the shiver out of her voice.

"Stomp them against the floor, as much as you can manage."

Meera tried hopelessly for a few times and then fell back, consumed by the raw pain shooting through her legs.

Aliya watched them wordlessly from the door. Moving like a shadow across the barn, she came to them, pulled out a bunch of keys and bent over Meera's feet. No sooner were the cuffs gone than Meera crawled away from Aliya, casting a scathing look towards her.

"So, this is what you are? Why am I not surprised?"

Meera's taunt got no reaction from Aliya as she turned towards Shezii to release his feet. Then she stood and looked at them both. "I cannot release your hands now, for obvious reasons," she spoke devoid of any emotion.

"What are you doing, Aliya … with a man like Maghrabi?" Shezii asked desperately. "We came with Awais Uncle to bring you back."

"I guess he is dead now," she shrugged. "Tomorrow, after our mission is complete, Maghrabi will kill you both too. If you want to live, pay attention to what I am about to say. I will find a way to leave you the keys to those," she pointed at their heavily chained hands, "… before I go. Head north and run—as fast as you can! In three kilometers, you will come to the village of Gagran. If you are lucky, you might get help there." She started to leave.

"Aliya, he is the one … Maghrabi," Shezii hesitated. "He is the one who held us hostage in Tel Aviv. He and his people blew up all those people. And you? Why are you with that terrorist?"

"You still want me to answer that?" She smirked. And then she stopped, detecting a movement in her peripheral vision. Without warning, she slapped Shezii hard across his face. "*I* am a terrorist," she screamed, "and that's all you need to know."

Then she turned and marched away, shaking in anger. Her eyes spotted Ganibhai shrink back into the shadows. *How long had he been watching? Had he heard their conversation?* She knew she had already played her hand and now she was ready to face whatever was the outcome. She was acutely aware that Shezii's presence had put her at a disadvantage. Yet, at this point, she also knew she couldn't let him simply die. She only hoped she had put up a good show for Ganibhai's benefit. She thought of confronting him but then she had more urgent matters to deal with. And one of them was getting back her sat-phone, which was now in Maghrabi's custody. Finally, she slowed down in front of his lair. The small, musty room was in semi-darkness and empty.

She peered in, cautiously looking for her sat-phone. *A quick in and out*. Just as she lifted her foot to enter the room, Ganibhai's face loomed in front of her. He caught her arm and yanked her quickly out and around to a secluded corner. As Aliya was about to protest, he placed a finger on his lips, gesturing for her to stay quiet. Slowly, he pointed back at the entrance. Maghrabi's sinister figure was swiftly headed towards them. He reached the room in long strides and entered quietly. Ganibhai stared at Aliya with raised eyebrows. They had just dodged a bullet.

82

"I know that boy," Ganibhai spoke softly. They were in the run-down storeroom at the back of the barn. It smelled of rat urine and was littered with old wood shavings gone dark and moldy over time.

Aliya stayed quiet.

"I remember seeing him with you outside the college." He paused for her reaction. There was none. "I was with Awais *bhai*. I knew something wasn't right, even then."

Aliya looked away.

"You have to answer me now. Your stupidity can get you and all of us killed. Tell me what are you up to?" Ganibhai's tone was forceful.

"Awais Sheikh alias Ashraf Shaheen was my mother's younger brother," she said flatly. "When he didn't appear at the safe house in Delhi, I thought he had developed cold feet after he came to know about me."

"You already knew about him?"

"Yes."

"What about that boy?"

"I have no idea how he landed here and why Awais was with him."

"Yet you are willing to risk your life for him." He shook his head. "I saw what you did for them."

"Now you know. Maghrabi knew too. My life is at risk while he is here, no matter what. And now, so is yours." She exhaled and continued, "We need to know what he is up to. For that, I need to connect with my agents outside. We don't have time."

Ganibhai recovered himself and made a decision. "I can get you a sat-phone. I always keep a spare hidden with me, just for times like these."

Aliya's eyes narrowed upon him. When had discipline under her leadership become so lax?

"I can get it for you. But you have to be careful. He may be tracking sat-phone activities."

"Why are you helping me?" she asked point blank.

"Because I know that monster Maghrabi has dangerous plans."

Ganibhai inhaled a lungful of frigid air and started relating the conversation between Maghrabi and an unknown entity. By the end of the narration, he could feel the dark chill of that night creeping up behind his neck.

"Are you sure he was talking about planning a new mission?" Aliya's brow was creased with concern.

"It wasn't just that." He folded his arms around him and shivered.

"What exactly did he say?" Aliya coaxed.

"This will curdle the blood of every kafir in Hind. That's what he had said." He paused and looked into Aliya's eyes, "And Bibi, I know one thing very well—if

Hindustan burns, my *Musalman* brothers will burn with it too. This is our home too, which he wants to destroy." Ganibhai's eyes were fixed beyond the small boxy window at the frosty chinars, swaying like dancing ghosts in the faraway jungle. A storm was on its way.

83

The bitter cold morning was absolutely still; even the birds had not left their cozy nests yet. But the truck carrying Major Ram Arya's team attracted the attention of a few stray dogs watching the outskirts of the village of Gagran. They followed the truck, barking aggressively for some distance till the truck entered the village. Akshara had triangulated the sat-phone's signal to the jungles beyond this sleepy hamlet.

The truck came to a stop in the center of the town and the Major commanded the team to get off. From there, it was on foot for approximately three kilometers. The team comprised twelve jawans of the Army's Special Ops that carried AK103 assault rifles. Major Arya had hand-picked this team for its quick thinking and vast operational experience in extreme war zones. A couple of them had previously participated in army actions against insurgent groups in the valley. The team took a warm-up run around the open space and came to a stop in unison near the truck. Major Arya summoned their attention with a crisp call for a quick, pre-operations brief. At a far corner, a lone teenager stood outside the village madrassa, watching the entire exercise quietly. After a little while, he snuck away back into the village.

"At ease, Team!" the Major commanded. "The final part of our approach to the target is through that trail leading into the jungle. It's a distance of 2.5 kilometers and we will cover it within 20 minutes. Any doubts?"

"No, sir." The chorus of reply was loud and instant.

"Alright then, let's form three groups. We will approach using a parallel sweep maintaining a sideways distance of not more than ten meters. We are operating against some of the most dangerous terrorists. They will be cornered and desperate. So, be ready for an ambush."

"Yes, sir." Once again, the chorus echoed and the team adjusted its weapons and communication packs, readying for its trek through the jungle.

Just then, the youngest and highly decorated sharp-shooter of the group, Captain Faiz Hassan dropped to his knees and stayed down, with his hand on his brow. Something sharp had hit him just above his right eye. He stared at his bloodied hand and then noticed the sharp-edged stone that lay nearby. He looked up to find a small group of teenagers staring at the army men with open hostility. In their hands they tightly gripped stones.

"Sir, we have hostile elements," Captain Hassan urgently addressed Major Arya, who was already moving in the direction of the group. The team stood alert, but their weapons were down. These were young civilians.

"Get back into your homes. We don't want to hurt you." Major Arya raised his voice to reach the youngsters. In response, several stones landed next to him and a few went flying past, missing him by an inch. He gestured at his team to approach and physically restrain the small group of boys. But then, he stopped and raised his hand immediately to halt his team. Then he turned and bolted towards them. "Get into the truck. Now!" he shouted.

Behind those handful of teenagers, a larger, menacing group of villagers had gathered, including women dressed in traditional Kashmiri *pherans*. And they all held stones in their hands.

The first flurry of stones hit the retreating soldiers within seconds. A few were hit although not seriously. Major Arya had been aware of the numerous incidents of stone-pelting in the Kashmir region in recent times, but he hadn't expected to face it firsthand. And definitely not in this remote little village.

Once in the bus, they ducked below the seats as the stones kept coming. The windscreen of the bus was cracked extensively and few windows had shattered.

"Sir, they are getting close," Captain Faiz Hassan spoke over the screams of the villagers, as a large stone hit the window near them and glass shards flew everywhere. The stone-pelting group had now swelled to at least 50 villagers. "Should I fire a few rounds in the air?" He sounded frustrated. The wound above his eye had been hurriedly patched but the swelling was prominent.

Major Arya nodded at Captain Faiz Hassan. "Just don't kill any of them."

The Captain quickly moved under the window and opened fire, taking care that no bullets ricocheted to hit any of the villagers. The sound of the gunfire reverberated in the air and there was silence for a few minutes. And then there was a renewed attack from the villagers and the body of the truck rang with the incessant sound of stones.

Captain Hassan peeped up from the window and sank back quickly. "Damn! There are more of them now." He looked up as one of the team members was crawling towards them. He spoke into the ears of the Captain and retreated to his position.

"What is it, Captain Hassan?"

"Sir, it seems like one of the jihadi group operatives is from this village. They must know of the terrorist camp in the jungle. If that's the case, then they won't stop. I know these people."

"What do you suggest?"

"We should open fire before they overturn the truck and set it on fire. Because that's what happened to an army truck last week in Pulwama."

"We don't have clearance for that." The Major shook his head. "Besides, we can't open fire on civilians."

"These civilians are aiding the terrorists." The defiance in the Captain's voice bordered on desperation.

Major Arya was just about to command Captain Faiz Hassan to stand down when his phone rang. It was Rajeev Bakshi.

"Major Arya, turn back with your men immediately."

"Sir?"

"Yes Major, get back here at the command base. I need you in Srinagar before the convoy leaves for the event today."

"But what about the terrorist base camp? We are less than three kilometers away."

"There is nobody there, Major. You will find it empty."

"Sir, I don't understand." Major Arya winced as one of the stones hit the window above him and a loose shard of glass grazed his face.

"Get out of there, now. I will brief you once you are here. And Major, hurry!" The call was disconnected.

Major Ram Arya gestured at the driver who was crouched near the driver's seat. Ducking below the windscreen, the driver put the truck in reverse gear and slowly started pulling back. The villagers, encouraged by the retreating enemy moved forward but then fell back as the truck gathered speed, and after a neat turn, sped away from their village.

84

The weather-beaten Toyota Qualis bumped along steadily towards its destination, followed by two similar vehicles. They all carried bogus number plates of Jammu & Kashmir and their occupants were all tense and silent. In the trunk, hidden underneath a stack of brand new Kashmiri willow-wood cricket bats and old clothing, were assault rifles and machine guns.

Aliya looked out at the passing villages and had a distinct feeling that they were moving towards Srinagar. They had left the base more than two hours ago and had been avoiding main roads as much as possible. But what had alarmed her was the fact that they had cleaned out the base before leaving. This meant they were not going back there. Maghrabi had instructed two of the operatives to take Shezii and Meera to their new base. In a deliberate move, Maghrabi had kept this location from Aliya and she knew her enquiries would have only led to a confrontation she didn't need at this point. She still had no idea about his plans, but she was not going to be the one to blink first. Not yet at least. She had to wait for the right time.

She finally knew that plans had been changed totally when their vehicles missed the turn towards Hazratbal.

Her nagging doubt that they were no longer headed towards Gandhi Bhawan Center at the Kashmir University campus, as per the original plan, was confirmed.

If they were not going to the location where the leaders were going to hold the conference, then where were they headed? She looked at Maghrabi who was riding shotgun. He was staring ahead and his neck muscles were strained. Aliya had a distinct feeling that the entire team knew about the plan apart from her and Ganibhai.

"You have to brief us about the plan if you want us to be a part of this mission," she finally addressed Maghrabi.

Maghrabi turned his head and smiled.

"The target has been changed," he answered cryptically.

"Who is the new target and what is your plan?"

Maghrabi turned in his seat and bored into her with his hypnotic oily eyes. Then, in three brief sentences he told her. The target. The plan. And the objective.

Aliya sat back, quietly absorbing the information. Her face was blank but her hand had clenched into a tight fist. Ganibhai had gone visibly pale.

Maghrabi was giving detailed final instructions to the driver. The convoy of vehicles continued their steady approach towards the point of action.

85

At The Lalit, Project Jai Hind's command center was buzzing with frantic activity. Defense Minister Arjun Jaisinghani was in the house. Clearances were being carried out for the staff serving the minister and the VIP visitors scheduled to pay him a visit. An equal amount of security measures had been deployed at the Gandhi Bhawan Center, where the meeting between the Defense Minister, the Chief of Rashtriya Sewa Samiti and the Kashmiri leaders was to take place. A unit of black commandos was deployed there already and was in the process of sweeping the location. A second unit was to accompany the minister's convoy from the hotel to the venue.

Rajeev Bakshi looked up to find Major Arya approaching. In his hand was a piece of paper.

"This is it," said the Major, sitting down and sliding the sheet over. "Mossad confirms a marked increase in the activities of bank accounts linked to *Tehrik-e-Islam*. Sixty million dollars have been deposited in these accounts over the last 48 hours."

"Anything specific concerning our mission?"

"Our man in Pakistan reports that two days ago, Al-Gazzar had a talk with a senior official in the Pakistani

Defense Ministry. Apparently, he is actually an ISI man." He paused and shrugged. "The timing of deposits is telltale."

"Something is still not fitting in," frowned Rajeev. "Funding cross-border terrorism via extremist factions is one thing, but targeting the Defense Minister of India?"

"Sir, can I ask you something?" the Major spoke quietly.

"Yes?"

"You knew that the camp had been abandoned by the terrorists. What was the source of that tip-off?"

"Actually, it came from the Defense Minister himself," he spoke in an off-hand manner. "And you better not enquire about his source."

"Defense Minister Jaisinghani?" he murmured with a look of mild surprise on his face. Obviously, there had been developments he wasn't aware of.

"Yes. Come on. Let's update the minister before he leaves for the event. This is important."

"So, he isn't agreeing to cancel the meet?"

"Actually, if I were in his place, I wouldn't cancel either. Come." Rajeev was already walking away and the Major followed immediately.

Both men filed out of the room and proceeded through the corridors towards the master suite housing the minister. As they approached, the security personnel stepped away respectfully.

The minister was on his phone, finishing a call. He nodded at the men to take a seat in the suite's anteroom, which had been turned into a meeting space and office after a careful sweep for listening devices or any other security threats.

"So, Rajeev, are we ready to leave?" he spoke brusquely. He seemed charged up and ready to go.

"Yes sir, but we just needed a few minutes to update you about an important and verified intelligence we have received."

"Go on."

Major Ram Arya quickly and concisely delivered the report to the minister. By the time the briefing was over, the minister's expression was no longer relaxed. He leaned ahead, his hands clasped in front of him. He looked at the two men in turn and spoke.

"I hope we aren't overlooking something," his eyes were screwed in concentration.

"Sir, rest assured, all security measures are in place. We have checked and double checked everything at the hotel and the venue. And I will be personally accompanying the convoy along with the commandoes," Rajeev Bakshi said.

"I am not talking about myself. What about Sohan Rajwat?"

"Sir, even after several requests to stay here at The Lalit, Rajwatji chose to stay with one of the senior Rashtriya Sewa Samiti officials, in his old bungalow at the outskirts of Srinagar. He said he didn't want to hurt the official's feelings because this official is a Kashmiri Pandit and was forced to abandon his home during the ousting of Kashmiri Pandits in the 1990s," said Major Arya.

"Major, immediately assign a team to accompany his vehicle to the venue," the minister stood up impatiently.

"The team assigned to him is already stationed at his residence. But since he declined our security cover, we ordered the team to stand down."

"He declined? Let me speak to him." Then he dialed a number. The call was answered instantly, "Good morning, Rajwatji. Where are you?" the minister asked and then listened quietly for several seconds. "Sure, I will see you at the venue." He disconnected the call and turned towards the men.

"He has already left his residence for the venue. Without the security." The minister's voice was somber, as if he was being forced to deliver some bad news. "Ask the security team to catch up with his convoy, right now," he ordered.

Major Ram Arya could sense that the minister had a hunch, which he wasn't yet sharing with them. In his mind, he once again ran through the possible security threats and measures taken to neutralize them.

86

The Toyota Fortuner was speeding towards its destination at a steady pace, followed by another sedan carrying the team of panel members representing the Rashtriya Sewa Samiti and accompanying its Chief, Sohan Rajwat. The drive was a pleasant one with roads lined by deodards and pine trees, interspersed with little Kashmiri villages, and often accompanied by small rivulets which would turn into full rivers during peak summer. The morning was crisp with bright sunlight and held just enough chill in the air to give the atmosphere the feel of an air conditioner set at just the right temperature.

The mood within the contingent was positive. The possibility of taking the first steps towards resolving the Kashmir issue and returning the valley to its earlier peaceful glory was uplifting. Especially for Sohan Rajwat, who found this to be a landmark event both personally and for the Rashtriya Sewa Samiti as an organization. It would establish Rashtriya Sewa Samiti as a true national entity and if things went well, he would be speaking about these successful peace talks at the next UN convention as a representative not only of India but of its entire Hindu population.

Sohan Rajwat rolled down the window to take in the fresh, pine-scented air. His co-passenger and fellow samiti worker of three decades, Shyamal Kher smiled at this enthusiastic gesture, "Careful *shriman*, you will catch a cold. This mountain air can be very tricky."

"Not possible, Kher *sahab*. After all, this air belongs to my country. It can't hurt me." Rajwat inhaled the air deeply.

"That's true."

"Your house is really beautiful, Kher. I am glad to have stayed with you."

"Rajwatji, if it wasn't for you, I wouldn't be returning to this house after all these years."

"See, this is where you make a mistake. You need nobody's permission—this is your house and Kashmir is your home. I just made a few calls and moved one file."

Shyamal Kher was about to respond when the SUV dropped speed suddenly. A small lamb had strayed onto the path. Rajwat smiled at the cute little fellow as it bleated and bounded off. The vehicle resumed its journey but Shyamal Kher's face wore a concerned look. "Looks like our colleagues will get stuck."

Rajwat turned back and smiled, amused by the scene. A large herd of wooly sheep had followed the lamb and were now blocking the second car behind them.

"Don't worry, they have plenty of time. They will catch up," he assured Kher and pulled out his notes for the meeting. He wanted to be prepared to answer every question with a solution, not just false assurances.

Shyamal Kher fell silent. He knew his leader did not wish to indulge in any more small talk now.

The car had resumed its momentum and was proceeding smoothly. Sohan Rajwat had just about pulled out his pen when a solid impact hit them with loud sounds of crunching metal and screeching tyres. The first thing he felt was being tossed around in his seat and the pen leaving his hand. It was a gift from his dead father. He half expected the car to stop moving but it had gone into an unending tailspin. He was thrown against Shyamal Kher who seemed to have fainted. Finally, the car toppled sideways and after skidding for a few meters, came to a stop on its side. He felt Kher's weight pressing against him as his head lolled in an unnatural manner. The impact had snapped his neck. Rajwat looked ahead to find the driver bent sideways over the steering wheel, hanging by his seat-belt, showing no signs of life.

Panicking, Sohan Rajwat pushed the dead man aside and opened the door on the other end. He crawled out over the door to collapse on the asphalt. The air was filled with the smell of diesel, smoke and burning tyre. He knew he was badly hurt, especially his shoulder, which felt like it was dislocated. A deep gash on the side of his face bled profusely and the front of his cream raw silk shirt was already red, the material absorbing the blood like a sponge. Rajwat was unable to locate the source of all this blood flowing from his own body.

The right side of the car was badly crumpled. Something heavy had rammed into it, causing it to lose control and go into a tailspin. The damage looked as if another vehicle had rammed into it from the right. And then, it all swam into focus. Him denying the security, the appearance of the herd of sheep, being separated from the second car. But the warnings of all his well-wishers rang the loudest in his ears. There were people who did not want these peace talks to go through. People who thrived on war and terror. Those who did not want him, a Hindu leader, in Kashmir.

Sohan Rajwat saw his cell phone lying a few feet away. Desperately, he tried to get up and reach out. But a hard, blunt object landed brutally across his chest. Aflame with pain, he let out a scream and fell back onto the hard asphalt littered with glass shards.

When he finally opened his eyes, a black masked man was staring down at him with an AK47's barrel pointed at his face. Sohan Rajwat closed his eyes again. He did not react as pairs of strong hands roughly dragged him and dumped him in the back of a SUV. A musty blanket was thrown over him and he was thankful for the darkness it brought. For some reason, he just wanted to sleep, peacefully.

87

The Lalit hotel went into a tizzy of activity as a convoy of armoured cars and Jammu & Kashmir police jeeps entered its open gates with blaring sirens and flashing lights. The convoy came to a halt at the main porch while a CRPF contingent truck took position at the main entrance.

The Defense Minister was back in the house, having cancelled the scheduled peace talk.

The local media had already arrived and was being held back by the CRPF jawans from entering the hotel. The media crowd at the gates was expected to swell by thrice, as national and international channel representatives were expected to arrive soon. And they all had only one question they wanted answered.

Where was Sohan Rajwat and what were the government's plans to get him back?

The news had spread like even wildfire before any well-worded press statement could be released to buy time. The Rashtriya Sewa Samiti's office was promising to punish the perpetrators of this dastardly act severely. No extremist organization had yet claimed credit for it, but there was no dearth of speculations being made by the media.

Arjun Jaisinghani strode purposefully through the lobby, flanked by Rajeev Bakshi and Major Ram Arya. Instead of proceeding to his official suite, they headed straight towards the command center. They were already at Gandhi Bhawan when the news had reached them, just before the meet could begin. Hurried apologies had to be issued and a national emergency was cited, before they could extricate the minister from the organizers without offending them or causing bad press about the last-minute pull out by the government. But in the process, they had lost precious time. It was now four hours since Sohan Rajwat had been abducted.

The trio entered and the chaotic command center went quiet. Its occupants stood up before the head of the defense forces.

"Sit down please and get back to your work," the minister ordered. "Has *Tehrik-e-Islam* reached out yet?" he asked Rajeev and Major Arya.

"There have been no claims made by them yet," Major Arya answered.

Jaisinghani closed his eyes. "Rajeev, how did they know of Rajwat's arrival and travel plans?"

"Sir, apart from us and Rajwatji, nobody knew about his travel and stay." Then he looked at Major Arya, "Of course, Prasanna knew about it too."

"Don't ignore the fact that some Rashtriya Sewa Samiti officials might have also known about it." The minister had not missed the insinuation but was not ready to entertain any more speculation without solid evidence.

The three men noticed Akshara approach nervously.

"What is it?" Major Arya asked.

"This message just arrived in my secure email ID. I suggest you look at it someplace private."

The men quickly moved to the next room and Akshara carried her laptop. She inserted a pen-drive and opened an unnamed media file on her screen. The video message began to play.

It was a tight close-up of a masked face which stared into the camera for a couple of seconds with angry hateful eyes before it started reading the scripted message in heavily accented English.

"*Tehrik-e-Islam* has declared a war upon the *kafirs* of Hindustan. The *Musalmans* need their rightful place in Hind and will not tolerate anyone who denies them. If Hindustanis want to continue living in Hind, they must accept Islam as their only religion. The *Musalmans* of Hind will restore Islam to its complete glory here. So, accept Islam, or run, or die. And to show to the world that we mean it, we have their Hindu leader, Sohan Rajwat in our custody. We will release the video of his beheading within the next ten hours along with this message to the Hindus that this land of Hind is now ours and ours alone. *Inshallah ... Allahuakbar*!"

The video ended abruptly with static and everyone sat still for a few moments. It wasn't a mere stake of claim for Sohan Rajwat's kidnapping. It was a warning. A warning of a nightmare that was about to begin, which every Indian would be forced to watch with open eyes.

"Rajeev, we can't let this video get out. There will be mass riots and our country will burn," Arjun Jaisinghani huffed, pacing the room. "If anything happens to Sohan Rajwat and this video is released, then Hindu extremists will turn upon Indian Muslims like mad dogs. The retaliations would also be severe. India will go into a state of civil unrest."

Rajeev Bakshi and Major Arya exchanged worried glances. They knew that the chain of events narrated by the minister would actually occur if Sohan Rajwat was not brought back. Alive and unhurt.

"Whoever is behind this hasn't done it for the rise of Islam or the betterment of Muslims. If anything, it will hurt the Muslims of India badly. This reeks of an agenda of hatred and destruction," Major Ram Arya growled.

"In the current circumstances, there is only one way to save our nation from burning. Find Sohan Rajwat and bring him back." Defense Minister Arjun Jaisinghani got up and exited the room without any further word. The two men stood up but stayed rooted to their spots.

"From the timing of us receiving the video, I think they are within two hours of driving distance," Major Arya said, getting back to their current situation quickly.

"Or they could have pre-recorded the video. They could be just 20 minutes away or possibly four hours away—and getting further out." Rajeev Bakshi shrugged his tense shoulders.

"I do not think they will leave Kashmir as they won't find the requisite support and network elsewhere. I will initiate a sweep of the entire Kashmir state, concentrating on abandoned, empty places. It's only about 132 kilometers in length and 32 kilometers in width to be covered."

"Ten hours is not enough to complete that exercise, but you can start immediately. And after the stone-pelting you and your team experienced, you should know better than to expect support from the locals. It will take a miracle for us to succeed. I will sound a red alert with the security and para-military forces, along with the state police. They need to be on high vigil." Rajeev Bakshi picked up his phone and walked back to the command center.

Major Arya stared at his phone restlessly. A miracle was desperately needed now.

88

The old two-storey wood and stone structure stood abandoned at the edge of a short cliff just outside the little village of Dachee Gam in Pahalgam. Long ago, it had boasted of its own approach path, which was now a mere mud trail hidden in bushy vegetation, leading towards the house. Weeds grew out of the crevices in the building's structure and the wood of the windows was weather-beaten and chipped. The house had the stillness of death, apart from the golden yellow leaves dancing in the wind that passed through its porch. The only reminder that it had once been a home was a rusted swing in the courtyard.

For as long as Dachee Gam's less than 300 inhabitants could remember, the house at the edge of their village had never been visited by its owners who had left more than 50 years ago during the post-independence partition, never to return to the valley. To the villagers, it was a forgotten story from a time long before them. And they had no need to revive it, as the house lay quietly hidden, out of their way and lives. So they had no reason to believe that the house had come alive on that particular day.

No one had seen the tyre marks and the two vehicles parked in the jungle beyond the house and the village, nor the hooded figures that had arrived quietly, dragging a body shrouded in a blanket. The house had no electricity or running water, but its current visitors were used to conditions far more challenging. The house had been chosen randomly out of the available options only because it was in the middle of an otherwise peaceful location in the valley and was least likely to be on the list of potential terrorist hubs circulated among the armed forces or the Jammu & Kashmir police. In any case, the visitors weren't planning to stay long.

The back of the house was abuzz with quiet yet urgent activity. The room was being readied. One of its sides had a door to a back porch, which further opened onto a vast expanse of jungle. On the other side, the stage for the beheading of Sohan Rajwat had been carefully set up to incite maximum viewership among the jihadi followers and to instill maximum fear in the hearts of its opponents. A green screen with *Tehrik-e-Islam*'s slogan of *baqiya wa tatamadad,* proclaiming the rise and expansion of the Islamic regime, had been put up against a wall. A halogen lamp and a hand-held video camera mounted on a folding stand had been focused at the center of the screen to ensure that no clues of the location were revealed. Now, only Sohan Rajwat remained to take his place in the spotlight. For now, he lay semi-comatose in a corner of the room, his hands cuffed and eyes and mouth covered with duct tape. Two of the operatives were standing guard above him, munching dried fruits with an air of executives at a working lunch.

Aliya eyed the arrangement with the aloofness of a professional and then exited the room. In the main hall, Maghrabi sat on a broken couch covered with sheets, so that no proof of their presence there would be left behind. Aliya sat down opposite Maghrabi and locked eyes with him.

"I still have no instructions from the leader about the change of plans. How do I know that you have clearance for this? I need to speak with the leader. Hand over my sat-phone," she spoke flatly.

"You don't need to do anything. I am the leader now. Nobody will speak to anybody outside until this mission is over." He smirked and then downed two tablets with a swig of water. Aliya knew those were high power Tramadol tablets, an addictive pharma-opioid used in the trade of terrorism for its ability to change how the body and brain reacted to any pain or stress. This drug was also taken by jihadis for a kick, before conducting long hours of torture on their subjects.

Aliya stared at him for a few seconds and then got up. Maghrabi's snake-like eyes followed her as she moved out of the hall. In the next room, Shezii and Meera lay on the floor, chained and gagged. Their escape plan had failed the moment Maghrabi had announced the shift to a new location.

One of Maghrabi's armed operatives was standing guard. She avoided looking at Shezii and shot a curt instruction at the guard to stay alert before walking towards one of the front rooms. The windows of the house were boarded up, allowing only chinks of evening light in. At the far end of the room, she found Ganibhai waiting for her.

"There's not much time left now," she spoke in a low voice as she came to a stop next to him.

Ganibhai nodded and after carefully scanning the rooms behind, silently handed her a device wrapped in cloth.

"Go now. And keep an eye on them. May Allah watch over you." Aliya took the package and slipped out of the side door of what had once been a kitchen.

Ganibhai quietly moved back into the house. He had to hold the fort for the next ten minutes. The beheading of Sohan Rajwat and the two young hostages had been scheduled for half past seven. It was nearing five in the evening. *Black Sand was right,* he thought. *There was very little time left now.*

89

Rajeev Bakshi stared at his team working frantically. It was the best team he could have ever expected to work on this case but their window of opportunity was fast closing. Seven hours had elapsed since the abduction of Sohan Rajwat and *Tehrik-e-Islam* was notorious for keeping their hostages alive for a maximum of 12 hours, under constant torture. He thought of Meera and stood up impatiently. With every passing hour, the chances of getting his daughter back were getting bleaker too, as her captors had no history of releasing any hostages alive.

Hoping that he hadn't made the worst mistake of his life, he looked around for Major Ram Arya for an update but could not spot him at the command center. Rajeev had just picked up his phone to call the Major when it vibrated. Alarmed by the identity and the timing of the call, he answered instantly. From the other end came a crisp instruction by the minister, summoning him to the office. Rajeev pocketed the phone, picked up the case dossier and strode out of the room towards the minister's suite.

Rajeev was expressly waved into the tense suite office. Both Major Arya and the minister stood in the middle of the room. They turned in unison towards him.

"Come Rajeev. We have actionable intelligence," the minister's tone was both grim and urgent.

"We have the location and schedule of the beheading of Sohan Rajwat," Major Arya filled in his boss.

"And the source of this intelligence is?"

"Rajeev, some of this is highly classified information for now. Let's just focus on bringing back the children and saving India from becoming unstable." The minister placed a hand on his shoulder. "You will have a detailed brief later. From me. Personally."

Rajeev nodded silently. "Where's the location?"

"An old house outside Dachee Gam village. The beheading is at 7:30 p.m. Two and a half hours from now. The video will be aired on *Al-Jazeera* within minutes of being recorded." Major Arya spoke fast but with emphasis.

"I will notify the air base right away. Is your team ready Major?" Rajeev didn't need any further elaboration.

"Yes sir, the tactical team comprises five special forces officers and two officers from the NSG."

Rajeev turned towards the minister, "Sir, we will need the HAL Dhruv helicopter for the team's air-drop."

"It will be expressly assigned, Rajeev." Arjun Jaisinghani nodded.

"Well, we are just in time then. What's your plan of action, Major?"

"Akshara is working on enhanced satellite images of the house right now. As soon as we have them, we will chart the exact approach. But there is a jungle right behind it. The plan is to get the team air-dropped two kilometers outside Dachee Gam and then approach the target through the jungle by foot. The falling dusk will work in our favor, and as per current timelines we can hit the house by 6:30 p.m. latest."

"Okay Major, once you have the heat signatures from the building, do confirm the number of its occupants."

"Yes, sir." Major Ram Arya knew that the question was more than a tactical query. It was a father hoping that his daughter was still alive.

Rajeev Bakshi walked out of the room. The one thing nagging him was the source of the information. *What was Major Arya doing with the minister before reporting to him about this development*? This was the second big lead that had come from a source beyond Project Jai Hind's pool of resources. *Was the minister mining the information from a direct source?*

There were too many questions circling in his mind but the ground reality was that their enemy had managed to stay one step ahead of them. He only hoped that *Tehrik-e-Islam's* batch of good luck was coming to an end soon.

90

Sohan Rajwat felt a sharp jerk through the dark haze he was floating in, forcing him to open his eyes into little slits. The slap landed harder across his face this time, making him yelp with pain. His eyes burned under the harsh light of the halogen lamp. He was beginning to slip away when the slap hit him again. Hot dark spots swam in front of his eyes as one of the operatives stepped up with a filled syringe and injected it into his arm with practiced ease. An almost dead subject would not have made for a good beheading video for the bloodthirsty jihadis. Slowly, Rajwat's eyes began to open and the pain became sharper as the injected adrenaline coursed through his blood. Finally, his eyes focused on a face in the shadows, beyond the blinding hot light.

Maghrabi peered down at Sohan Rajwat with a tilted head and eyes filled with gleeful madness. As his senses returned, Rajwat blinked around the room and came to terms with his predicament. *He was going to die*.

He noticed the rifle-strapped chest of a jihadi who stood before him, tinkering with a camera. Two others towered beside him. He whimpered with fear as he saw the one on his left holding a long, heavy blade.

Aliya watched the preparations in silence. Ganibhai stood against a wall behind Maghrabi. Shezii and Meera lay chained on the floor next to him. Ganibhai caught Aliya's gaze and tilted his head ever so slightly to the hostages, raising an eyebrow in question.

She looked away and ran through the situation again. She stood against four armed jihadis, considering that Ganibhai wasn't much of a combat person. Ordinarily, taking them down would not have been a problem. But they were alerted against her now, no doubt under Maghrabi's orders. She noticed their tense grip on the guns and their guarded stance.

Her firearm was secure in a holster clipped to the waistband under her shirt. It was best to leave it there as a last resort. In cases of gun fire in close quarters, half the fatalities were a result of ricocheting rounds. When the time came, she planned to use the smoke grenade securely tucked in her cargo belt. She eyed Ganibhai's sub-machine gun resting next to his side.

"It's time," Maghrabi looked at his watch and added, "Bring those too." Ganibhai tensed. Meera's chains clanked as she shrank into herself.

"Wait!" Aliya stepped in the way.

"What is it?" Maghrabi snarled.

"I cannot allow you to proceed unless I hear an approval from our leader."

"Are *you* going to stop me?"

"Yes, if needed."

"You still haven't realized, have you woman? You are a deserter now and that makes you a *kafir*. I could shoot you now but I think I have a better plan for you." Maghrabi let out a mirthless laugh and then turned towards the jihadis. "Tie her up too. She will be beheaded alongside this *kafir*. Let everyone know that *Tehrik-e-Islam* will not tolerate desertion," he thundered.

The nearest jihadi lunged at Aliya, not bothering to pull up his firearm. A fatal mistake. In the blink of an eye, she swung out of his way and behind him. Her hand slammed over the carotid in his neck. He fell forwards and did not move again.

In another blink, she was on to Maghrabi, but knew in the next instant that in her desperation, she had misjudged his brute strength. Before she could hit out, he had her in his deathly grip, his strong arm almost choking her throat. His other hand held a sharp knife pressed against her ribcage. She heaved and fought but he was too strong. Aliya felt the blood rushing madly to her face, as her breath became short. When the final wave of darkness was about to engulf her, she heard a familiar voice over the sound of rushing blood in her head.

"Let her go!" Shezii screamed. He was pointing Ganibhai's machine gun at Maghrabi. His jaw was clenched. His chains lay free by his feet. Maghrabi's eyes quickly scanned the room and his eyes narrowed as he saw Ganibhai hurriedly removing the chains off Meera.

"Let her go, *now*!" Shezii repeated.

Maghrabi lowered Aliya back to the ground but didn't let go. He stared unblinkingly for a few seconds and then a shrewd smile spread on his lips.

"You won't shoot," he smirked.

Shezii took a small step ahead.

"You don't have the courage," Maghrabi goaded him.

The two jihadis next to Sohan Rajwat had drawn their weapons and were awaiting his signal.

"Shoot him, Shezii! Shoot now!" Aliya gasped hoarsely.

Shezii hesitated, stunned by what she was asking him to do. He had never fired a real gun in his life, but he knew that he held a machine gun capable of releasing several rounds at one go. If he pressed the trigger now, the gun's fire would definitely hit Maghrabi. But it would also kill Aliya.

At his feet, Meera whimpered. From a corner, he saw Rajwat cowering and blubbering incoherently. Shezii looked at Aliya one last time and released the breath he was holding back. Then, his eyes shifting to Maghrabi's purpling face, he prepared to fire. Just then, a deafening blast hit the room. The air was ripped apart with shards of flying debris from splintered wood and mortar. Everyone was thrown to the floor. Loud gunshots echoed at close range.

It all happened in less than five seconds. Shezii was the first to recover and he sat up coughing. Major Ram Arya and his team emerged through the clouds of dust with their guns raised. They swept the room in an arc, expecting a counterattack that was not to come.

Two men lay dead against a wall, with gunshot wounds blossoming over their hearts. Maghrabi was on the floor, his brains scrambled in a pool of thick blood leaking from a wide hole across his temple. His lifeless eyes were still open.

Major Arya's team scanned the area for more weapons or bombs timed to go off later. Sohan Rajwat was released from his bonds. He broke down weeping on the officer's shoulder. Shezii quickly scanned the room, relieved to see Meera being helped up by Ganibhai. *Aliya!* he thought.

Major Arya noticed the back door was slightly ajar. He kicked it open. Shezii ran to him. Outside, darkness had fallen over a dense jungle. The wind howled like a restless banshee.

"Aliya! ... Aaaliyaaa!" Shezii screamed.

But there was no response. *She was gone.*

91

Even though it was close to midnight, a big cheer went up through the media and the crowd gathered outside The Lalit as the vehicles carrying Shezii and Meera, followed by an ambulance with Sohan Rajwat, entered its gates. The news of a successful military operation had already reached the media representatives, who were disappointed about not getting a sound byte from any of the survivors. A helicopter for medical evacuation from the hotel grounds had been ordered for Sohan Rajwat, considering his injuries.

Project Jai Hind's command center was decidedly jubilant. Akshara was smiling after a long time and one of the technicians had collapsed with exhaustion and fallen asleep on his desk. It was a celebration of their efforts and they were all superheroes, even though it was officially a military operation. Project Jai Hind simply did not exist in any official file or folder. But it didn't matter. They had beaten the bad guys and averted a disaster. And today, just for now, they were free to celebrate.

However, the mood in the Defense Minister's office was sombre and heavy with questions. Rajeev Bakshi sat on the couch with his arm protectively around a shrunken and pale but now composed Meera. The doctors had let go of Shezii after tending to his bruises and cuts, instructing him to rest and regularly follow up with the doctors. "We need to find her and bring her back," Shezii urged, looking at all present in the room. "She could be hurt and she is out there alone!"

"Shezii—," the minister began.

"Think of Sana aunty!" Shezii interrupted.

The minister shook his head and went on resolutely, "Aliya is not just a confirmed *Tehrik-e-Islam* operative, she was also the leader of this mission. Ganibhai has already confirmed this." He paused. "So yes, we will be looking for her, but only as a potential terrorist threat."

"If it wasn't for her, none of us would be alive. She risked her life. You know that, sir!" Shezii turned towards Major Arya, his face bleak with despair.

"I think you guys should be leaving now. Your parents are waiting for you, Shezii. And they are proud of you," Major Arya replied.

"Come on, Shezii, I have to call Faisal to tell him that I am bringing you back. He will want to hear from you directly." Rajeev got up and patted Shezii's head. Looking back, he added, "And Major, I expect all the loose ends will be tied up quickly." Rajeev helped Meera to her feet.

"Yes, sir," Major Arya replied.

"Sir, please!" Shezii stepped up to the minister, "She is not just a loose end! And I know you can help her."

He looked into his unrelenting eyes. The minister looked away, silently. Finally, realizing the futility of his words, Shezii turned towards Major Arya. "Would you please give her a message, at least?"

Major Arya nodded for Shezii to continue, "Tell her that I am sorry that I found her too late. Also tell her ... that I am so, so sorry that I did." His tone was bitter and his expression, dark as he turned to walk out of the room. Rajeev Bakshi followed wordlessly, along with a visibly shaken Meera whose wet eyes were bloodshot.

The moment they were out of the room, Major Arya collapsed into the chair in front of the minister. They locked eyes and stayed quiet until they could no longer hear the echo of retreating footsteps from the corridor.

"Where is she, Major?" There was a hint of impatience in the minister's voice.

"Sir, I have no idea. She was gone before we entered the room. Most likely, she escaped through the jungles behind the house. A search party was dispatched to comb the jungles ... after a strategic delay," he added meaningfully. "I have a feeling they won't find her."

"Are you sure she was the one who killed Maghrabi and thc other jihadis?"

"Absolutely. Plus, we have Ganibhai's testimony to that effect."

"Was she injured?"

"I believe she may have been stabbed earlier, but it seems not to have affected her much."

"So she escaped? After killing the jihadis?"

"Wasn't that the plan? She gave me the location of their camp via sat-phone with all the details in advance. And I can easily surmise where she got my private number from." He looked at Arjun Jaisinghani pointedly. "She knew that even if she turned herself in, she would be tortured and interrogated endlessly in some dingy prison. She had to run."

The minister sat back with a deep sigh. "You misunderstand me, Major. My concern for her has a bigger purpose. *This* is much bigger. Bigger than you … me … and Aliya."

"Sir, I have done as instructed by you, even defied the standard procedure by not reporting about it to my superior. You said she should not be hurt. And I followed your word without question. Don't you think I have earned my share of the truth?"

Arjun Jaisinghani fixed Major Arya with a stare. Finally, the minister had just started to speak when his personal unlisted mobile rang, sounding shrill in the quiet of the room. He stared at the screen and then shot a quick look at Major Arya. Then he answered tentatively, "Hello."

"It's me. I have to be quick. Is this line secure?" the voice breathed into the phone.

"Yes, it is. Where are you?" The minister sat up.

"It doesn't matter for now. But I will be in the capital tomorrow."

"What do you need?"

"Need to cross the border … as soon as possible."

"Where to?"

"Kabul, via Pakistan."

"And then …?"

"My final destination is the control center of the organization."

"Okay. Everything will be arranged. The courier will meet you in the capital tomorrow at the drop site with a fresh ID for the travel and other things," the minister answered tersely. They had to conclude the call soon now.

"One more thing."

"Yes?"

"As far as the world goes, I am dead already." With that the line disconnected.

The minister looked up at Major Ram Arya, who was sitting up alert.

"Was that her?" he asked in a low voice.

The minister nodded.

"What do we have to do?"

"Call for an official press briefing about the mission, Major."

"Now?"

"Right now. We need to inform everyone that Aliya Sheikh aka Black Sand, a deadly operative of *Tehrik-e-Islam*, was killed in the encounter with your team today."

"But sir ..."

"Do as I say, Major. I will personally update Rajeev about this. We all must maintain the same statement."

"Because *she* is asking *us* to lie to the world?"

The minister was quiet.

"Why, sir?" the Major stood up, his arms crossed.

"Because she is one of us, Major. *She always was.*"

And then the minister picked up the phone and dialed the Prime Minister's office.

92

Sana Sikandar Sheikh's face was hard and devoid of any emotion. Her shaking hands had gone white, tightly clutching the leading daily. The newspaper carried a front-page story about how a timely military operation had averted the beheading of Rashtriya Sewa Samiti's chief, Sohan Rajwat. It elaborated upon the ghastly plans of the dreaded Islamic extremist group *Tehrik-e-Islam* to create a civil war-like situation in the country. It also reported the grisly death of a radicalized foreign-educated Muslim girl from an affluent urban background. The girl who had chosen to embrace the dark side of Islam, only to be killed by the bullets of the Indian military.

"This? This is what I get in return for my years of upright conduct as a citizen of this country?" She finally banged the newspaper on the table and, in turns, looked at each of the grim faces around it. No one moved, no one dared breathe. "My little baby, she dies with 'terrorist' tagged to her name?" Her voice was on the verge of breaking down, but her countenance was full of cold malice.

"Sana, please!" Defense Minister Arjun Jaisinghani was for once without any suitable words for the situation.

"How could you let this happen? You let them kill her? You promised to bring her back," she snapped at the minister. "Maybe you ordered them to kill her."

"Sana, ma'am ... the circumstances under which—," Major Arya started to speak but was cut off by her.

"Don't you dare," she snarled, "I know her. She is my child. If only she had a chance to defend or explain herself, then maybe ...," her voice trailed off.

"Sana, please listen to me," Rajeev Bakshi, who had been quiet all the while, finally intervened. "Maybe you are right, maybe Aliya just got caught in an unfortunate situation. But the team was only doing its job and Aliya's presence at that place was itself questionable. I too risked my daughter's life by sending her in with Shezii. So I can totally understand your anger."

"No, you don't understand. You will never understand! And, you got your daughter back, Rajeev! So you don't get to play the peacemaker." Then she turned towards the minister and Major Arya and spoke bitterly, "This doesn't end here. You will be hearing about this news story with a fresh angle on my news channel shortly, *Mr. Defense Minister*." She waved the newspaper in her hand. "Maybe those human rights violation stories about JBP's government aren't false after all."

"Sana, you know that the military didn't go in with the sole purpose to kill Aliya. She was there with the jihadis and they were going to behead Sohan Rajwat. The team had no choice," Arjun Jaisinghani spoke evenly.

"Mr. Defense Minister, if I don't get possession of my child's mortal remains within the next 24 hours, I will make sure this government pays heavily for your callous attitude." With that dire warning, she got up and walked out of the room. None of the three men present in the room wished to speak after witnessing the heartbreaking outburst of a mother. Finally, it was Rajeev who broke the silence.

"Why don't we just tell her?" Rajeev Bakshi rubbed his forehead.

"And blow up Aliya's deep cover at *Tehrik-e-Islam*? *And* kill the chances she has worked so hard for in the last five years?" the minister spoke.

"But all this is really hard on Sana."

"She is a tough woman. I know she will bounce back."

"Pardon me, sir, but no parent can bounce back from the tragedy of losing a child."

"This isn't permanent, Rajeev. We just have to wait until the time is right and then I will personally explain it to her. Do you think it's easy for me to watch her like this?" The minister sighed.

"I must say, Aliya is an extraordinary agent, that too at such a young age. She is barely 22 ... when did we recruit her?" Major Ram Arya finally asked.

"We didn't have to. It was as if she was simply meant for it. As if her whole life had been leading to this point in time." The minister looked at the two curious faces and continued. It was a story whose time had come to be told. "RAW's London wing identified her when she took her first trip to Syria at the age of 18, immediately after the London Tube blasts. She took the usual London-Amsterdam-Turkey-Syria route."

"She wanted to become a part of ISIS?" Major Ram Arya asked.

"Not really. By then ISIS was already diluting itself into many regionally operating sub-branches. The training camps in Syria were actually providing radicalized and totally lost souls to terror outfits that were nothing but organized crime cartels operating in targeted bombings, political assassinations, kidnapping and cold blooded murders, some even black marketing ancient relics under the guise of Islamic jihad. Terrorism was now on sale, that too at a discount." The minister sipped some water before continuing, "After 14 months' on-site training, she finally got recruited with *Tehrik-e-Islam,* headed by the notorious Al-Gazzar based in the Cairo prison and returned to London as its sleeper-cell. By then, her lethal swiftness in close combat and a natural flair with weapons had earned her the title of Black Sand at the training camp in the Syrian desert. She quickly rose through the ranks of *Tehrik-e-Islam* by being the brain behind the funding and communications wing."

"So how did we know she was gold for us?" Major Arya asked, fascinated by the revelation.

"We did not, Major. Already an expert in counter-surveillance, she was the one who spotted our agent tailing her, at the crowded Piccadilly Circus square."

"And then?"

"At the right opportunity, she accosted the RAW agent and asked for a meeting with the London station head. She was brought in for a de-briefing and rest is history, as you know. Since she was already trained in weaponry and combat, all we needed was to prepare her for the role of a spy too. Needless to say, she was a natural double agent."

"I wonder what motivated her to such an extent," mused Rajeev Bakshi. He was the father of a girl the same age as Aliya after all.

"Ironically, it was her own mother," the minister said.

"You mean Sana Sheikh?" Major Arya was mildly surprised.

"She spoke about this to her handler, during a psych evaluation session. Her mother's isolation and loss after Kashmir, witnessed by her during her formative years, affected her in a big way. It drove her to work against all extremist and radical Islamist organizations. And she was at it as soon as she had a bit of freedom as a quasi-adult, after her arrival in London to study engineering. Her trip to Syria was more about infiltrating the dark camps of Islamic terror. She wanted to bring them down, not join them."

"God bless her soul. Shezii is right, you know. If it wasn't for her, we would have a serious crisis at hand." Rajeev Bakshi rubbed the bridge of his nose.

"Things were going as per plan. The major glitch developed only with the arrival of Awais Sheikh and Maghrabi on the scene," the minister added.

"I think Al-Gazzar already knew of her relationship with Awais Sheikh," the Major said.

"We knew of Ashraf Shaheen's identity for a long time but Aliya had no idea about her maternal uncle being a part of the mission until the sleeper-cell was activated in Delhi. Awais's change of heart further complicated things, not to forget the meddling by Dr. Kamran Khan."

"But why would they choose Aliya for a mission in India? To be specific in Kashmir, her place of birth?" Major Arya asked.

"She was due for another rise on the ladder but Al-Gazzar first wanted to put her through a final test. To see if she would be willing to operate against her own country and her own blood relation if the situation so demanded. Maghrabi was inserted into the equation only as a check-point to begin with."

"But I guess he had something much more sinister on his mind and with Awais's defection, Al-Gazzar panicked and put Maghrabi in charge of the mission," Major Arya said thoughtfully.

"Yes. After this mission, Aliya was supposed to have the ultimate honor of meeting with Al-Gazzar. We knew that with her tip-off we would have easily neutralized the mission in time. This mission in Kashmir would have failed no doubt, but it would have gotten noted as a well planned and executed hit in the records of *Tehrik-e-Islam*, albeit with minimum collateral damage for us," the minister concluded.

"So where is she going now?" Rajeev Bakshi asked finally.

"To the eye of the storm," the minister smiled. *To finish off what she started.*

93

Three Weeks Later
Khan el-Khalili Market
Cairo

For someone with a trained eye, the man would have appeared restless, with a nervous tick. He was moving purposefully through Khan el-Khalili's souk street, hardly paying any attention to the bright stalls flanking the narrow alleys, selling everything from incense and sheesha to chandeliers and traditional brass pots. He had an air of someone running late, as sweat traced his temples. Once again, he impatiently checked his watch as he squeezed past a bunch of noisy American tourists, his face contorted with irritation.

Finally, the venue of his important meeting was in sight. A not so popular Arabic coffee shop, tucked away behind a shop selling Egyptian souvenirs and antiques. He slowed down and looked around. It was an obvious and amateur counter-surveillance move, but then he had to be sure. He approached the coffee shop tentatively, waving off the sheesha smoke emanating from the cluttered establishment with small round tables placed close to each other. He settled on one of the tables and eyed the two men at the adjacent table. *There was little possibility of any clandestine talk here. Definitely not for the conversation he had in mind.* He shifted uncomfortably. He knew he was taking a risk. If they ever came to know, they would make sure that he and his entire family disappeared from the face of the earth. But the prospect of leaving his depressing job as a prison guard at the Tora prison and moving from Egypt to France with his family was something he could not ignore. Moreover, he could not bear the thought of being a nameless guard at the notorious Tora prison for the rest of his life.

Even though *Tehrik-e-Islam* paid him regularly for tending to the needs of Al-Gazzar, the money was tainted, and nearly not enough for taking care of his young wife and two girls. And he also knew that it couldn't last forever. Not after the call he had received last night from an unregistered number. The woman had a job for him. A job that required a dangerous betrayal. But in return he could have the golden life of his dreams. He had even allowed himself the luxury of deaming about opening a kiosk selling *shwarma* rolls in a small French town.

Suddenly, his phone buzzed. It was the same unregistered number.

"I am here already," he answered in a hushed tone.

"Leave from there, *now*. Meet me outside the main gate of Al-Hussein mosque in ten minutes." The woman's voice was calm and authoritative.

"How will I know it's you?" he asked hurriedly.

"I will find you." The line went dead.

He got up in a rush, toppling the pretty brass water

carafe on the table. Mumbling an apology to the owner, he sneaked out. The Al-Hussein mosque was not very far, but he was beginning to get edgy. He reached the main gate of the mosque with three minutes to spare. Much to his dislike, it was teeming with locals visiting the mosque and vendors selling dates and sherbets. He stood awkwardly, feeling exposed, until he was approached by a *khatun* in a black *abaya*. She handed him an open pack of dates.

"Eat those and keep walking with me," she whispered.

He complied without question and they walked a short distance across the road to a parapet under a date palm tree. She sat down first.

"Sit," she commanded.

He sat down gingerly. He had never sat this close to any woman not related to him in his life.

"Here." She handed him a package. "There are four new passports in there with new IDs and air tickets for you and your family. Details of the Swiss bank account in your new name are also in there." She paused to look around. "You will travel on your original passports until Amsterdam. That's where you will change IDs and use the new passports to board a flight to Paris. And then you will burn your old passports, understood?"

He nodded slowly.

"Remember, your Swiss bank account is under the name of your new ID. Inside the pack, there is enough cash to last you a month. You will access the Swiss account only after that. Am I clear?"

"Yes," he croaked.

"Good. Now tell me about Al-Gazzar and his prison schedule."

Then he spoke at length, about his tormentor's life in prison—when he slept, how he prayed and what he ate. After he stopped, she was quiet for a beat before she spoke.

"Tomorrow, just before the *Fazr Namaaz* is offered at dawn, you will give me unregistered access to Al-Gazzar's solitary confinement cell. And you will ensure that all CCTV cameras are offline at that time. Tomorrow will also be your last day of duty at Tora prison."

He looked into the dark eyes through the *hizaab*. They had a fire burning in them. He nodded under their hypnotic spell.

"And then you will leave and no one will ever see you again."

"Yes."

She got up to walk away. But then she turned and spoke casually, "You should know that the secret services of at least four countries are working together to offer you this chance as a price for your defection from *Tehrik-e-Islam*. So, should you decide to change your mind at the last minute, it would not end well for you." And then she moved fast and quick, disappearing into the crowds.

He sat stupefied for a few moments, staring at the package in his clammy hands. Then he thought of his little girls attending a western school and smiled. Tomorrow would be his last day at the Tora prison. Also, his last day in Egypt.

94

The Morning After
Delhi

The mid-morning sun had barely broken through the sky on an unexpectedly stormy day of June in Delhi. The clouds hung dark and low and the trees were windswept. The Defense Minister's office was partly in shadows, bathed only in the ambient light of a television running on mute. The staff was strictly instructed to not enter the minister's office. The rich aroma of coffee filled the room and three pairs of eyes were firmly fixed on the TV screen. *Al-Jazeera* was running a live segment with breaking news. The very news for which they had been waiting restlessly for the past two hours.

"What time is it in Cairo now?" the minister asked.

"They are three and a half hours behind, so ... 8:00 a.m." Major Ram Arya checked his watch.

"So the operation went well." The minister smiled.

"Yes, from the looks of it." Rajeev Bakshi responded with a triumphant smile of his own. "We are awaiting an official report from the *Mukhabarat*. But our Egyptian station head has already confirmed the mission as successful."

"Has the Egyptian government issued any official statement yet?"

"Not yet. But considering that *Al-Jazeera*'s media reps are stationed outside the Tora prison to report live, it should follow soon. The news is out already. They can't keep it under wraps," Major Arya shook his head.

"What's the inside story?" Arjun Jaisinghani sat back in his chair.

"Had a chat with Maryam Bilal, *Al-Jazeera*'s Bureau Chief in Egypt, ten minutes ago," Major Ram Arya added. "I know her personally as she covered an operation in Kashmir alongside our team in 2012."

"What did she have to say?" Rajeev Bakshi leaned in.

"Apparently, Al-Gazzar was found dead in his cell by the guard on first shift who brought in his breakfast this morning at 6:30 a.m. His throat was slit, but not the carotid artery, mind you. The cut was to the trachea, and deliberate, it appeared."

"So, he did not die instantly. He died drowning and choking on his own blood," Rajeev narrowed his eyes.

"A befitting end," the Major shrugged. "As per the initial reports, he had been dead for not more than an hour when he was found."

"At dawn? You mean just before or after the first prayers?" the minister asked.

"Yes, sir. The primary suspect is the night-shift guard who used to service Al-Gazzar's solitary cell, as no one else had access to it. Also, the CCTV cameras were found to be deactivated." Major Arya paused and then added with a smirk, "As expected, the guard is missing. He has vanished, along with his family."

"Hm, are they buying this story?"

"Not that it matters, but it is being touted as a case of inside rivalry. The general opinion is that the guard was bought over by those who wanted Al-Gazzar dead. Not every comrade of *Tehrik-e-Islam* believed in his style of functioning. With his death, the position for the new chief is now open."

"This may be the theory for now but the forensic report will speak otherwise. It won't connect the guard to the crime scene. And, as far as I know, she wouldn't have left a trace," the minister observed.

"Nope. They won't find any trace of her, forensic or otherwise. It will, at best, be a trail which will go cold in due course, with the missing guard as the only probable suspect. Not that any service or force really cares about finding the killer of one of the most notorious terror kingpins," Rajeev Bakshi scoffed.

"True. With Al-Gazzar gone, *Tehrik-e-Islam* will be fragmented. Soon, it will only be a toothless shade-monster without any bite in it. And we will be one step closer to decimating these hate-mongers for good." Major Arya threw a punch in the air.

The three men raised their coffee mugs slightly.

"So, what now?" Rajeev eyed the minister.

"We wait and watch. Meanwhile, PMO is of the opinion that Project Jai Hind is a brilliant team. Also, that it should continue status quo. And Rajeev, one more thing, Mossad got in touch with RAW last night.

Be prepared to take up bigger international assignments soon." Arjun Jaisinghani's tone was conspiratorial.

"Very well, sir." Rajeev smiled back. "But what about her? Aren't we going to bring her home now?"

It was an unspoken understanding to not take her name in reference to the case any more. As far as the world was concerned, she was gone for good.

Arjun Jaisinghani inhaled deeply and looked at the two men seated across the table.

"The best homecoming is in finding your calling, my friends. And in that sense, she is home already." The minister had a faraway look on his face. "She belongs to the world now. We will see her, no doubt, but only as a migratory bird, visiting for a purpose. And for now, her purpose is not here. She has a lot to do ... and she is only getting started."

Rajeev Bakshi and Major Arya exchanged glances and nodded ever so slightly. As men working for the clandestine services of their country, they knew that glory was not a reward they could ever expect. What they did was risky and demanded a huge price. In return, it only doused the passionate fire burning within them little by little. In that alone, they found their deliverance. But the fire burning in the young woman they were discussing was a fire from hell. *It burned brighter than any of them and it was going to take a long time to douse it.*

95

Six Months Later
Delhi, IGI Airport

Meera brought her newly acquired sedan to a smooth halt at the departure gates of the Indira Gandhi International Airport. She got off and quickly scanned the flight information display board and sighed. The check-in for British Airways' direct flight from IGI to Heathrow had already been announced. She hid her disappointment behind a cheerful smile as Shezii came around the car with his luggage and placed his arm around her shoulders.

"Your driving has improved. Nobody died today," he teased.

Meera made a face and mock-punched him on the shoulder.

"I am going to miss you," he said with a sad smile.

"Liar," she chided.

"No seriously, Meera." Shezii's face wore a hurt look.

"Just because it's an internship, don't think that they will go easy on you. Anderson Orr is one of the leading architecture firms in London. They will keep you very busy. But don't you dare miss my Facetime calls." Meera's tone was bright. She couldn't afford a meltdown now.

"I won't." Shezii smiled. "But yeah, I think I got lucky on this one. I didn't know I would get a call from them this quickly."

"Why not? You are the brightest student at Madhav Raje Institute of Technology. I am so proud of you," she said, hugging him tightly.

"I will be back for the summer break." His tone held a promise.

"I will be waiting," Meera said simply.

Shezii turned and looked deep into her eyes, without uttering any words.

"What happened?" Meera asked, uncomfortable under his gaze.

"Nothing ..." He looked away.

"Don't you go silent on me now, Shezii. Not when you are about to board an overseas flight." She pouted.

"Thanks, Meera ... for standing by me. And believing in me, when no one was willing to listen."

"Well, in the end, you weren't wrong." She smiled.

"If it wasn't for Aliya, I wouldn't be standing here, ready to board a flight to London," Shezii said.

"I wonder where is she now."

"*If* she is alive." Shezii's expression was one of remorse. "They just left her alone to fend for herself. And then, so easily declared her dead."

Shezii was allowing himself to talk out loud about his feelings after a very long time. Meera's deep melancholy at their separation was affecting him in unexpected ways. She was something he wanted to cling on to with all of his being and she was also one of the reasons he had to go away. He loved her, in a way that he couldn't allow himself to make her the target of his rebound love. But he wasn't very good at saying goodbyes. His mom and dad knew this too and for that very reason, they had left Meera with the job of dropping him to the airport.

"Think of the coincidence. You are going to the very place from where she had returned," Meera chirped after an uncomfortable silence.

Shezii nodded. He had worked very hard to keep that thought out of his head. But in the end, Meera was the one who always spoke her heart. "Anyway, I better get going now." He eyed the lengthening queue at the departure gate.

She nodded silently and let go of him.

He turned and hoisted his backpack and pulling at the luggage, started his casual saunter towards the departure gate.

"Hey Shezii ...," she called out.

He turned and stood rooted to his place, a question in his eyes.

She walked up to him and peered into those eyes.

"You know, we never lose those we truly love. When it gets dark, they make their presence felt through a sudden thought or a lost dream or a forgotten song. And when the sun shines, they come back to us like a shadow that can never leave. Remember ... the one that lives in your heart can never die." Meera's eyes shone through her tears.

Shezii held her shoulders and placed a light kiss on her forehead. Then he turned quickly and walked away. He was looking forward to the journey ahead and to London.

Maybe, just maybe, it would bring him closer to his calling. He entered the gate and located the British Airways check-in counter at the far end of the hall.

The queue at the counter was mercifully short. And as he approached the counter, the pretty check-in executive looked up at him and flashed a charming smile.

"So, what's taking you to London, Mr. Shahzaib?" she asked.

Shezii stared at her unblinking, transported back to that last time when Ms. Tishby had called him by his formal name. After all these years, finally, he hadn't flinched at the sound of his own name. In fact, he loved it.

"Actually, I am going to look for something I have lost." He smiled and picked up his boarding pass. His flight was on time.